Acclaim for the Novels of Opal Carew

"A blazing-hot erotic romp . . . a must-read for lovers of erotic romance. A fabulously fun and stupendously steamy read for a cold winter's night. This one's so hot, you might need to wear oven mitts while you're reading it!"

—*Romance Junkies*

4 stars! "Carew's devilish twists and turns keep the emotional pitch of the story moving from sad to suspenseful to sizzling to downright surprising in the end. . . . The plot moves swiftly and satisfyingly."

—*RT Book Reviews*

"Fresh, exciting, and extremely sexual, with characters you'll fall in love with. Absolutely fantastic!"

—*Fresh Fiction*

"The constant and imaginative sexual situations keep the reader's interest along with likable characters with emotional depth. Be prepared for all manner of coupling, including groups, exhibitionism, voyeurism, and same-sex unions. . . . I recommend *Swing* for the adventuresome who don't mind singeing their senses."

—*Regency Reader*

"Carew pulls off another scorcher. . . . [She] knows how to write a love scene that takes her reader to dizzying heights of pleasure."

—*My Romance Story*

"So much fun to read . . . The story line is fast-paced with wonderful humor."

—*Genre Go Round Reviews*

"A great book . . . Ms. Carew has wonderful imagination."

—*Night Owl Romance Reviews*

"Opal Carew brings erotic romance to a whole new level. . . . She writes a compelling romance and sets your senses on fire with her love scenes!"

—*Reader to Reader*

4 stars! "Written with great style . . . A must for any erotic romance fan, ménage enthusiasts in particular." —*Just Erotic Romance Reviews*

"Plain delicious in its sensuality. Opal Carew has a great imagination, and her sensual scenes are sure to get a fire going in many readers."
—*A Romance Review*

4½ hearts! "Humor, angst, drama, lots of hot sex, and interesting characters make for an entertaining read that you will have a hard time putting down." —*The Romance Studio*

"Opal Carew has given these characters depth and realism. . . . A thrilling romance, full of both incredible passion and heartwarming tenderness, and Opal Carew is an author to watch." —*Joyfully Reviewed*

"Wonderfully written . . . I highly recommend this tale."
—*Romance Reviews Today*

"An outstanding novel . . . I encourage you to read this exceptional book." —*The Road to Romance*

"This book is extremely hot! Ms. Carew had me squirming in my seat while reading this story. . . . This book was so great I want to read more stories by this author." —*Coffee Time Romance*

Also by Opal Carew

Pleasure Bound

Bliss

Forbidden Heat

Secret Ties

Six

Blush

Swing

Twin Fantasies

Total Abandon

Opal Carew

St. Martin's Griffin
New York

This is a work of fiction. All of the characters, organizations, and events portrayed in this novel are either products of the author's imagination or are used fictitiously.

www.stmartins.com

Library of Congress Cataloging-in-Publication Data

Carew, Opal.
Total abandon / Opal Carew. — 1st ed.
p. cm.
ISBN 978-0-312-67459-5
I. Title.
PR9199.4.C367T67 2011
813'.6—dc22
2010042918

10 9 8 7 6 5 4 3 2

With love to
Mark,
Matt, and Jason

Acknowledgments

As always, thanks to Rose, Emily, Mark, and Colette.

I'd also like to thank my brother, Ed, and his wife, Linda, for the many times I've spent enjoying their lovely home on the lake. Thanks for the boat rides, swimming, barbecues, and long summer evenings spent in great company in a beautiful setting. The cottages in this book aren't real, but I was inspired by the delightful area where you live.

Also, thanks to Leeann Burke and Reece Butler, whose generosity enabled me to attend the New Jersey Romance Writers conference and receive a wonderful award. (The Golden Leaf for *Forbidden Heat* in the Single Title category.)

Total Abandon

One

"I can't believe you've gone an entire year without sex. And by choice."

Sandra grimaced at her friend's comment. She tightened her fingers around her champagne flute. Many times she'd regretted telling Aimee about her resolution, but in fact, her confession to Aimee had forged a closer friendship between them. A friendship that had helped her through some tough times over the past year. Especially the loneliness.

Aimee held up her glass. "Happy anniversary." She grinned. "A year well behind you."

Sandra clinked her champagne glass against Aimee's, then sipped the bubbly wine. Not that a failed marriage was something to celebrate.

She glanced around Maelstrom's Bar, wondering when Devlin would arrive to join them. He'd called to say he'd be a little late because he'd had to attend an afternoon meeting on the outskirts of the city. That meant he had to brave the rush-hour traffic driving back downtown to meet them.

Once he got here, he'd have some trouble finding parking, too, since the bar was in a busy area.

Sandra pushed her long hair behind her ear as she shifted on the upholstered seat. It was Friday evening and the bar was filling up fast, but she and Aimee had walked over right after work and grabbed one of the cozy curved booths near the window.

"So, you're sticking with your story that your ex wasn't a complete loser? Because I'm all ears if you want to dis him. It'll help get it out of your system."

"No, Eric was just the wrong guy for me."

Not that it hadn't hurt to find he no longer loved her. Or really, that he had never loved her. They'd dated since high school, and for many years, they'd mistaken being comfortable with being in love. But neither of them had wanted the marriage to fail—to admit *they* had failed—so it had taken ten years for them to finally realize that divorce was the only answer. They simply weren't happy together. They were great roommates, but their connection had broken down years ago—if it had ever been there in the first place.

Aimee pursed her lips. "Okay then. Moving on. Tell me what you're looking for in a man."

She leaned toward Sandra and her lips turned up in a crooked smile. Sandra could tell Aimee had had a little too much to drink. And Sandra probably had, too. Champagne tended to have that effect on her.

Sandra attempted to answer her friend's question, but when she tried to picture the man of her dreams, all she came up with was a blank.

Aimee seemed to understand her dilemma. She sipped from her glass, then giggled. "I have an idea. Let's make a list."

She opened her purse and pulled out a pen, then grabbed one of the small square cocktail napkins the waitress had left on the table with the appetizer platter. Aimee wrote down the numeral one followed by a dot.

"Okay, I want you to think about"—she giggled—"you know . . . men . . . and what you'd really like."

"What I'd like? I guess I'd like a guy who's really sensitive, with a good sense of humor and . . . well, a sense of adventure."

Aimee pointed at her and winked. "That's what I'm talking about. Adventure." She sipped her drink again, then set down her glass. "Forget that Mr. Sensitive stuff. Think about Mr. Muscle-Bound-Hunk meets Mr. Sexy-Bad-Boy and how he"—she winked—"or, better yet, *they* could make your dreams come true."

Sandra knew exactly what Aimee was talking about. Sandra had made the mistake of telling Aimee about one of her ultra sexy dreams, dreams that had been a frequent occurrence over the past few months. Fantasies brought to life in steamy erotic detail in the middle of the night, leaving her hot and frustrated in the morning.

"Before you settle down with Mr. Right, you need to get your mojo back. You know, enjoy the single life and see what's out there. Now"—she pointed at Sandra with her pen—"tell me what kinds of adventures you want to have. Your wildest, craziest fantasies. Let's write them down."

"I don't see the point in making a list." Sandra really didn't want her fantasies written out in black and white. That seemed too . . . sordid.

"Ah, come on. If you can dream about them, you can talk about them."

Sandra's cheeks flushed. "I don't think so."

Aimee patted Sandra's hand. "Honey, there's nothing wrong with having fantasies. And it's good to examine them. It'll help you know what really turns you on. Which is good since you're going to start dating again. Look, I'll get us started. You told me about that one where you were captured by pirates and carried off to their ship, so . . ."

Sandra watched as Aimee wrote *Be held captive* beside the numeral one.

"Now you," Aimee said, pen poised.

Sandra shrugged. "I don't know. I can't think of anything."

"What about that book you were reading a couple of weeks ago? It had bondage, didn't it?"

"Um . . . dominance and submission, actually."

Aimee smiled. "You'd like to try that?"

Sandra shrugged again. Aimee nudged her shoulder.

"Come on. Get into the spirit of it. I'm just trying to help."

Sandra took a sip of her champagne and gazed at Aimee's deep blue eyes. She did want to help. Sandra sighed.

"Okay. Well, I'm not sure about the bondage and domination stuff. I'd have to know the guy pretty well."

"Well, yeah." Aimee nibbled on one of the chicken wings, then picked up the pen again. "Okay, let's leave that one a little open."

She wrote down item number two as *Experiment with bondage.*

"What else? Think about some fantasy that has really intrigued you that you know you'll never try but wish you could." She grinned. "And don't be shy."

One fantasy immediately popped into Sandra's head. She'd caught part of a show on sexual fantasies and she'd been intrigued by one woman's fantasy about being with a stranger. To her surprise, that had turned on Sandra immensely. Which was just crazy, especially since the only man she'd ever been with was her ex-husband, Eric.

"You've got one. I can see it in your eyes. Spill it."

Sandra pursed her lips. "Well . . ."

"If you go, I'll go."

Sandra nodded. "It's . . . well, being with a stranger."

"You mean a one-night stand?"

"No, more like making love with someone and not knowing who it is."

"So, like, some sexy guy is making out with you and you can't see who it is? That's pretty intense."

Aimee wrote down item number three as *Make love to a sexy stranger while blindfolded.*

"Now yours," Sandra said.

Aimee wrote item four on the napkin, then turned it toward Sandra so she could see.

Have sex with two men at the same time (maybe more).

Sandra felt her cheeks heat. "That's some list we have there."

Aimee laughed. "It's only four items. We're not done yet."

"I think I am."

"Okay, then. I'll just put some down for your consideration."

Aimee jotted several more items on the napkin as Sandra watched. Finally, she turned it so Sandra could read it.

1. Be held captive.
2. Experiment with bondage.
3. Make love to a sexy stranger while blindfolded.
4. Have sex with two men at the same time (maybe more).
5. Be a love slave.
6. Have a love slave.
7. Be a voyeur.
8. Try exhibitionism.

"Want anything else?"

Sandra nearly jumped at the waitress's voice. She wanted to snatch the list from Aimee and stuff it in her purse, but the young woman didn't even glance at it.

"Yes. How about a couple of piña coladas?" Aimee said.

Sandra smiled and nodded. She loved piña coladas.

The waitress picked up the empty champagne bottle from the table and placed it on her round tray, then grabbed the two empty flutes. She disappeared into the crowd.

Sandra picked up a piece of zucchini from the appetizer tray and dipped it in the dressing, then took a bite. The waitress returned a few moments later with their drinks. Sandra took a sip.

"It's about time." Aimee glanced over Sandra's shoulder.

Sandra glanced around to see Devlin approaching their table. His glittering gaze locked on her as he walked toward them with his usual relaxed gait, a charming half smile curling his lips.

Although she couldn't see the color of his eyes in this light, she knew they were as blue as the sky at dusk, dusted with golden specks, and surrounded by a midnight blue ring. The raspy shadow across his jaw gave him a definite masculine allure, and he'd tied back his medium brown shoulder-length hair, which was typical on a workday. His relaxed casual-Friday outfit consisted of well-worn jeans and a brown tweed blazer over a brown striped shirt.

Sandra slid farther into the booth to make room for him, and he sat down beside her.

His gaze fell to the table. "What's this?"

Oh, damn. Sandra tried to grab the cocktail napkin as he plucked it from the table—the napkin with the list scribbled on it—but he snatched it out of reach and began to read.

His grin broadened, revealing his strong white teeth. "Well, this is quite the menu. Are there pictures to go along with it?"

"You are so bad." Sandra's hand brushed across his broad chest as she tried to reach the list, but he held it farther away from her. She stretched her arm more, trying to grab the small square napkin, but his arms were longer than hers. Suddenly, she realized she was practically draped across him, her chest against his, and she became intensely aware of his muscular arm beneath her fingertips, her breasts pressed against his solid, ridged chest, his face far too close to hers. Kissably close.

And kissing wasn't something she intended to do with Devlin. He was her friend.

She drew back and tugged the sides of her shirt down, then smoothed it over her hips, her lips pursed.

Now would come the teasing.

"Is this your weekend to-do list?" he asked, eyebrows raised.

"Well, maybe you and I can talk her into it," Aimee said with a wink. "I've convinced her to stretch her imagination a little. Now we need to convince her to go a bit wild."

Devlin grinned, his amused gaze settling on Sandra.

"Especially now that she's lifted her ban on sex." Aimee rested her chin on her hand. "A whole year without." Aimee shook her head and gazed at Sandra. "I don't know how you lasted so long."

Devlin watched Sandra's cheeks blush softly. He didn't know how he'd lasted so long. From the first time he'd met her, he'd been crazy about her. Aimee had told him Sandra had recently divorced and how tough it had been on her, so he'd decided to tread carefully. He'd gotten to know her, becoming her friend, making sure to give her plenty of time, hoping when she was ready, she'd agree to go out with him. Then he'd show her why the two of them were perfect for each other.

But timing was everything. The woman hadn't been with anyone else since high school, and she was clearly on the rebound. The first few guys she dated wouldn't—shouldn't—lead to something permanent. He needed to wait it out awhile longer, let her get a taste of the single life. Then once she was firmly ensconced in the dating world, he'd swoop in and make his move.

Sandra held one of Devlin's arms and Aimee the other as the three of them stepped outside into the warm summer's evening. Sandra took a deep breath and realized she felt more than a little light-headed.

"My car's around the corner," Devlin said as he tugged her to the left.

"I'm glad we've got you as our designated driver," Aimee said. "It beats taking the bus at this hour."

Sandra took the bus to work and no express buses ran at this hour, so it would have been a long commute. Sometimes Aimee drove her car, but Devlin hadn't even asked. Aimee and Sandra had both had enough drinks that he would ensure neither of them drove. Even though Sandra didn't need a guy looking out for her, it was kind of nice that he did. Devlin was a good friend.

He opened the front passenger door and Sandra climbed in. Aimee got into the backseat—the usual arrangement, since he would drop off Aimee first. As he drove, Sandra relaxed in the front seat, her head against the headrest. Suddenly she realized they'd stopped—she must have dozed off—and Aimee was getting out of the car.

"I'll be back in a minute," Devlin said. "I'll just make sure she gets in all right."

Sandra watched Devlin walk Aimee to the door of her apartment building, wondering why the two of them weren't dating. Devlin was such a great guy, and available. Aimee really was missing out. Sandra sighed. Maybe she should say something to Devlin.

A few minutes later, Devlin opened the driver's door and slid into the seat beside her. He pulled the car into traffic again.

"So, the year's finally over." He glanced toward her, then back to the road. "Are you looking forward to dating again?"

She shifted in her seat. "Not really."

"Any particular reason?"

"Well, I'm out of practice, for one." She glanced over at him. "And don't say it's like riding a bike."

He chuckled.

"I guess I'm worried I won't find anyone who wants to date me." She fiddled with her hands in her lap. "And then I'm worried that if I do date someone, it won't go well . . . I won't know what to say or do. That kind of thing."

"I'm sure you won't have any problem finding someone—probably a lot of someones—who would love to date you."

He gazed across at her. Was it her imagination, or was there a heated interest in his eyes? Butterflies quivered through her stomach, but she realized it was most likely her imagination. Probably the alcohol hazing her judgment.

"And if you want to go on a practice date or two—"

"You'll volunteer? But that wouldn't really be the same thing. You and I are comfortable together. There wouldn't be any of the awkwardness of being with a stranger."

Devlin smiled but shook his head. "No, I was going to say that I could set you up with someone. Maybe introduce you to a couple of my friends over drinks, to see if you hit it off in a casual sort of setup."

"Oh." As much as she'd protested, she'd actually liked the idea that Devlin wanted to do some test dates with her. The idea that he wanted to pawn her off on his friends disappointed her for some reason.

He pulled in front of her building and parked the car, then walked around it and opened her door. She stepped out of the car and, as she breathed in the fresh night air, felt a little woozy. Devlin took her arm.

"I think someone celebrated a little too much tonight." He took her hand and rested it on his elbow, then walked with her to the front door of her apartment building.

She rarely had more than a glass or two of wine with dinner, or a single cocktail in an evening, so the champagne and piña coladas had definitely gone to her head. She pulled her key from her purse and pushed it into the front door lock and turned it. Devlin opened the door.

"I'll see you up," he said.

She walked beside him across the air-conditioned lobby.

He summoned the elevator and they stepped inside. As the doors closed behind them, Sandra realized how small a space it was and how tall Devlin was standing beside her. And how broad his shoulders were.

And how safe she felt around him.

His arm brushed hers, and she realized he hadn't actually moved toward her; she'd listed a little to the left and now leaned against him slightly. She should move away, but it felt cozy leaning close to him like this. Her good friend. Her buddy.

Her sexy, extremely masculine buddy.

The elevator dinged and the doors opened. She stepped into the hallway and walked toward her apartment, Devlin by her side. The lights of the city glittered below them as she walked toward the big window at the end of the hallway, where her apartment door was. Devlin took her key from her fingers and pushed it into the lock, then turned it.

"You want to come in?" Sandra asked impulsively.

Two

Sandra's stomach fluttered at the thought, which was crazy because he'd been over a dozen times before. Of course, always with Aimee. They were sort of a threesome, friendship-wise. But right now, looking into his striking blue eyes, she thought of a threesome of another sort. Threesomes like Aimee had suggested on their list. Sexy, erotic threesomes.

But right at this moment, she'd be fine without the third. Just Devlin and her.

She locked gazes with him and tipped her chin up.

Devlin stared at Sandra, who gazed at him with warm olive green eyes, her full lips looking soft and kissable. His stomach clenched, and he couldn't help himself. He leaned in and captured her lips. Oh, God, they were every bit as soft as he had imagined.

Her arms curled around his neck and she drew closer to him. Her soft breasts pressed against him. He wanted to shove away his jacket and pull her tight to his chest, to feel if her nipples were hard with desire, just as his cock pulsed to life at her proximity.

Damn, he wanted her.

Her tongue slipped between his lips, gently exploring, and he groaned, then sucked it into his mouth. Everything about her was so soft and warm. His body hardened even more. He felt his resolve weakening, his need for her growing.

Her hand stroked down his back, then wrapped around his butt and squeezed. His cock lurched to full attention.

She had never, ever done something like that before. Through the haze of desire, he remembered how many drinks she'd had tonight. Three since he'd shown up at the bar. He didn't know how many before that.

He couldn't take advantage of her. And that's what he'd be doing if he continued this now. With great power of will, he eased away from her.

"Let's get you inside."

Her eyes lit up, and he realized she'd misread his comment. Still, he opened the door and guided her forward, then closed the door behind them.

When he turned back, he saw her bent at the waist, unfastening the strap on her shoe. Her very round, very sexy derriere was right in front of him, her short, flowing skirt barely covering the essentials. He wanted to reach out and stroke her lovely round ass. His cock twitched. What he really wanted to do was lift that skirt to reveal the luscious curves underneath, to stroke her naked backside, then draw her against him. His cock ached with need.

She shifted to unfasten her other shoe and swayed a bit to the side. He grasped her hips to steady her and she eased back against him.

The bulge in his pants nestled snugly into the heat of her delightful backside. She shifted a little as she tugged at her shoe, and he tightened his hands around her hips. She was driving him crazy with need.

"Sorry. The strap is stuck."

"Let me help," he offered.

She stood up and turned around to face him. She pushed her long, glossy black hair behind her ear and started to lift her knee, raising her foot in the air. Worried she'd topple over, he crouched down in front of her and captured her foot. Conscious of her long shapely legs in front of him, he unfastened the ankle strap on her high-heeled shoe, then drew it from her foot.

She smiled, her eyes twinkling delightfully. "Thanks."

She placed her foot on the floor, then walked away from him, a definite sway to her hips.

"Want some coffee? I just got a new Hawaiian blend in decaf."

"Uh . . . no, I'd better go." If he stayed here any longer, he might just give in to his intense desire.

She stopped and turned around. "Are you sure?" She walked toward him, then trailed her fingers up his lapels and gazed into his eyes. "I thought maybe you might want to stay and talk about that . . . uh . . . that list Aimee and I made up earlier." She smiled as she tugged on his shirt collar, then rested her hands on his shoulders. "Do you think I should maybe try out any of those things? I've never had a man tie me up. I think it could be pretty sexy."

His breath caught at the thought of Sandra tied up. Naked. *Lying on his bed.*

His hands started to tremble and he rolled them into fists to stop himself from grabbing her and tossing her over his shoulder, then carrying her off to the bedroom.

The delicate scent of her mango shampoo filled his senses. Intoxicating. She lifted her chin, bringing her lips closer to his, holding them mere inches from his own. Expectantly.

He couldn't resist. He captured the lips she so willingly offered again. So soft. So alluringly sweet. He wrapped his arms around her and glided his tongue into her velvety mouth. She tasted of sweet pineapple, coconut, and rum. He swirled his tongue inside her mouth and her tongue joined his, then plunged inside his mouth. He almost gasped at the urgent need flooding through him.

He wanted her. Badly.

She tugged on his jacket and pulled it from his shoulders. It fell to the floor. Then she pushed at his open shirt as she nuzzled under his chin. Her soft lips caressing his raspy skin sent quivers through him. His shirt dropped to the floor, leaving him in only a T-shirt, and she grasped his hand and lifted it. He felt her round, firm breast against his palm, beneath the thin fabric of her soft silk blouse. The nipple peaked to a hard bud.

His groin flooded with heat as he caressed her.

Oh, man, what was he doing? He'd promised himself.

If he moved ahead with this now, took her to bed as his hormones demanded, he'd ruin everything. He'd mess up any chance he had of winning her for the long haul.

And that was too important to blow for one night of passion, no matter how sweet the experience would be.

Summoning all of his willpower, he drew his hand from her ample breast and released her lips. Her eyes, still closed, quivered a little, then her eyelids opened. She stared at him, her olive eyes dazed.

"Sandra, I've really got to go."

Slowly, comprehension seeped in and Sandra drew herself back. "Oh. Um, okay. Sorry."

"Sandra, you and I . . . this . . ."

"No, I understand." She stepped back, her cheeks flushing.

He grasped her hand, stopping her escape. "No, I don't think you do. Look, we're friends and I wouldn't want to do something to ruin that." His heart thundered in his chest. He wanted to say more, to be more reassuring, but he had to get away from her before he caved. He squeezed her hand. "Okay? Are we good?"

She gazed at him, her chin trembling a bit, but finally she nodded.

"Yeah. We're good." She shifted onto her tiptoes and kissed his cheek. "You're a good friend, Devlin. Thanks."

He nodded and picked up his shirt and jacket. "Anytime, friend. You going to be okay?"

She nodded. "Yeah. Of course. Thanks for the ride home."

She followed him to the entrance and he opened the door.

"See you next week," she said.

"Sure thing."

As she closed the door behind him, leaving him in the abandoned hallway, he wondered if he'd just made the worst mistake of his life.

Sandra leaned against the door and sucked in a breath.

Oh, damn, how embarrassing. What the hell was I thinking?

She pushed herself from the door and walked to the bedroom, her cheeks still burning.

Devlin was her friend. And now she'd gone and thrown herself at him. How could she face him again?

Especially since he was so clearly not interested.

She stripped off her clothes and pulled on her pajama pants and cotton camisole. She went into the bathroom and grabbed her hairbrush, then gazed in the mirror as she pulled the brush through her long black hair.

For a little while there, she'd thought he'd been interested. She'd been sure she'd seen more than a spark of interest in his eyes. But clearly that had been the piña coladas affecting her brain.

She picked up her toothbrush and squeezed some toothpaste onto the bristles. She began to brush her teeth with vigorous strokes. What an idiot she'd been. If he'd been interested in her, he would have shown her by now. Sure, he knew she'd sworn off relationships after her divorce, but that never stopped a guy from trying when he wanted a woman.

As her friend, maybe Devlin was more inclined to respect that boundary, but wouldn't he have hinted at his interest somehow?

She rinsed her mouth and stuffed the toothbrush back into its stand.

If he had been interested. Which clearly he wasn't.

She strode into the bedroom and climbed under the covers. Now, if she could just forget the sting of her embarrassment and fall asleep, maybe tomorrow she could forget the whole thing. Or, at least, act as if she'd forgotten about it. Devlin, sweet guy he was, wouldn't bring it up again. He was that kind of wonderful.

Remembering the kisses they'd shared, the feel of his muscular body against hers, her insides warmed again and, at the memory of his hand on her breast, her nipples ached. Oh, God. She had actually taken his hand and . . .

She pulled the covers over her head. How could she ever face him again?

As soon as Devlin got into his car and closed the door, he grabbed his cell phone and tapped in Aimee's phone number.

"Hey, Aimee. I didn't wake you, did I?"

"You kidding? You know I'm a night owl. So, did you make a move on Sandra?"

His heart skipped a beat. "Why would you ask that?"

"Oh, like I haven't known you've had a thing for her from day one."

He saw no reason to deny it. Aimee had a way of reading people.

"You've never mentioned it."

"Why should I? You knew how Sandra felt about starting a relationship and you respected it."

"Does Sandra know that I'm interested?"

"No. A guy would have to send her an engraved invitation with his intent before she'd believe he wanted her. So are you planning to pursue her?"

"Yes, but not yet. I want to form a real relationship with her. She won't be ready for that with the first guy she goes out with. After swearing off men for a year, she'll want to do some . . . I don't know . . . experimenting before she settles down with one guy." Roughly, he figured he should give it about six months.

"So you want to give her time to sow a few wild oats, then you'll sweep her off her feet?"

"I'm not sure about that."

"Well, don't underestimate sweeping a gal off her feet. It's really quite romantic."

Romantic. He liked that.

"So how can I help?" she asked. "That is why you're calling me, right?"

He smiled. Aimee really was sensational. If he didn't have it so bad for Sandra . . .

"Well, I was thinking about that list you and Sandra made tonight," he said. "Maybe we could get her to fast-track through her sexual exploration by doing the items on the list."

"And you'd like me to arrange this miracle somehow."

"Well, that would be nice."

"And how would you feel knowing Sandra's off having a threesome with a couple of other guys? Won't you be jealous?"

"Sure, but I'll live. And, say, if you could arrange it so I could watch . . ." He trailed off, a grin on his face.

"Well, sure, why not? It's not as if it's going to be hard to get her to follow the list in the first place. What's that one small addition?"

He chuckled. "That's the spirit."

After he ended the call and slid his cell phone back into his pocket, he settled into the driver's seat and stared out the windshield. Rather than the cars parked across from him in the apartment building parking lot, what he saw were images of Sandra naked, between two men, crying out in pleasure. His fingers curled around the steering wheel as his groin tightened in need.

He glanced up at Sandra's window on the eighth floor. The light was out. She'd be in bed by now. Probably in some skimpy, slinky teddy.

His cock pushed painfully at his jeans.

He should just open the car door right now and stride up there. Tell her what he wanted and take his chances. The memory of her responding to his kisses, her body responding to his touch, sent his hormones skyrocketing.

Why wait when every indication told him she wanted him right now?

Three

Sandra glanced up at Devlin's handsome face.

"You're here."

He drew back the covers, revealing her naked body. Had she peeled away her pajamas since she fell asleep?

The heated look in his eyes sent her insides melting. He sat on the bed beside her, then leaned in and kissed her. His hot lips brushing against hers took her breath away. She arched forward and he wrapped his arms around her, then drew her close. He explored her mouth with his probing tongue, urging her lips apart, then gliding into her mouth. She stroked his tongue with hers, then sighed as he sucked her tongue deeper into his mouth.

He lay down beside her and stroked her breasts. Her nipples tightened into hard buds. Then he tasted one, stroking his tongue over the tip, driving her insane with need. She glided her fingers along the back of his head, then released the leather tie that held his hair behind his head and stroked her fingers through the long strands. She'd wanted to do that for so long.

He slid to her other nipple and sucked lightly. She gasped at the intense pleasure.

She stroked down his solid chest, then to his belt buckle. She released it, then his fly and tucked her hand inside. His erection pulsed with life as she encircled it with her fingers.

She sat up and stared at his wonderfully large cock. She pressed her lips to the tip and licked, then swallowed his cockhead whole.

"Sandra, that's fantastic. You are fabulous at that."

She beamed and dove down on him, taking him deep into her throat without a single gagging sensation, even though he was big and thick. She sucked and licked, then bobbed up and down.

"Oh, God, sweetheart. That is incredible. I'm going to . . . Oh, God."

In a rush, hot liquid flooded her throat. She swallowed and smiled up at him. She'd never gotten her ex off that quickly.

She grabbed his pants and pulled them down, then tossed them off the bed. He tugged his shirt and T-shirt over his head in one quick movement. He drew her into his arms and kissed her, her naked breasts crushing against his rock-solid chest. Her beaded nipples driving into his ridged flesh.

She pressed her hands against his chest and he lay down on his back. She arched her leg over him and wrapped her hand around his straight-as-an-arrow cock and pressed it to her slick opening, then slowly lowered herself onto him.

Oh, God, it had been well over a year since she'd had a man inside her. And now Devlin was gliding into her. Deeper. And deeper.

Finally, she rested on his groin, his cock embedded in her. He twitched and she thought she'd fly over the edge right then and there.

He stroked her breasts, sending tingles rushing through her. She leaned forward so he could take one in his mouth. It was such sweet heaven to be touched by a man again. She moaned at the exquisite sensation of his hot lips covering her hard nipple, and his hard cock filled her so full she thought she'd explode.

She lifted her hips, then lowered herself again. Pleasure swelled through her. She glided up and down. She sucked in a breath at the intense sensations writhing through her.

"Oh, dear God, Devlin, make me come."

He wrapped his hands around her hips and lifted her, then lowered her again. Lifted and lowered, augmenting her rhythm.

The phone began to ring, but she ignored it. Bouncing up and down on Devlin's big cock. Gazing into his delightful, star-speckled blue eyes.

Ring.

Pleasure burst through her, washing through every cell.

Ring.

Devlin seemed to dissolve. The phone rang again. Light filtered into her eyes. The orgasm that had seemed so close only a second ago also seemed to dissolve. Her vagina clenched, but Devlin's big cock had also dissolved.

Oh, God, no. It was only a dream!

She gasped for air, her body twitching with need. She stroked between her legs and found her clit nestled in the damp folds. She stroked it, then gasped and moaned as the orgasm finally overtook her. Her body convulsed, and she collapsed on the bed.

The phone stopped ringing.

As she stared out her sunny bedroom window, catching her breath, she remembered what had really happened last night. How she had thrown herself at Devlin and he had turned her down.

Damn, what a crappy way to start the morning.

As Sandra gazed out the sunny window of the restaurant, she saw Aimee walking toward the door. A moment later, Aimee entered the restaurant, glanced around, and waved at Sandra. She walked toward the table.

"Hey, there." Aimee hooked the shoulder strap of her purse over the back of the chair, then sat down. "Did you order for me already?"

"Pastrami on rye and a diet cola." Sandra sipped her own diet cola, a vice she had picked up from Aimee. She really didn't need the caffeine.

The waitress arrived at the table and placed plates loaded with food in front of them. Aimee's sandwich and fries and Sandra's chicken wrap with a side salad.

Aimee picked up a long, slender fry with her fingers

and took a bite. "Mmm. These things are way too good. And really hot. Just the way you like them. Want one?"

Unable to resist the delicious aroma, Sandra grabbed a fry and took a bite. Heaven. She swallowed, then pushed her fork through a chunk of salad. One fry was her limit.

"So, do you want me to pick you and Devlin up for the movie tonight or do you want to drive?" Aimee asked.

Sandra's chest constricted. "Oh, well, um . . . I think I'm just going to stay home tonight. You two go ahead."

The thought of facing Devlin after last night mortified her. She knew she had to find a way to get over it eventually, but that wasn't going to be soon.

Aimee put down her sandwich. "Okay, what gives?"

Sandra realized she'd stabbed her fork into the salad multiple times, gathering several chunks of lettuce on the tines. She glanced at Aimee.

"What do you mean?"

"Did you and Devlin have a fight or something?"

"No."

"First, you insist we go shoe shopping today instead of joining Devlin at the art museum for the new Escher exhibit, which I know you wanted to see. Now you want to blow him off when you know he's been looking forward to that new thriller movie for weeks."

Sandra shrugged. "I just need some alone time."

"Aw, honey. Is it about the divorce?" Aimee rested her hand on Sandra's. Her deep blue eyes gazed into Sandra's with sympathy. "Did the anniversary bring up bad memories?"

Sandra appreciated her friend's comforting gesture.

"No, it's not that, I . . ." She bit her lip. "It's just that . . . I sort of made a fool of myself last night with Devlin."

Aimee's well-shaped eyebrow arched upward. "Really? How?"

Sandra's cheeks burned in embarrassment.

Aimee grinned. "Hmm. With cheeks that red, I've gotta know. Give."

"When he dropped me off last night . . . I . . . sort of kissed him."

"Boy, if you're not sure, you are definitely out of practice."

Sandra picked up her diet cola and swirled it around, sending the ice cubes tinkling against the glass.

"Aimee, you're not helping."

"Okay, so what happened then? Did you guys . . . ?" Aimee's eyes glittered in amusement.

"No. He . . ." She stared down at her plate. "He couldn't get away from me fast enough."

"Really? Hmm. I find that hard to believe." Aimee took a bite of her sandwich.

"Well, believe it."

Aimee chewed for a few seconds, then swallowed. "Okay, so now what? You going to avoid him forever?"

Sandra gazed at Aimee sheepishly. "Can I?"

Aimee laughed melodically. "No, I won't let you get away with that. He's a great guy. And you guys are friends." She patted Sandra's hand. "But I will allow you a reprieve. We'll skip the movie tonight and, to help you out even more, how about you and I go up to my cottage next weekend. It's a long weekend, and the weather's supposed to be fabulous. We'll enjoy three days of sunshine, water, and relaxation. That should give you lots of time to forget all about any nonsense between you and Devlin, and the following week we can all pick up where we left off. What do you say?"

A weekend at Aimee's cottage. Sandra had never been, but had heard many stories from Aimee about the good times she'd had there. And where better to spend a glorious sunny long weekend than at a lakeside cottage?

Sandra's hair whipped wildly in the wind as the small boat, with Aimee behind the wheel, raced across the sunlit water. Sandra glanced at the cottages along the treed shoreline. Off to the right, several teenagers enjoyed a large swim raft, some sunning themselves on top while others swam around the edges. Shrieks rang out as the ones in the water splashed the others, then several dove into the lake, probably with revenge in mind.

"Over there." Aimee pointed to a small island beyond the end of the channel where the shores widened. "We're coming up on Silver Lake, and that's the island where the cottage is."

Aimee shared the cottage with her sister. It had belonged to their parents, but they hardly used it anymore and found it not worth the maintenance headache, so they'd given it to their two daughters.

"An island all to yourself. That's pretty cool," Sandra said.

"Well, it's a tiny island, and it's not exactly all to myself.

There is one other cottage, but it's on the opposite shore, so it's pretty private."

Sandra liked that. Aimee had told her there was a lot of waterskiing, canoeing, and other water sports in the main lake, but most people didn't come in too close to the island because of the danger of rocks. There were better places to go in the large lake, so the traffic around them would be practically nonexistent. Sandra enjoyed the idea of a quiet weekend on the water without swarms of people around.

"Do you know the people who own the other cottage?"

"It used to be owned by the Reeds, friends of my parents, but they didn't get up all that often anymore, so they sold it last year. To a friend of their son's. His name's Craig. In fact, I used to date him."

"Oh." Sandra pursed her lips. She didn't think she'd want to date someone she shared an island with. When the relationship ended, things could get dicey.

As the boat approached the island, Aimee slowed down. Sandra spotted a neon orange buoy off to the left, and another couple way to the right. Aimee headed straight ahead toward a wooden dock. A sleek maroon boat was tied on one side of the dock.

"I guess that means someone is at the other cottage this weekend," Sandra said. "So you dated the owner. Is this going to be awkward?"

"No way. Craig and I are still good friends. We dated for a while last summer, but it didn't last long after that. It may not be love, but we get along really well."

Aimee's face lit up with a smile and she waved. Sandra

glanced toward the shore and saw two men walking along the dock, each carrying a tall-necked brown beer bottle in his hand.

"That's Craig," Aimee said. "And that's his friend James."

The way Aimee looked at Craig, Sandra wondered just how well Aimee and Craig got along. Of course, she might just be imagining the hunger in Aimee's eyes, reflecting her own hunger for a strong, sexy man.

"We still run into each other the odd time during the summer and we always have a good time together. You'll like him. James, too."

James, too. Suspicion reared up and Sandra's eyes widened. "You sneak. This is a setup, isn't it."

Aimee grinned. "Well, maybe a little bit. But I just figured it would be a way for you to meet a couple of nice guys in a casual setting. No pressure. And if you decide you don't want to spend time with them, we'll just keep to ourselves."

Yeah, right. No pressure. They were on an *island* together. No other people for miles.

Sandra's gaze locked on the two men standing on the steadily approaching dock. They were both tall, just over six feet, the one with the short, sandy hair slightly taller by about an inch. The dark-haired one wore a shirt draped open, revealing his masculine chest, while the other wore no shirt at all. Sandra couldn't peel her gaze from his tight, sculpted abdominals. She didn't know which one was Craig and which one was James and, quite frankly, it didn't matter. From what she could see, both were drop-dead gorgeous.

Just Sandra, Aimee, and two exceptionally hunky guys

for the entire weekend. Her pulse began to race and tingles danced along her nerve endings. This weekend was going to prove more of a distraction than she had anticipated.

As Aimee brought the boat alongside the dock, the shirtless man with sandy brown hair handed his beer to the other man and grabbed the side of the boat and pulled it closer to the dock. Then he tossed a loop of rope over the cleat on the front of the boat, and hooked it back, neatly tying the boat to the dock. Sandra's gaze fell on the large tattoo of a tiger, which prowled up his right arm and along his muscular shoulder.

"Got a load of stuff, I see." He stepped into the boat and picked up the huge cooler, then hefted it onto the dock.

"Thanks, Craig. This is my friend Sandra. Sandra, this is Craig." Aimee nudged her head toward the other man. "And that's James."

Craig's sandy brown hair was short and straight all over, the spiky tips almost glittering with golden highlights, probably from a lot of time spent in the sun, judging from his dark tan. James had his back to them as he placed the beer bottles on the other side of the dock, but Sandra could see that his dark brown hair was short on the sides and full and wavy on top.

Sandra smiled. "Hi." She grabbed her small wheeled suitcase and lifted it.

James turned around and stepped toward the boat. "Here, let me." He took the bag and placed it on the dock, then offered his hand to help her from the bobbing boat.

Her gaze locked with his as her fingers nestled in the confines of his strong grip. Awareness flashed through her. Of his strong masculine body, his arms and chest bulging with muscles. Of his glittering blue-gray eyes that nonchalantly perused her body. Of the attractive dimple in the center of his chin as he smiled at her.

Her eyes widened as recognition struck.

"James Connor?"

Four

Incredibly sexy, wickedly tempting James from college.

Sandra had spent her entire freshman year trying to ignore her wild infatuation with this man. He had been her lab partner in chemistry, and the chemistry between them had been sizzling. He'd been a constant source of hot sweaty dreams for which she'd felt no end of guilt because she was dating Eric at the time. Had been for five years.

Eric hadn't wanted her to go to college so far from home—so far from him—but she'd assured him she would be true to him. Even though she had kept that promise, she'd always felt guilty about her intense attraction to James. An attraction she'd never forgotten.

James' smile broadened. "Sandra Blair. It's been a long time."

From the heat in his eyes, Sandra could tell he hadn't forgotten, either.

"You two know each other?" Aimee asked.

James still hadn't released Sandra's hand, and the heat

simmering through her at his touch was becoming overwhelmingly distracting.

"We knew each other in college."

Aimee smiled. "Did you guys date?"

He squeezed her hand. "We would have if I'd had my way, but she was dating a boy back home."

"I see." Aimee tossed her duffel bag to Craig, then took his hand as she stepped onto the dock, too. "So you two will have a lot of catching up to do."

"Definitely," said James.

He finally released Sandra's hand, then placed her bag on top of the wheeled cooler. Craig piled Aimee's bag on top of Sandra's, then grabbed the long handle and pulled it along the dock. James retrieved the beers and followed his friend.

Aimee and Sandra fell into step behind him, which gave Sandra an excellent opportunity to notice James' tight, well shaped butt as he walked in front of her. Every bit as gorgeous as she remembered it.

Aimee caught her staring and winked at her, a big grin claiming her face.

The cooler wheels bumped along the uneven ground as Craig dragged it up a well-worn dirt path heading through the trees to the right. After a couple of moments, a cottage came into view: rich stained wood with a deck around two sides, and huge windows overlooking the water. Stairs from the deck led down to a stone patio with a picnic table, and beyond that there was a beach. A hammock hung between two trees off to the left.

Aimee trotted ahead of the men and unlocked the back

door, then they all headed inside. The living area was light and airy, with comfortable chairs and a couch, a full kitchen overlooking the living and dining area, and all of it with a great view of the lake.

James pulled the bags off the cooler and set them near a hallway that probably led to the bedrooms, and Craig dragged the cooler into the kitchen.

"Do you want us to help unpack?" Craig asked.

"That would be great. I'll get Sandra settled in," Aimee said. "Come on. I'll show you to your room."

Sandra grabbed the handle of her suitcase and drew it behind her as she followed Aimee down the hall to a bright bedroom with a double bed, a pine dresser and side tables, and sky blue bedding. A rattan chair and footstool sat by the window where she could relax and read.

"This is really cozy."

"I aim to please." Aimee sat down on the bed. "So what's the deal with you and James? How could you not go out with such a hunk?"

"Like he said, I was already dating Eric."

"You were engaged back then?"

"No, but we promised each other we wouldn't date anyone else."

"So you were celibate all through college?"

"No. I still saw Eric several times each term. And summers, et cetera."

Aimee's eyes widened. "Oh, my God. Is Eric the only guy you've ever been with?"

Sandra nodded. "Pretty much."

"Wow. Well, I think we ought to do something about that." Aimee patted the bed beside her and Sandra sat down.

"You were attracted to James in college, right?" Aimee asked.

"Um. Yeah."

"I mean, from the look on your face when you recognized him, I'm guessing *really* attracted. Right?"

Sandra simply nodded her head.

"Okay, so do you think you and he might . . . I mean, do you think there's the possibility of starting a serious relationship?"

"Oh, no. I mean, he is a really special guy but . . . it's too soon. I haven't even started dating again after my divorce. Jumping right into anything serious wouldn't be a good idea."

Aimee nodded. "Yeah. Okay. That makes sense. Just in case, though, I want to tell you. James and I dated, too."

"You and James?"

"Yeah. Just in case you and he start dating, I want you to know right up front."

Sandra nodded. Aimee had dated James. She had probably gone to bed with him. Her stomach clenched. Of course she'd gone to bed with him. What sane woman wouldn't, given the chance?

Aimee stood up. "Well, I'll leave you to settle in right now. I was going to invite the guys to dinner. That okay with you?"

"Yeah, of course."

She was looking forward to getting to know James again.

Remembering the feel of his hand around hers and the resulting tremors through her body, she realized a part of her hoped that something would happen. After all, it had been a long time since a man had touched her and . . . she'd often dreamed of what it would be like to feel James' arms around her. To feel his lips against hers.

"Aimee?"

Aimee stopped at the door and glanced back. "Yeah, honey?"

"I just wanted to know . . ." She sucked in a deep breath. "What was he like?"

"James?" She grinned wickedly. "He was sensational!"

Sandra finished unpacking her bag, then walked down the hall to the kitchen. The aroma of onions and steak cooking made her mouth water.

"Hey, honey, we're out on the deck." Aimee's voice drifted in from the screen door beside the kitchen.

Sandra glanced outside to see Aimee peering in at her. James stood beside her.

"Grab a beer and join us," Aimee said.

Sandra went to the fridge and pulled out a strawberry beer, then poured it into a glass. She stepped outside into the warm evening. The sun hung low on the horizon. Craig stood at the barbecue, flipping the steaks, still shirtless. Her gaze lingered on the tiger tattoo prowling up his thick bicep and over his broad shoulder. She dragged her gaze away and glanced at

James, who picked up a wooden spoon and stirred the onions and mushrooms sautéing in a pan on a side burner of the fancy barbecue. His open shirt revealed his taut muscles beneath.

She licked her lips, more from the display of delicious male flesh than from the aroma of food. She sipped her beer, then set the glass on the table, which was fully set, including a salad and a basket of bread.

James grabbed the frying pan from the burner and scooped the onions and mushrooms into a bowl, then set them on the table. Craig placed the steaks onto individual plates. Aimee picked up two and brought them to the table, and Sandra grabbed the other two.

They all sat down to enjoy the meal.

"So you're divorced." Craig took a swig of his beer, then set the bottle down.

"That's right." Sandra stabbed a chunk of lettuce in her plastic salad bowl and put it in her mouth.

"I imagine it must be pretty hard to get back into the dating scene after that."

Sandra nodded, then gazed over the lake, as smooth as glass in the calm evening light. A loon let out a mournful cry in the distance.

"Sandra decided to wait a year before she jumped back into the dating game again." Aimee put one arm around Sandra and squeezed her. "So fair warning to both of you. We celebrated the one-year anniversary last week, so this beautiful woman is now available!"

Aimee's enthusiasm made Sandra smile, but her cheeks flushed with heat. She felt like she was about to be auctioned off.

"What do you do, James?" Sandra asked, desperate to change the topic. In college, they'd taken a few electives together, but she couldn't remember his major.

"I'm an industrial engineer. I work for a consulting firm and we do a lot of work for big companies to streamline their operations."

"That sounds interesting."

He smiled. "What do you do?"

"Oh, well, Aimee and I both work in the marketing department of TeleNorth. We work on their Web site."

"Yeah, I do the boring coding part," Aimee said. "Sandra can do that, too, but she's also the artistic one and does all the graphic design."

"What about you, Craig?" Sandra asked, not wanting to leave him out.

He grinned, his brown eyes twinkling. "I'm a construction worker."

Sandra's gaze took in his broad chest and shoulders. She could imagine those muscles bulging and rippling while he swung a huge sledgehammer, his skin glistening with sweat. Her gaze drifted to his hands, wrapped around the brown bottle in front of him. They were big and masculine and she couldn't help wondering what they would feel like touching her body.

Aimee batted his arm and laughed. "Don't listen to

him. He's an architect and he owns his own construction company."

"How long have you and Aimee known each other?" James asked, his gaze on Sandra.

"About a year," Sandra said. "I met her just after my divorce. Eric and I lived in Toronto for most of our marriage, but when we split up, I decided to move back to Ottawa, where I grew up. I met Aimee at work." She took a sip of her beer. "I guess you've both known Aimee for a while."

"We all met up here, actually. About four years ago," Craig said. "Sammie Reed often used to have big parties and barbecues at the other cottage when his parents still owned it. He'd invite people from Beneton Lodge and the surrounding campground. You know, where the marina is. There are a lot of trailers there on a seasonal basis. They're a pretty sociable group."

Sandra wondered what Aimee thought about all kinds of people invading her island.

Aimee laughed. "We had some great times. We should do something like that this summer."

Craig grinned. "That's a great idea."

"What do you think, James?" Aimee asked. "You in?"

"Sure thing." James smiled at Sandra. "But not this weekend."

Sandra stared into his gorgeous blue-gray eyes with the navy ring around the edges, and her breath caught at the heat simmering there.

Sandra pulled on her camisole and loose boxers and climbed into bed. A pleasant breeze wafted in through the screen and the sound of crickets filled the air. Moonlight washed the bed in a soft glow.

She was tired so had finally excused herself to head off to bed since Aimee was a night owl and seemed in no hurry to end the evening.

The sound of the patio door gliding open drifted in from outside, then footsteps along the deck.

"It was really great seeing you again, Aimee." Craig's deep voice came clearly through her open window.

"It was nice seeing you, too."

Silence, followed by a faint sigh, made Sandra's ears perk up. They must be at the end of the deck, which was only about a foot or so from her window, but around the corner. They probably had no idea she could hear them.

"I've missed you. A lot," Craig said. "Are you sure you don't want to come back and join me tonight?"

"I'm tempted, but this weekend is about helping Sandra. If both you and James showed an interest in her, it would build her confidence. I thought you'd find her attractive."

"I do. She's a beautiful woman. So you don't mind sharing me?"

"Oh, do you like the idea of sharing?" Aimee asked teasingly.

Craig chuckled. "If you're talking about a threesome, I'm in."

Sandra's eyes widened and her fingers tightened around the bedclothes. Oh, no. Aimee wouldn't.

"I'm not talking about me and—" Aimee's words were interrupted by the sound of the patio door sliding open.

"Sorry, I'm not interrupting anything, am I?" James asked.

"No, of course not." Aimee's voice moved away as she talked. "I'll walk you to the path."

Sandra could hear footsteps on the wooden steps of the deck.

"Oh, damn," Aimee said.

"What is it?" James asked.

"Sandra's window is open."

Sandra's breathing stopped. Great. Now Aimee knew Sandra had heard their conversation.

"Good night, guys. Thanks for cooking dinner." Aimee's voice grew closer to the cottage.

"No problem," Craig said. "We'll see you tomorrow."

Sandra heard the sliding door glide closed and a click as Aimee locked it. A moment later, she heard a tap on her bedroom door.

"You awake, Sandra?"

For a split second she considered pretending she was asleep, but immediately discarded the idea. "Yeah. Come on in."

The door opened and the light from the hall streamed into the room. Sandra sat up and turned on the bedside lamp.

"You heard?"

Sandra nodded.

"You know, I didn't mean anything by it. I know you can find guys on your own. I . . . just wanted to help."

Sandra nodded. "I know."

Aimee stepped into the room and walked toward the bed. "Are you mad at me?" She sat down beside Sandra.

Sandra smiled. "Of course not." She wrapped her arms around Aimee in a big hug. "You've been a great friend. You've been there for me through the whole aftermath of my divorce. I love that you want to help me out." She released Aimee and smiled sheepishly. "I just hope the guys don't think I'm some kind of pathetic loser." Especially James.

"Are you kidding? You said you heard us outside. Craig is hoping for a threesome."

Sandra rolled her eyes sideways and grinned. "Yeah, well. He's a guy. That goes without saying."

Aimee grinned. "He finds you attractive."

"I'm sure he just said that in hopes of talking *you* into a threesome."

"No way. You're not getting away with that. He found you attractive. And you know James does."

Sandra shrugged, not sure how to accept the compliment.

"You know, since you and James already have the hots for each other, he'd be perfect to . . . you know . . . jump into action with."

Sandra's cheeks burned. "Um, I don't know. I wouldn't feel comfortable just jumping into bed with a guy I haven't seen for more than ten years. It's not even like we've done it before. In fact, we're practically strangers."

"Well, we have three days. You guys can take that time to get to know each other again."

Sandra shook her head. "Not going to happen."

Aimee lifted her feet onto the bed and leaned against the headboard beside Sandra. "You know, that idea about the threesome—"

"Was a joke. I know."

Aimee stared at her for a moment, her eyes entirely too serious. "You know, all those items on the list . . . You've got to admit, those fantasies are hot. You can't tell me you haven't thought about living any of them out."

"Come on, Aimee. You don't really mean to suggest that you and me and Craig—"

"No, honey. I mean you and Craig and *James*."

Sandra's breath caught as shock bolted through her.

But as the blood thundered through her veins, she had to admit that was an inspired idea.

Aimee's face beamed and she leaned closer to Sandra and nudged her arm. "Oh, my God. You're considering it."

"No, I'm not."

"You are, too. Oh, honey, just think how sexy it would be. Two gorgeous guys, both totally intent on giving you pleasure. They'd go for it, you know. I'm sure they would. And since you're on the pill now and the guys have been recently tested, you don't even have to worry about pesky condoms, so if you want to enjoy some water activities—"

"Aimee, stop it. I could never do that."

Sure, she'd gone on the pill again, but that was so she was ready when she met someone. Started dating. Not random sex at the cottage.

Aimee grinned. "Never say never."

"Anyway, you and Craig—"

"Are old news."

"You didn't sound like old news out there when he kissed you."

Aimee's mouth formed an O. "You were watching?"

"No, but sometimes silence speaks volumes. And that silence when he told you he'd missed you . . ." Sandra shrugged.

"Sandra, I really think you should consider a threesome with James and Craig. I know we were letting our imaginations run wild when we wrote that list, but if it's something that turns you on, I think *you* should try running wild for once. And the four of us are alone on this island. No one else would need to know. The guys wouldn't tell anyone." She squeezed Sandra's arm. "And definitely don't let my past relationship with Craig get in the way."

"I can't just have sex with two guys who are practically strangers. It would be hard enough with one—"

"Yeah, it would be *hard* all right."

Sandra ignored Aimee's suggestive comment—and the images of long hard erections that quivered through her mind, sending her hormones swirling.

"I couldn't just go off with both of them."

"Okay, I get it. A threesome is a bit overwhelming. What about something else on the list? Since you keep saying they're strangers, there's always item three. I could tell the guys about the list and—"

"Oh, God, don't you dare."

"You know, they'd totally get it. It's a perfect opportunity."

"Aimee."

Aimee took her hand. "Okay, just think about it."

Sandra shook her head. "You are a total nutcase."

Aimee grinned. "That's why we get along so well."

Five

Craig stared at Sandra over the picnic table, his hands around the beer bottle in front of him. Big masculine hands. She could feel her breasts swell at the need to feel those hands on her breasts.

"Go ahead, Sandra. You know you want to." Aimee, who sat beside Craig, smiled at her with that cute quirky grin of hers, showing the dimples in her cheeks.

"Do what?" Sandra asked.

"This!" Aimee lurched to her feet and ripped open her blouse, revealing round, full, and very naked breasts.

Her big dusky rose nipples puckered as she grabbed Craig's hand and placed it on one of her breasts. Craig wrapped his other arm around her and kissed her, his hand still fondling her breast. James stepped behind Aimee and she drew back from Craig as James' hands curled over her breasts and stroked, then cupped them.

Sandra's breasts ached to be touched like that.

"Go ahead, Sandra." Aimee smiled, then dropped her

head back against James' naked chest and sighed. "It feels so good."

Sandra wanted to. Why shouldn't she?

Somehow both men were naked now. Aimee climbed on top of James' lap, her back to his chest, his hands cupping her breasts. Her hard nipples peeked between his fingers.

The tiger on Craig's arm and shoulder seemed to pulse with life. She wanted to touch it. The picnic table melted away and she stepped toward Craig, then ran her hand along the tiger's back. Although it was tattooed on his skin, it felt like real fur. The animal made a rumbling sound as she stroked. It then prowled over his shoulder and down his chest, toward his rock-hard, fully erect penis. The animal licked the penis, then curled around it as a cat would someone's leg. It licked again, then bounded away.

Sandra's gaze remained locked on that huge cock. Oh, God, she wanted to climb on top of it and ride it until her whole body shattered into a cataclysmic orgasm.

"Do it, honey," Aimee encouraged. She eased herself to her feet and wrapped her hand around James' enormous cock, then held it as she lowered her body onto it.

Her blood boiling inside her, Sandra ripped open her dress and dropped it to the ground. Now she stood totally naked in front of them, her breasts rising and falling with her labored breathing. She stepped forward and wrapped her hand around Craig's big cock. Solid. Rock-hard. She desperately wanted it inside her.

Craig stroked her hair back from her face, then curled his

fingers around her head and drew her toward him. His lips met hers sweetly, with a wonderful tenderness. She closed her eyes and lost herself in the intimate kiss, accepting his tongue inside her mouth, stroking it with her own tongue. His hands covered her breasts and she gripped his shoulders for support.

Yearning soared through her, overwhelming her senses. She pressed her hands on his chest. He lay down and she climbed on top of him. Wrapping her fingers around his hard cock, she positioned herself over him, then she lowered herself down. Oh, God, he felt incredible as he glided into her, penetrating deeply. She rested on top of him, her knees on either side of his hips, and reveled in the feeling of his hardness inside her, stretching her impossibly tight.

Without even moving, her body quivered, close to orgasm already. She raised herself, then lowered again. He wrapped his hands around her hips and rolled her over, then thrust deeply. The trembling in her body increased as pleasure washed through her. He drew back and surged forward again, filling her deeply. She gasped and rode the rising wave. Orgasm was so close.

He drew back and thrust again. She clung to him, then gasped as pleasure catapulted through her. Her whole body trembled and convulsed. As the orgasm claimed her, the feel of Craig's body on hers melted away. She opened her eyes, still quivering in pleasure, and realized she lay in the bed alone.

Another dream. A hot, totally awesome dream!

A tap sounded at Sandra's door.

"Hey, sleepyhead. Can I come in?" Aimee asked through the door.

Sandra glanced around but couldn't see a clock in the room.

"Sure. What time is it?" Sandra asked, her voice scratchy. She cleared her throat as she pushed the covers back and sat up.

"It's eight." Aimee opened the door and entered the room, a bright smile on her face and a steaming mug of coffee in her hand. The aroma tickled Sandra's senses. Mmm, that's what she needed right now. As if reading her mind, Sandra handed her the cup.

"I thought you could use this."

"Thanks." Sandra took the cup and sipped. The coffee had a subtle acidity balanced with the rich flavors of milk chocolate and hazelnuts. Definitely the Mexican blend she'd brought along as part of her contribution to the food this weekend.

"I thought we might go for a swim before breakfast. You game?"

Sandra thought about diving into cold lake water so early in the morning and shivered. She much preferred swimming in a heated pool. "I don't know. How's the water?"

"Invigorating."

Sandra's face puckered. "You mean cold."

Aimee grinned impishly. "Well, you can have a shower instead, but the only one we've got is outside."

Damn. Hose water would be even colder than the lake.

Actually, it would probably be *from* the lake, but she was sure it would feel colder. And she'd have to wear her bathing suit, since she was absolutely not going to shower outside naked.

"Fine, I'll go for a swim."

Aimee patted Sandra's leg. "It's a glorious morning. You'll love it."

"Yeah, sure I will."

Aimee laughed at Sandra's dubious tone.

Sandra loved the outdoors, but she did not love being cold and wet in the morning. She preferred swimming in the afternoon, when the sun was blazing hot.

She took another sip of her coffee, then pushed her feet to the floor.

"Give me ten minutes."

"I'll wait for you on the deck." Aimee left the room.

Sandra opened the drawer and riffled through the contents for her favorite bikini in a tropical floral print of reds, oranges, and greens. She tugged it out, then headed for the bathroom.

Ten minutes later, Sandra followed Aimee along a path through the trees.

"Why aren't we just going to the beach out front?" Sandra had assumed they'd go swimming at the lovely sandy beach only yards from the front of the cottage.

"This place is more private. You'll like it."

The path led them out of the trees to another beach, but here the shore circled around, forming an enclosed bay not visible to the open lake or the other shore. Sunshine glazed the glassy surface of the calm water.

"Isn't it beautiful?" Aimee dropped her straw bag and towel on the beach.

"It is." Sandra set down her towel and untied the sarong she wore over her bathing suit, then laid it on top of the towel.

Out in the middle of the bay was a swim raft with a ladder on one side. She'd love to come out here in the afternoon and swim out to the raft, then lie back and work on her tan.

Aimee untied the belt of her short red terry cloth coverup and dropped the garment on the ground. Sandra's eyes popped open as she realized Aimee wore nothing underneath the robe.

Aimee stepped into the water up to her ankles. "Are you going to join me?"

Sandra stepped into the water, too. It was cool, but not as cold as she'd thought it would be. The long hot days of the past couple of weeks had done a good job warming it up. She waded in to her knees.

Aimee laughed. "I meant why not lose the bathing suit."

Sandra glanced at her uncertainly.

"It's not like there's anyone around, and it really feels great swimming with the water against your bare skin."

Sandra glanced down at her skimpy bikini. "It's not like I don't have a lot of bare skin now."

Aimee waved away her words. "Not the same thing." Aimee waded deeper into the water. "Come on. Give it a try."

Sandra glanced around. It was pretty private here. Reluctantly, she reached around behind herself and unfastened her bikini top. She removed it quickly and tucked it inside her sarong, just in case anyone happened by. *As if that would be my main concern.* She tucked her thumbs under the waistband of her bikini bottoms, but she just couldn't bring herself to do it. Shedding her top out in the open was hard enough.

She turned and raced into the lake, then dove in. Her nipples hardened at the cool water. She swam out until her feet didn't touch the bottom. Aimee swam toward her, then treaded water beside her.

"Nice, eh? There's a big rock over here somewhere that you can stand on." She swam away, then circled around for a bit. "Here it is."

Aimee stood up, revealing her naked breasts above the water, which caressed her hips just below her navel.

"Well, what a beautiful sight."

Sandra sucked in air at Craig's voice. She glanced toward the beach. Both Craig and James stood watching. Rather than diving back into the water, Aimee placed her hands on her hips and posed.

"Well, thank you."

Sandra wanted to cover her own breasts, but she had to tread water. Anyway, the guys couldn't really see her under the surface like this.

"Why don't you gentlemen come and join us?" Aimee asked.

Immediately, Craig tugged on his T-shirt and started pulling it up, but James grabbed his arm.

"Hold on," James said. "What about you, Sandra? Do you want us to join you?"

She glanced at Aimee and licked her lips. It wasn't up to her to spoil her friend's fun. "I . . . uh . . . well, I was just heading back to the cottage so . . . if you'll give me a minute . . ."

"Of course." James nudged Craig with his elbow. "Turn around."

"Huh?" Craig asked, his gaze firmly on Aimee's breasts.

"I said, turn around for a second."

Craig glanced at Sandra, then smiled. "Oh, sure."

Both men turned around. Aimee pushed herself from the rock and swam toward Sandra.

"Listen," she said, when she was close enough that her voice wouldn't carry to the shore, "I'm sorry if I made you uncomfortable. I've got to admit, and I don't know if it's all the fresh air, seeing Craig again, or maybe it's that darned list we made—probably the last—but I really want a man right now. And there are two willing ones right here. You sure you don't want to stay? You probably need this more than I do."

Sandra thought about her dream last night. She definitely needed to get laid, but . . . she couldn't just . . . do it.

Her cheeks flushed and she shook her head. "No, this is not for me, Aimee. I'll just go back to the cottage."

"Aw, honey, I don't want to ditch you like this."

"Don't worry about it. Really."

Aimee swam a little closer. "Listen, I have an idea. I can understand why you might not want to jump in whole-hog. But why don't you . . . you know, watch."

"What?"

"Remember number seven on the list? Or was it eight? Voyeurism. This way you can do something a little risqué, but not stray too far outside your comfort zone."

"Can we turn around yet?" Craig called from the shore.

"I'm going." Sandra turned and swam toward the shore.

"Okay, but think about it," Aimee said, then called to Craig. "Give her another minute."

Sandra's feet touched bottom and she covered her breasts with her hands as she walked toward the shore, even though the men still faced away. She had to walk past them to get to her things and they'd see her in their peripheral vision.

"Um . . . could you guys turn a little more to the left?" Sandra asked.

Craig started to turn toward her.

"No!" she cried. "The other left."

Immediately, he turned the other way. Sandra dashed to her stuff and grabbed her sarong and quickly wrapped it around her body and tied it over her breasts so it formed a strapless dress.

"Okay, you can turn around. I'll just head back now."

The men turned around and James smiled at Sandra. Craig nodded her way, then his gaze spun back to Aimee, who was swimming toward the rock again.

"Hey, guys." Aimee stood up on the rock and waved at them, her wet breasts glistening in the sunshine. "You don't mind if Sandra stays and watches, do you?"

Craig thrust off his shirt. "That's okay with me."

Sandra glanced away as he unbuckled his pants and thrust them down. Seconds later, she heard footsteps splashing through the water, then a bigger splash as he dove in.

Sandra turned and started to walk away.

"Wait, Sandra," James said.

Six

Sandra stopped and glanced around. James picked up something from the sand and held it out to her.

Oh, damn. It was her bikini top. She hadn't noticed it fall on the beach when she'd grabbed her sarong in such a hurry.

She snatched it from him and rolled it in her towel. Her nipples swelled at the thought that he knew she was nearly naked under the thin fabric of the sarong.

"I'll walk back with you, if you want, or . . ."

At his pause, she gazed at his face.

"We could stay and watch," he continued.

She shook her head, her cheeks burning. "No, I . . . uh . . ."

"You know, it might be a good way to ease into the sexual arena again. Watching allows you to participate while keeping a distance. It's not as threatening as getting personally involved."

She turned toward the water and saw Aimee and Craig

locked in a deep kiss, their naked bodies pressed close together. Aimee's full soft breasts crushed against Craig's hard muscular chest, his big arms wrapped around her. The tiger tattoo made his bulging bicep seem even larger. Her insides ached. She wanted to be Aimee. She wanted to feel a man's hard body against hers. To feel his hands stroke every part of her.

She tried to drag her gaze away, but it stuck like glue.

"It's okay," James said. "There's really nothing wrong with watching. They said it's okay and I'm sure it's adding to their excitement." James spread his towel on the sand and sat down, then patted beside him in invitation.

Despite her uncertainty, Sandra sank onto the towel, her gaze locked on the couple on the rock in the middle of the water.

Craig had moved behind Aimee and his hands covered her round breasts. Her nipples peeked from between his fingers as he stroked and squeezed. Sandra's own breasts ached to be touched. She wanted to stroke her nipples. She glanced over at James sitting beside her, also watching the action on the rock, and she itched to reach for his hand and place it on her breast.

Craig lowered himself into the water and swirled around Aimee until he faced her, then he clung to her waist and began to feast on her breasts. Sandra almost moaned at the thought of his hot mouth on her own breast.

"Pretty hot stuff, eh?" James said.

Sandra just nodded. Her breasts pulsed with need. She wanted to slide up beside James, as close as she could get.

To feel his hard thighs next to hers. To climb in his lap and—

He raised his arm, inviting her to scoot closer. She knew exactly what he was hinting at and she hesitated, but she couldn't ignore the burning in her body. As soon as she shifted closer, he took her elbow and guided her in front of him until she sat between his long legs, her back against his solid chest, watching the action. She could feel his bulging erection pressing against her behind. Her breasts ached for his touch, but he simply slid his hands around her waist and watched the couple in the water.

Craig stepped onto the rock and stood up. His raging erection stood tall and proud. Aimee wrapped her hand around it and smiled.

"You've got it bad for me, don't you, sweetie." Aimee stroked that wonderful long cock several times.

Sandra could feel James' cock twitch against her. She couldn't stand it anymore. She stroked her fingers over his hands, then lifted them and placed them over her breasts. His strong fingers closed around her mounds of flesh and she almost moaned at the sublime feeling. Her insides melted and she felt slick moisture between her legs.

Oh, God. She wanted to roll back, strip off her suit, and invite him in. She could just imagine his cock gliding into her. Deep. And so powerful inside her.

Aimee stroked Craig's long cock several times, then she wrapped her lips around him and lowered her mouth over him. Her hands wrapped around Craig's tight butt and squeezed as she bobbed up and down.

James' hands glided under the opening in the front of Sandra's sarong and he found her tight, naked nipples. As he toyed with them, she sucked in air at the exquisite sensations rocketing through her. He smiled at her and nuzzled her neck. She turned her face and he captured her mouth, his lips gentle and coaxing on hers. His tongue nudged between her lips, then glided inside, and all the while his talented fingers stroking her nipples until she nearly gasped for breath.

When he released her mouth, her head fell back against his chest and her gaze drifted back to Aimee and Craig. Craig now stood on the rock and Aimee floated on her back. Craig guided his large cock to her opening and drew her toward him, gliding inside her. Sandra's insides clenched in need.

Aimee wrapped her legs around Craig's waist and he thrust once, then toppled into the water. Both of them went under, then broke the surface, laughing. They swam to the swim raft about twenty yards farther out, then Craig turned his back to the ladder and curled his arms around it, his body still in the water. Aimee wrapped her legs around him, capturing him inside her again, then wrapped her arms around his shoulders.

Sandra could just imagine that long hard cock inside her. Her insides burned with need. She stroked her fingers over the back of James' hand, which still caressed her needy breast, and nudged his hand downward. He got the idea and glided over her stomach, then under the band of her bikini bottoms. As soon as she felt his fingers slide over her slick folds, she moaned, her eyes closing. Her head lolled back against him as he stroked over her slit, then glided inside with two thick masculine fingers.

She arched upward, loving the feel of him inside her. Stroking. Nudging deeper.

"Oh, that feels so good," she murmured.

He nuzzled her neck as he withdrew, stroked her slit, then found the little button hidden in her folds. As he stroked over her clit, she moaned, then in a sudden burst of pleasure gasped and cried out in ecstasy.

The orgasm swept her away, thrumming through her body in a sweep of sweet rapture. As the pleasure ebbed, she found herself sprawled on the towel in front of him. Her gaze snapped to the couple on the swim raft, but they were groaning their own release.

"Oh, my God, I didn't mean to . . ." Her gaze fell on the bulge in James' pants. "I mean, you didn't . . ." She sat up. "I should—"

He stroked her long hair back. "It's okay."

"But you . . ." She reached out her hand, but he caught it before she could stroke his bulging crotch.

"Sandra, it's okay. Really."

Oh, God. She couldn't believe she'd gotten so carried away.

Sandra leaned her elbow on the table and stared out the big window at the sunlight glittering on the lake. Three loons swam along the surface of the calm water. One dipped its head underwater, then smoothly glided beneath the surface. One of the others dunked its head in the water, taking a drink, and the other resurfaced several feet away.

The door opened and Sandra's gaze jerked to the entry. Aimee stepped inside, her dark blonde hair still damp from her escapade in the water.

"Hey there. You disappeared in a hurry." She tossed her bag on the floor, then slumped onto the chair beside Sandra's. "I was glad to see you decided to stick around and watch." She grinned. "Now we can tick number eight off the list."

"Seven," Sandra corrected.

"Okay. That's the spirit." She put her feet up on the chair beside her. "So where is the list anyway?"

"You stuck it on the fridge this morning."

"Oh, yeah." She pushed herself to her feet and retrieved the list, then set it on the round glass dining table. "You're definitely right. Seven it is." She grabbed the pen she'd left on the newspaper crossword she'd been working on that morning and ticked off number seven. "Great. I'm sure you can knock off a few more before we leave."

Sandra groaned. "Are you kidding? I can't believe I did the one."

"Well, in fact, weren't you halfway to doing number three? Not that James is exactly a stranger, and you didn't have a blindfold, but I'll go easy on you and count it if you want."

Sandra glanced at number three. *Make love to a sexy stranger while blindfolded.*

Sandra dropped her face to her hands, covering her burning cheeks.

"Oh, honey. What's wrong?"

"I just . . ." She raised her face and gazed at Aimee. "I can't believe I did that. I hardly know the man and I let him . . . And I didn't even . . . for him, you know?"

"Sweetie, don't worry about that. I'm sure the whole situation is a fantasy come true for him. And if you want to reciprocate, we still have the whole weekend ahead of us."

"Reciprocate? I don't think I can even face him again."

Aimee patted her arm. "You're blowing this way out of proportion. You both got turned on watching Craig and me, and you got caught up in the action. As I said, James was probably thrilled. He understands that you're still a little shy about getting involved in sex again. Don't worry about it."

"Easy for you to say. You're obviously way more comfortable with the situation than I am."

"Listen, honey, I've never done this before, either. Never put on a show before. But I'm comfortable around you and I thought it would help loosen you up a bit."

"Not a great choice of words," Sandra grumbled.

Aimee started giggling. "I didn't mean it that way, but okay. Why don't you let yourself become a loose woman? Just for the weekend. James is terrific. So is Craig. And man, Craig is an incredible lover." She nudged Sandra's elbow. "And James, too. I told you that. Maybe once you get down with the two of them, you'll give me a shot, too. I've never had a threesome, either."

"I can't have a threesome," Sandra said, tight-lipped. "I can't even have a twosome."

Aimee glanced at the list and tapped the pen several times.

"You know what? I have an idea." She pointed at number three with the tip of her pen. "Why not give number three a shot, but in the truest sense?"

"Meaning?"

"Meaning . . . we'll have you approached by a strange man—you won't know who—and he'll initiate sex. I'll take you out in the woods and blindfold you. He'll come up behind you and . . . then you'll do it."

"Out in the woods?"

"Sure. Why not? Or on the beach. Wherever. I'll arrange it."

"So basically, you'll have James or Craig come up behind me—"

"After this morning, it can't be James. He doesn't really count as a stranger now."

"Craig?"

"Okay, now you're just making it hard. The idea is you're not supposed to know who it is."

"Well, it's not hard to figure out that it'll be either Craig or James. They're the only men on this island."

Aimee grinned. "Well, maybe I can change that."

"You're *not* going to bring in a total stranger to have sex with me, just to make the fantasy real."

"Okay, I promise. I won't bring in a total stranger. Now, will you do it?"

Sandra really wanted to have sex, and that taste of a man's

touch this morning made her hunger all the more for the feel of a man deep inside her. But the hardest thing was for her to let go and just let herself be with a man. Maybe Aimee's idea was the best. It made sense that Aimee would ask James to be the one, but then, she might ask Craig instead, just so Sandra wouldn't be sure. The only thing predictable about Aimee was that she could be totally unpredictable.

The thought of James' stealing her away, then undressing her, and caressing her . . . then claiming her body completely, set a fire inside her. Then shivers started when she thought about the fact that she wouldn't know if it was actually James or Craig who would be touching her.

Refusal hung on her lips, but the powerful images burned through her. Her insides felt like a pressure cooker, churning inside. She desperately wanted to have sex. Why was she holding back? It's not like Aimee would tell anyone, and she was sure the guys would be discreet. Aimee would choose well.

"Okay, what the heck."

Devlin peered at the clearing from behind the bushes, holding a long-stemmed yellow rose in his hand. He knew it was Sandra's favorite type of flower. His cock had been hard from the moment he'd received Aimee's call this afternoon.

He'd thrown some things into his small duffel bag and driven up right away, arriving around four. James and Craig had come over to the marina in their boat to pick him up, then they'd had dinner together, giving them some time to get reacquainted. He'd met them at Aimee's cottage a few years ago and tended to see them three or four times during the summer.

Craig had graciously invited him to stay overnight at his cottage and offered to take him back to the marina tomorrow before dinner, all while keeping Devlin's presence hidden from Sandra. The guys were really into the idea of helping Sandra live out the items on her list. Since they knew Devlin was their partner in crime on this endeavor, they'd told him about the goings-on that morning.

The thought of Craig and Aimee having sex while Sandra watched set his groin aching. It turned out that Sandra knew James from college and, as he waited there, he was glad Aimee had asked him to come. While he wanted Sandra to spend a little time living the single life, he figured it was better that he stay within arm's reach. The last thing he needed was her forming an attachment to another guy before he could make his move.

As he watched, Sandra walked into the clearing, then turned and faced the large rocks as Aimee had instructed her to do.

He'd sworn to himself that he would wait for Sandra. Give her time to go out on a few dates, maybe even experiment with sex a little, if that's what she needed, before he got romantically involved with her, but Aimee's suggestion that he play out the sex-with-a-stranger fantasy revved his engine beyond clear thought. It did make sense, though.

He'd be able to be the first man she had sex with after her divorce, which totally appealed to him. And he would be helping her live out one of her fantasies.

And his own!

Devlin ensured his mask was firmly in place. Although, if all went as planned, she would never actually see him, he didn't want to take any chances. He'd even secured his hair under a light knit hat. If she saw or felt his hair, which was longer than both the other men's, she'd figure out who he was immediately.

He stepped out from the bushes and approached her from behind.

Seven

Sandra could hear him approaching, but she did not turn around. Excitement skittered along her nerve endings. His arm curled around her waist and he drew her back against his solid chest. He held a yellow rose in front of her. She loved yellow roses. A note was attached, which read: *I am your fantasy stranger.* She took the rose from his hand and pressed it to her nose. Her eyes closed as she breathed in the sweet fragrance.

"It's beautiful."

She knew he wouldn't say anything. That was part of the arrangement, to keep his identity secret. He slipped a piece of black cloth across her eyes, then tied it behind her head, leaving her in total darkness. Then he took her hand and led her away. It was strange walking through the woods with no idea where she was going. Having to trust this stranger completely.

The ground changed beneath her feet. Became softer. Sand.

They walked a little farther, then he stopped. His arms encircled her and he drew her close to his body. His lips met hers in a sweet, gentle kiss. His hand stroked across her cheek, then he cupped her head and deepened the kiss, his lips moving on hers with more urgency. This was so totally hot, so totally wild . . . not knowing who this man was yet being held by him, kissed by him. And knowing how much more would happen between them very soon.

His tongue pushed between her lips and she sucked it deep into her mouth, urged on by her deep consuming need. He groaned and stroked his hands along her back as he devoured her mouth. She arched her body, crushing her breasts against him, driving her arrowlike nipples into his chest.

Emboldened by the anonymity of her blindfold, she grabbed the hem of her camisole and tugged it over her head, then unsnapped the front clasp of her bra and peeled it away. She couldn't see his expression, but she could feel his hot gaze on her. Admiring.

At least, that's what she imagined.

His hands cupped her and she sighed with delight at the feel of his big warm hands covering her breasts. Were these Craig's big hands? Touching her just as she'd imagined?

His mouth covered one taut nipple and she moaned in pleasure. She dragged her hand down his taut stomach to the bulge in his pants, then stroked over it. She fidgeted with the button and succeeded in unfastening it. Next, her fingers found the zipper tag and she tugged it down, then slipped her hand inside his pants and found the prize. His big thick cock. Oh man, it was huge. She wrapped her fingers around it and drew it free.

She ran her hand up his body to his cheek, found his lips, and kissed him again. Then she nuzzled down his neck. She released buttons on his shirt with her free hand, still gripping his big cock in her other hand, and kissed down his bare chest. Once she reached his navel, she dipped her tongue inside, then she sank to her knees and wrapped her other hand around his cock, too.

"It's so lovely and big. I wish I could see it." She grinned. "I am definitely going to taste it." She leaned forward and found the tip of him with her mouth. She kissed and explored the tip of his cock with her lips, then lapped at him with her tongue.

"Mmm. Delicious."

Leaning closer, she opened her lips and took his whole cockhead inside. It filled her mouth. It was so big. So hard. And she wanted to suck him until he exploded in her mouth.

Her stranger's hands tucked around her head and stroked her hair. She swirled her tongue under the crown as her hands stroked his shaft. Sucking on his cockhead, she tucked one hand under his balls and cradled them in her palm while stroking her thumb over the tight spot behind his balls.

He groaned and drew back a little.

She released his cock. "I want to make you come. Like this. Please don't hold back."

She swallowed him again, then dove as deep as she

could, taking at least half his lengthy cock into her mouth. She squeezed as she drew back, then sucked as she stroked that sweet spot behind his balls. She bobbed up and down, squeezing and sucking, determined to make him come. He stiffened, then groaned. Hot liquid filled her mouth as he erupted.

Once he was done, she smiled. He drew her to her feet and kissed her, his lips moving on hers with passion, yet at the same time she could sense a deep tenderness.

When he drew back, she gripped his shirt on both sides and pulled him back for another kiss, driving her tongue deep into his mouth. He sucked on it, pulling it even deeper. Once he released her, they both gasped for air.

She unfastened her jeans and pushed them to the ground, then stepped out of them. Dragging her hands up her body, she smiled. She cupped her breasts and squeezed, then toyed with her nipples, feeling intensely wicked but courageous, given she couldn't see him at all. That gave her a certain freedom.

"I want you to fuck me." Oh, the coarse words made her blood boil.

He dragged her against his body and captured her lips in a breathtaking kiss. His arm scooped under her legs and he swept her up, then she felt herself lowered onto the ground. Something soft. An air mattress?

She lay back, her head on a pillow. Man, he'd thought of everything. His fingers hooked in her panties and they slipped away. She heard the rustling sounds of him fumbling with his clothes and them falling to the ground. A second later, he parted her legs and his mouth teased along her inner thighs. Then he covered her. His tongue dragged along her damp slit . . . then grazed over her clit. She arched upward, pushing herself against his mouth. He drew her legs farther apart, tucking her knees over his shoulders, then began to feast on her in earnest.

His tongue dipped inside her, followed by his fingers. One. Then two. He licked upward and his tongue found her clit again. As his fingers stroked inside her, he licked her clit, then began to plunder it. The dual sensations fueled her rising excitement. Pleasure swamped her senses, rising as he continued to stroke and tease.

"Oh, God. That's . . . Oh, it feels so good." She wrapped her hands around his head—covered by a knit hat—and held him close to her.

He sucked on her clit as his fingers worked inside her. Waves of pleasure pummeled through her and—

She gasped, then moaned as she plummeted headlong into an intense orgasm. He kept sucking and stroking as she rode the wave to incredible heights . . . then slowly floated back to earth.

She lay back, gasping for air.

"That was . . . oh, so good."

He lay down beside her and cradled her against his body.

"Hey, Stranger Man, that was good, but we're definitely not done yet." She grasped in the darkness until she found his cock, which was rock-hard and ready to go. "I want some of this."

He stroked her cheek, and she paused at the incredible tenderness. He kissed her. Sweetly. Lovingly.

His touch, his tenderness, made her heart ache. She felt a deep connection with him, something she hadn't expected. It was only supposed to be about the sex. Sex with a stranger.

But it felt good. And she wanted him.

"Fuck me," she murmured, needing to lighten the mood. "Slide that big cock of yours inside me and trigger some fireworks."

He nuzzled her ear, then shifted sideways. Then he was over her. Something hot and hard brushed her thigh, then glided along her slit.

"That's right, Fantasy Man. Give me all you've got."

With that, he drove forward, his thick long cock thrusting deep inside her. Stretching her. Filling her impossibly full. She clung to his shoulders as he lay still, his cock fully embedded inside her. It twitched and she groaned. It was incredibly erotic.

Oh, God, I don't even know who this is, yet his cock is inside me and, any second now, I'm going to come. Again.

He drew back and drove forward again. She hung on to his shoulders. When he drove forward the next time, she arched to meet him. His cock dragged along her inner passage, sending thrilling sensations bursting inside her. She squeezed him and he thrust faster. Deeper. Harder.

"That is so . . . oh. So good."

He thrust again, then swirled. She gasped. Deep. He swirled. She felt light-headed. Her nerve endings seemed to quiver with electricity. He drove harder. Faster. Tremors raced through her. Her heightened senses exploded in a surge of intense pleasure. Joy rushed through her and she clung to him, gasping in air, then wailing as a potent orgasm claimed her. Body and soul.

He exploded, groaning as he pumped inside her, intensifying her pleasure.

Finally, they both collapsed in complete and utter satisfaction.

As she snuggled against him, he stroked her cheek, holding her tight to his body with his other arm. Then he kissed her cheek gently.

She never wanted this moment to end. Held in this stranger's arms, in the afterglow of their intense lovemaking.

She desperately wanted to take off this blindfold and find out which man it was.

But she wouldn't. She'd promised. And she didn't want to do anything to ruin this moment.

Sandra yawned as she trod down the hall toward the kitchen, tying her robe as she walked.

"Good morning." Aimee, sitting at the dining table, smiled as she looked up from her book. "There's coffee made."

Sandra poured herself a cup and sat down beside Aimee, wondering if her friend would ask her about her adventure last night. But Aimee simply sipped her coffee, then put her book down and went to the sink to rinse out her mug.

"I thought I'd go for a swim again this morning. I figure you'd probably want to skip it today."

"Oh, why do you think that?"

Did Aimee think she still regretted yesterday morning's playing? After making wild and passionate love with James—or Craig—last night, she'd totally shed her qualms about yesterday morning. She felt more adventuresome. More accepting of her sexual self.

Aimee smiled. "Well, I'm not asking about last night, but . . ." She walked across the kitchen and picked up something from the counter.

A long-stemmed yellow rose, just like the one sitting in the bud vase by her bed right now—given to her by her fantasy man.

"This was waiting outside the door this morning." Aimee handed her the rose, which was wrapped in clear cellophane and tied with a yellow satin ribbon. It even had a little water reservoir on the bottom of the stem to keep it fresh.

"Ohhh. It's beautiful." Sandra's face broke into a broad smile as she took the flower and sniffed the lovely fragrance.

"Hmm. I'd say things went really, *really* well last night." Aimee grinned. "But I'm not asking."

"That's good. Because I'm not telling."

Aimee laughed heartily. "You've got to be kidding. Your face is telling everything." She turned and sashayed toward the hallway. "By the way, don't forget to read the note."

Sandra hadn't noticed the small pastel yellow envelope attached to the ribbon. She drew out the card. White with a fancy little heart in the top corner.

Time for item eight? Use the shower outside and I'll admire you from afar.

Fantasy Stranger

Her gaze darted from the card to the list still attached to the front of the fridge. She couldn't read it from here, but she could tell by the shape and length of the words what number eight was. Exhibitionism. That was one Aimee had added, and she'd done a fine job of it herself yesterday.

Aimee returned with a towel and headed toward the door. "I'll be gone for an hour or so."

"Um, Aimee?"

"Yeah, hon?"

"The shower you told me about . . . the one outside?"

"Yeah?"

"Is it usable?"

"Of course. Just be careful of the temperature. My sister sets the hot water heater at max, so you could scald yourself if you're not careful."

"Hot? I thought it would just be hose water."

"Are you kidding? When my parents built this place, they knew my sister and I would track sand in from the beach, so Dad decided to put the shower outside. He also knew there was no way we'd use it if it was cold. We loved it. We could take a shower with our bathing suits on." She grinned. "But don't worry, there's a shower curtain you can pull around for privacy."

Too bad Sandra hadn't asked yesterday instead of just

assuming. Of course, if she had, she would have missed her sexy morning adventure on the beach. Which had led to her totally sensational adventure last night.

"Okay, thanks."

Aimee walked to the door, then turned around again. "Does this have anything to do with the note your fantasy man sent you?"

Sandra sniffed her rose again. "Umm. Maybe."

"Okay, then." Aimee walked to the table and picked up her book. "Maybe I'll stay out a little longer. I wouldn't want to rush you." She grinned. "The shower is just out the side there." She pointed to the wall opposite the sliding door.

Sandra watched Aimee stroll to the door and step out onto the deck.

"See you later," Aimee said, a little loudly, as she closed the door, then she disappeared down the steps.

Sandra leaped to her feet and raced into her bedroom, then pulled off her pajamas and tossed them on the bed. She glanced toward the dresser, thinking about her royal blue satin robe, but she'd left it at home. All she had here was her serviceable, but definitely not sexy, mint green terry robe.

She could put on her bikini and . . . what? Shower in her bathing suit like Aimee when she was a little kid? Or do a striptease by taking it off under the shower? Well, that could work, but knowing her, she'd fumble with the clasps and totally wreck the erotic mood.

And the whole thought of showering—fully naked—in front of her Fantasy Stranger while he watched from a secret place was beyond simply erotic. Wild and tumultuous sensations surged through her body. Her breasts ached and her insides melted into a gooey mess, need thrumming through her. It was all she could do to stop herself from dropping to the bed and getting herself off right now.

Who knew I'd be so turned on by the thought of showing off my body to a man?

Then she thought about the list. *Well, Aimee, for one.* That woman had amazing instincts.

Sandra grabbed her fuchsia floral beach towel and wrapped it around her naked body, then pushed her shoulders back and headed for the door. Seconds later, she stepped outside into the bright morning sunshine, greeted by the cheerful twitter of birds. Sandra walked down the wooden steps and headed to the opposite side of the cottage.

As soon as she turned the second corner, she saw it. A section of the cottage wall was done in slate, with a cedar platform only a few inches above the grass extending outward, a cedar bench against the wall, and a rainwater showerhead above. An earth-tone shower curtain hung on a curved rod, forming an extended half circle.

Devlin heard the sliding door open and stood up, his presence obscured by the bushes. Aimee had told him Sandra usually got up around ten o'clock, so he'd arrived at nine-thirty and had been reading for about an hour. Aimee had left a few moments ago, so he'd put aside his book to await Sandra's arrival.

He watched as Sandra stepped around the corner of the cottage, the morning sun glistening on her long black hair.

She wore only a bright-colored beach towel wrapped around her body. No straps over her shoulders. Was she wearing a strapless bathing suit beneath the towel or nothing at all? His heart rate quickened at the thought of her naked body covered only by the towel.

Soon he would see her naked again. Last night had been incredible, making love to her for the first time. Seeing her naked body, touching her intimately. Hearing her moan with the pleasure he gave her. He had ached to tell her who he was, for her to know it was him making love to her. But that would have ruined everything. He needed to stay focused on the plan so he could ultimately win her heart. Not just be a short-term affair.

Sandra glanced around, wondering if her Fantasy Stranger was already nearby. What if he wasn't? There was no way she could know. Except for the hot prickle down her spine. It didn't matter whether it was her imagination or an actual sense of the man's presence. It made her feel sexy and wicked. Because he knew why she was here.

Clinging to her towel, she walked toward the wooden platform, then stopped just before stepping onto it. Remembering what Aimee had said about the water, she reached across to the tap marked with red and turned it. Feeling his gaze on her, she felt the water until it ran warm, then turned on the cold-water tap, adjusting it until she got the temperature just right.

She turned her back to the cottage and her gaze trailed along the thick wild bushes. The thought that he was out there, watching her, sent tingles through her. She drew in a deep breath, then with a dramatic sweep of her arms opened the towel, revealing her totally naked body.

At first, her skin danced with goose bumps. She knew she could just step into the shower to heat up, but she wanted to linger here a little longer.

To let him see her.

Eight

Devlin sucked in a breath when Sandra flung open the towel. Oh, God, she was beautiful. Her full round breasts stood firm and proud, the dark rose nipples puckering into tight nubs. He dragged his gaze down to her waist, so slim, then down the gentle slope of her hips. Her thick black pubic curls had been trimmed to an adorable little heart shape.

She didn't immediately step under the water. Instead, she raised her arms and stretched them behind her head, pushing her naked breasts forward. Her puckered nipples pointed straight toward him. She flipped her long hair over her shoulders, then lowered her arms, looking exceptionally sexy and feminine. His gaze strayed down her body as she turned around and stepped onto the wooden platform. Water streamed over her hair and back, and her delightfully round derriere, glazing her body in moisture. Teasingly, she dragged her fingers along the edge of the shower curtain, toying with it as if she were going to pull it around.

Would she do that to him? Tease him with such a sensational display of her naked body, only to hide it behind a curtain while she showered?

But she released the curtain and turned around, a smile lighting her face.

The water flowed over her body, as if caressing her. He remembered the feel of her soft skin when he'd caressed her last night. Of his fingers stroking over her breasts, then inside her. His tongue gliding over her private folds.

Her hands caressed her breasts, stroking in circles. Her nipples peeked out between her fingers as she caressed those beautiful breasts, then squeezed. He longed to touch them, to take the hard nipples in his mouth and tease them until she moaned out loud.

She ran her hands down her stomach, then over her hips. His gaze strayed to the little black furry heart, but she turned around. His disappointment quickly dissipated as her hands stroked over her buttocks, then she bent at the waist and touched the ground, allowing him a great view of her sensational ass.

Still bent at the waist, she widened her legs and his hormones jumped into overdrive at the sight of her intimate folds, water sluicing over them. So wet and inviting. He quivered as she stroked her fingers along her calves, then continued up her inner thighs. He had to stop himself from striding up behind her, then reaching around and cupping her wonderfully soft breasts while he pushed his hard, aching cock into her wet opening.

He wrapped his hand around his rigid shaft, desperately wanting to feel her heat enveloping him.

Sandra was sure she could feel the heat of her Fantasy Stranger's gaze on her. Touching herself like this in front of him made her feel wicked. And sexy.

Slowly, she stood up, then turned around, her shoulders back, displaying herself proudly. Was he turned on watching her? Was his big cock long and hard? Was he touching it?

His invisible touch seemed to burn through her. She ached with need. Wanting to feel his cock. Wanting it to glide deep inside her. Just like last night.

Remembering the glorious sensation of his huge cock stretching her slick passage, she ran her hand over her stomach, then lower. She stroked her fingertips through the small patch of damp curls, then lower. Her other hand stroked up her wet body to her breast. She squeezed the tight nipple, almost gasping at the intense sensation, remembering his mouth covering her. Sucking on her hard nub.

The fingertips of her other hand stroked along her slit, sending quivers through her. On shaky legs, she backed up a few inches and sat down on the cedar bench. Wanting to give him a better view, she spread her knees wide as she stroked her intimate folds. Heat careened through her.

What if he came bounding out of hiding and dragged her into his arms? His cock would be hard, extending upward. He could drive it into her in one long stroke.

She would so love to feel that right now.

The water poured over the front of her body in thick drops as she stroked faster, her fingers quivering. Then she drove a finger inside. Her head fell back against the slate as pleasure surged through her. Her thumb found the little button tucked in her folds and she teased it.

Oh, God, it felt so good. She squeezed her nipple. At the intense sensation, she pinched it harder, then stroked between her legs faster. She closed her eyes, remembering her Fantasy Stranger pressing his cock to her opening while she'd lain beneath him, blindfolded. His cock had pushed into her, stretching her with its girth.

She gasped as blissful sensations shot through her. She moaned, long and deep, as the orgasm erupted inside her. Hot. Fast. Intense.

Devlin's gaze remained glued to Sandra as her fingers pulsed into her intimate folds. His cock, engorged, close to bursting, filled his hand as he stroked it. God, she was such an incredibly sexy woman. He wanted her so badly.

She gasped, then moaned, her face a picture of ecstasy as the orgasm washed through her. His groin tightened and then he groaned quietly as he felt the release, hot liquid gushing from him.

Sandra's hands stilled and she sucked in air. Oh, wow. That had been incredibly sexy. She never would have thought showing off her body like that would be so wildly erotic. She didn't even know for sure who her Fantasy Stranger was, yet knowing he'd watched her touching herself . . . *arousing* herself . . . had been an intense aphrodisiac.

She felt wicked and extremely sexy.

Was he still out there watching? Her hand glided leisurely up her body, then cupped her breast. Had he come when she had?

She hoped so.

She thought she'd heard a groan in the bushes, but it might have been her imagination.

She drew in a deep breath. Slowly, she stood up, her knees still a little shaky.

One thing was for sure, this weekend had changed the way she looked at sex.

Sandra sat on the deck in her bikini, stretched out on a lounge chair, staring over the water, her book by her side. She'd tried reading, but delicious thoughts of a sexy stranger kept distracting her. Finally she'd abandoned the book to enjoy the heat of the sun on her body and the gorgeous surroundings.

"Hey, you look pretty relaxed." Aimee walked up the steps, finally returning from her morning swim.

Sandra wondered if that swim had been with Craig, including a repeat performance of yesterday morning's activities on the swim raft.

Assuming, of course, that Craig wasn't Sandra's Fantasy Stranger. Which she was pretty sure he wasn't. She had a strong feeling it was James.

"The fellows suggested we go to their place for dinner tonight. That okay with you?"

Sandra smiled. "That would be great."

She really wanted some time with James. She had yearned

for him for such a long time. It had been excruciating when she'd been in college. Wanting him. Wishing they could be together. And feeling terribly guilty about that wish.

Now she was single, exploring her sexuality, and she had the opportunity to satisfy the intense craving she'd had for him for so long.

She might have already made love with him as her Fantasy Stranger, but she wasn't sure. And no matter what, she wanted to experience his lovemaking face-to-face. Especially after this morning. She'd reached orgasm, but it wasn't the same as being touched by a man. Having his cock deep inside.

Her internal muscles tightened at the thought and her insides ached.

"You want a drink?" Aimee asked.

"Sure. How about one of those hard lemonades?"

"That's a great idea." Aimee slid open the door and went inside, then returned a moment later with two bottles of pink liquid and handed one to Sandra. Aimee sat down and took a sip, then set hers on the table between their chairs, a quirky grin on her face.

"What?" Sandra asked.

"I noticed another item checked off the list."

"Yeah, well." Sandra sipped the tart liquid, feeling the burn of the alcohol as she swallowed, then shrugged lightly. "So the list wasn't such a bad idea after all."

"Hmm. So you ready to tackle item four?"

A threesome

"Uh, no. I think two men is a little over-the-top for me right now, but . . ."

"Yeah?" Aimee's grin broadened. "What?"

"Maybe one guy . . . tonight . . . would be . . ." Goose bumps quivered along her arms. "Kinda great."

"You got it. You pick one and I'll keep the other one occupied."

Sandra laughed. "Don't you care which one?"

Aimee smiled and shook her head, her short layered blonde hair fluttering. "Nope. They're both great-looking. And they're both"—she held her hands about a foot apart and grinned—"big."

Sandra's eyes widened. "Really?" She nibbled her lower lip as she toyed with the label on her bottle. "So . . . which one is bigger?"

"Well, that would be Craig."

Sandra remembered her Fantasy Stranger's huge cock stretching her as it glided into her. Since that was probably James, she wondered just how big Craig's cock must be.

Man, had she been missing out!

After dinner, Sandra and James went out on the deck to watch the sunset. The sky flamed with rich gold, orange, and red, setting the placid water ablaze with color. They sipped their wine as they watched the colors slowly fade, giving way to darkness.

"Where do you live these days?" she asked.

James had asked her a lot about herself over dinner, but she hadn't found out much about him. And she wanted to learn all about him.

"I live on the east end of the city, in that new development out by the river."

"That's a nice area." And it was only about an hour from her place.

The moonlight glimmered on the water and crickets chirped.

"I love it there. I've got a big backyard and a beautiful view of the river out the back of my place. Also, there's this great park nearby. I'm into radio-controlled airplanes, which I design and build myself, and on the weekends I often take them out there with a few of my buddies. I fly the real thing, too. I just got my pilot's license last year."

He'd said he was an engineer, so it made sense he'd like gadgets, but it amazed her that he could design and fly airplanes. She pictured herself in the cockpit with him, looking down at the world below as they jetted off for a weekend getaway.

He smiled. "Maybe you'll come out and join me sometime. I'll teach you how to fly—the big planes or the small ones. Whichever one's your speed."

"That would be great."

She took another sip of wine and they stared over the water for a bit. She felt a little awkward, like she was on a first date, and she hadn't dated for a long, long time. James seemed quite comfortable with the silence, but to her it dragged on and on.

"So what else have you been up to since college?" she finally asked.

"Me?" He grinned. "Pining after the woman who got away."

More like learning how to be an incredible flirt. Not that she minded. If anything, she was enjoying the attention. She laughed. "So did you ever get married?"

He stared at his glass for a few moments. "No. I came close once, though. We went out for about four years, even talked about marriage." His leaned back on the deck chair and stretched his legs out in front of him. "But when it came right down to it, I couldn't imagine spending the rest of my life with her. We had great chemistry, and we had a lot in common, but it just didn't feel like that was enough."

"Why?" She wished she had been so astute before falling into marriage with her ex.

He shrugged. "I don't know exactly, but she felt it, too. We had a long talk about it. We're still friends. Actually, after we ended it, she met someone else, and two years later they got married. I guess we just weren't meant to be together."

"So you believe there's one right match for every person?"

"Not necessarily one. Maybe there's more than one person we can make a life with, but I think when you meet one of those special people, you'll find a deeper connection."

She stiffened a little.

He chuckled. "Don't panic. I know you're not looking for a relationship right now. I'm happy to keep it casual. Just take time to get to know each other again."

The heat of his gaze warmed her. There were definite possibilities here.

He stood up and took her hand, then drew her to her feet and led her to the edge of the deck. "It's a beautiful evening. Look at that water."

Leaning against the wooden railing of the deck, Sandra glanced across the lake, the moonlight illuminating the glassy surface. Crickets chirped merrily in the background and the stars shone brighter than she'd ever seen them in the city. A soft breeze brushed lightly across her arms and a scattering of goose bumps danced across her skin, but the latter was because of her intense awareness of James beside her, his tall, masculine physique so close to her. She sipped her wine.

"It is a beautiful view," she said.

But not as beautiful to her as James, who was so sexy. So incredibly male.

She set her wineglass on the flat top of the railing and glanced up at him, her gaze catching his. His intense blue-gray eyes glittered in the moonlight and her heart skipped a beat. Not only was he an amazingly sexy man but he was also so understanding and easy to talk to. A lot like Devlin in that way.

But she wanted more from James than friendship right now. Her insides quivered as she thought about him kissing her. Stroking her. Making love to her.

She wanted him to tear off her clothes and ravish her. She wanted to feel him inside her. To gasp as he thrust into her and drove her to ecstasy.

As if he could read her thoughts, his eyes darkened and his lips lowered, brushing hers lightly at first, then his arms wrapped around her and he drew her against him. She kissed him back, hungrily, wanting to be closer than she could possibly get. She pressed her body tight to his and thrust her tongue into his mouth. He groaned, then tightened his arms around her, crushing her to his body. Her nipples ached with need as they thrust into his chest. She could feel a bulge growing through his jeans, pressing into her belly. She wanted to touch it. Oh God, she *needed* to touch it.

Their lips parted and their gazes locked. He searched her eyes, clearly worried he'd gone too far. But couldn't he tell how much she wanted him? She brushed her lips against his briefly, then grabbed her glass and gulped the rest of the wine before setting it down again. The heat washed through her, boosting her courage.

She rested her hand on one of his shoulders and ran her fingertips along his cheek, then down his square jaw. She kissed the dimple on his chin, then nibbled the slightly raspy texture of his jaw. She pushed herself on her tiptoes and nuzzled his neck, then pressed her lips near his ear.

"I am *very* turned on. I really want you."

"Sweetheart, the feeling is definitely mutual." He drew her close again and captured her lips. "Do you want to go inside? To my room?"

She thought about going back into the cottage. Facing Aimee and Craig, then scooting away to James' room. She felt hot and sexy now. She was afraid the interruption would ruin that. Maybe steal away her courage. She'd waited so long, and everything was so perfect right here. Right now.

"No, I want to stay here."

James grinned. "Why you little scamp. You like the idea we might be caught."

She glanced toward the sliding glass door. She couldn't see Aimee and Craig inside. They were probably sitting on the couch. Probably in a clinch.

"It's not that. I just don't want to ruin the mood." But was that all it was? With all the talk of watching, and being watched . . . What if Aimee and Craig were watching them right now? There was a certain thrill at the thought of the other couple seeing them. Watching them while they kissed. And more.

Especially if she was wrong about James being her fantasy stranger. If it was really Craig . . . the thought of him seeing her with James had a strange and definitely sexy effect on her.

His mouth widened into that sexy broad smile of his, showing even, white teeth. "Whatever you want, sweetheart, you've got it."

She stroked her hands over his shoulders and down his chest, heat thrumming through her at the feel of his hard muscles beneath her fingers. "What I want is"—she leaned in and kissed his chin—"to touch you."

"Go for it, sweetheart."

Sandra pressed him backward until his back was against the wooden wall of the cottage. She drew her hands down his chest, over his abs. She could feel the hard rippled muscles through his fine cotton shirt. She passed his belt, then stroked over the impressive bulge in his chinos. The feel of his hard erection under her palm thrilled her. She had touched her Fantasy Stranger like this. Felt his hard cock in her hand.

Was James the same man?

A compulsive craving shattered her control and she squeezed him, then dropped to her knees and tugged down his zipper. She reached inside the cotton twill fabric and through the slit in the front of his underwear until she felt his hard, naked shaft.

Oh, God, it felt so good. Hot. Rock-hard.

He wanted her.

And that was a huge boost to her confidence.

She freed him from the cotton prison and stared at the broad mushroom-shaped head of his impressively long cock. She stroked her finger over the tip, then around the underside of the corona, admiring him. She hadn't seen her Fantasy Stranger. She couldn't tell if James was him or not.

She leaned forward and licked under the edge, then upward, the tip of her tongue stroking over his cockhead. She swirled around the small opening, then opened her mouth and took his large cockhead inside her mouth.

His fingers stroked through her hair.

"Aw, damn. Sweetheart, that's fabulous."

His encouraging words boosted her confidence even more. She sucked. He groaned.

Oh, God, she wanted to make him come.

She pressed her tongue against him, squeezing him against the roof of her mouth, then she glided down. His broad head pushed deeper into her mouth.

"Sweetheart, that feels so good." He stroked her hair, his touch sending quivers through her.

She glanced up at him and caught a glimpse of his eyes, half closed, full of desire. She sucked on him while she stroked up and down his shaft with her hand. He tipped his head back and his cock twitched in her mouth. She glided up, freeing more of his shaft to her hand, then down again.

"I'm so close. Maybe I should—"

Gazing up at him, she asked, "Are you really going to come?"

"If you keep that up, yes."

She smiled, then squeezed his rock-hard cock in her hand. "Bring it on."

She swallowed his cock again, then moved up and down, taking him a little deeper this time, and squeezing his hard flesh inside her mouth.

"Oh . . . God . . ."

He tensed and suddenly she felt a stream of hot liquid fill her mouth. Elated, she sucked harder. He pulsed and pulsed. Then he slumped back against the cottage wall. She released him, a big smile on her face.

"Man, sweetheart, that was incredible."

She stood up and pressed against him, her smile still stretching her face wide. "Thank you."

She captured his lips, hotter than ever. He embraced her and his tongue glided into her mouth and explored thoroughly. Intense need pummeled through her. Her nipples, hard and puckered, pushed against his hard chest. Every movement caused friction and sent her hormones swirling into overdrive.

She drew back, breathing heavily.

"God, I am so turned on." She took his hand, desperate to feel his touch, and pressed it against her needy breast.

"I can tell."

She grabbed the hem of her tank top and tugged his hand underneath, so there would be less fabric between them.

"Make love to me. Now."

He kissed her, then grabbed her hand and tugged her with him along the deck, away from the sliding doors. He led her around the corner of the cottage, then down the stairs. A wooden picnic table sat on the stone patio beside the building. Although it could be seen from the kitchen window, it was not visible from the living room, where Aimee and Craig probably still sat, immersed in each other. And the kitchen light was off. Of course, they could still be watching, and that possibility actually added to Sandra's excitement.

This whole idea of the list had turned on some eager adventurer inside her.

She stripped off her jeans and her tank top and sat on the picnic table, her feet on the bench seat. James' eyes glittered as she reached behind her and unfastened her bra. She stripped it off, then tossed it onto the table beside her.

"You are gorgeous." He stood in front of her and reached for her breasts reverently. His hands covered her hot mounds and her nipples pressed into his palms.

She almost groaned in need. He stroked her for a few

moments, then he knelt on the bench seat and licked the tip of her hard nipple. Intense pleasure rippled through her.

"Oh, yes." She stroked her fingers through his dark wavy hair and held him close.

He sucked. Tingles danced through her, right to her core, and she moaned. He moved to her other nipple and sucked, sending her head spinning, while he stroked her abandoned, wet nipple with his hand. Her insides tingled with need. She felt the wetness pooling inside her.

She released his head and tucked her fingers under the elastic of her panties and wriggled as she shifted them downward, still under the onslaught of his talented mouth. Still sucking her hard nub in his mouth, he stroked down her stomach and between her legs. When his fingers glided along her slit, she moaned.

He released her nipple and grinned at her. "You do want me."

"Oh, God, yes." She stroked over his pants, then grabbed his cock. "Right now."

He shifted to his feet while her hand continued to stroke his long cock.

"Well, a gentleman never keeps a lady waiting."

He pressed his hands to her waist and turned her ninety degrees. Her legs dangled over the edge of the table and he pulled her panties the rest of the way off, then stepped toward her, positioning himself between her thighs.

She sucked in a deep breath. This was really going to happen. The first time she'd made love with a man . . . at least, face-to-face . . . for well over a year.

He stroked her slit, sending thrills soaring through her. Then he flicked her clitoris and she groaned. He wrapped his hand around his cock and positioned it against her wet opening. It seemed poised there forever.

"Please," she whimpered. "Do it." She needed him so badly.

The broad smile on his face turned tender and he eased forward. His cock glided inside her. Stretching her. Filling her.

She sucked in a deep breath as his cock pushed deeper. Her need rocketed out of control. She wrapped her calves around him and pulled him tighter against her. Long and hard. Her inner passage adapted to his large cock. She squeezed internal muscles, thrilling at the feel of his hard flesh inside her.

Waves of dizziness wafted through her. She wrapped her arms around his strong shoulders. Could it be she was this close to orgasm already? She could almost believe that even the slightest movement would—

He kissed her, then drew back and glided into her again. Pleasure swelled through her. He drew back and thrust again. She clung to him and moaned as intense desire merged with potent pleasure. Rocketing through her. Carrying her to a special place of heightened awareness and crystal clear feelings. She gasped and electrical sensations sheared across her nerve endings as she plummeted into ecstasy.

James continued to thrust into her, his big cock stroking her pleasure on and on. Hot liquid erupted inside her and he groaned. Still he thrust.

The intensity of her pleasure eased, flowing to a sense of joyful contentment. She dropped her head against his chest and sighed. He stroked her hair, then gently down her back. Then he just held her. For several long moments they stayed like that, in the warmth of the night, in each other's arms.

Finally, she drew back. "Thank you."

"I think that's my line." He kissed her forehead and smiled. "You are something else. I don't think I've ever met a woman who is so responsive."

She smiled as she grabbed a handful of his shirt and pulled him toward her for a kiss. His lips met hers and she thrust her tongue inside his mouth, just as his cock was still snuggled inside her.

What had just happened had been incredible . . . ecstatic . . . orgasmic. This man was sensational. But, as her body calmed from its joyful high and coherent thought set in once again, she realized something very important.

James was *not* her Fantasy Stranger.

Nine

Sandra climbed the deck steps as James went to grab some wood for the fireplace from the pile at the side of the cottage. It was a warm evening, but he'd suggested that a fire would be cozy and romantic.

She opened the sliding door and stepped into the cottage, her mind running over what had just happened with James. If he wasn't the one who'd played her Fantasy Stranger last night, it must have been Craig. A man she hardly knew.

Her ex-husband had been the only man she'd ever made love with before this weekend had started. She'd only ever been with one man. Now, in the space of twenty-four hours, she'd tripled that number.

Her cheeks burned at the thought of facing Craig now that she knew he was—

At a muffled sound, her head spun toward the couch. Her cheeks burned hotter as she saw Craig's bare, well-sculpted ass and Aimee on the couch in front of him, naked from the waist up, her lips wrapped around Craig's cock.

"Oh, my God. I'm sorry." Sandra cupped her hand beside her face like a blinder and averted her gaze.

Aimee laughed. "Don't worry about it, honey. You already saw us do *everything* yesterday morning anyway."

It was true—the memories of watching them coupling on the swim raft quivered through her—but this felt more intimate. She'd walked in on them when they'd been expecting privacy.

Or had they? They could have gone into Craig's bedroom. Maybe they liked the idea of being caught, too. Maybe they'd even been watching James and Sandra while they'd made love outside.

The thought of them watching while James had glided his cock inside her sent a tingle of excitement through her. She glanced at the couple, Aimee sitting on the couch, Craig standing in front of her, the delightful tiger tattoo encircling his arm just as Aimee's fingers encircled his big erection. Aimee smiled in Sandra's direction. Sandra's gaze locked on the big hard shaft in Aimee's hand.

Even though Sandra had just made love with James, hormones flooded through her. Like a starving woman at a feast, she licked her lips. She remembered what that cock had felt like in her mouth. What it had felt like gliding inside her.

Aimee smiled broadly. "Honey, why don't you come over here? This cock is so big and hard. I could use some help."

Sandra nibbled her lower lip, but found herself drifting toward the couch, her gaze glued to Aimee's hand moving up and down Craig's long shaft. When Sandra reached the couch, she settled down beside Aimee, her gaze still locked on Craig's erection. Finally, she tugged her gaze free, then allowed it to stray upward, along his tight, hard abs, along his sculpted, bulging chest muscles, to his face, his lips turned up in encouragement.

Aimee took Sandra's hand and guided it to Craig's cock. As soon as her fingertips touched the hot kid-leather skin, she stroked lightly, then wrapped her fingers around his shaft. Aimee smiled and licked one side of the cock. Sandra couldn't help herself. She leaned forward and dragged her tongue along the erection, too.

"What's going on here?"

At James' voice, Sandra lurched back. Her gaze locked on his, but he just smiled.

"That's pretty hot." He closed the deck door behind him and walked to the chair across from the couch and sat down. "Mind if I watch?"

Aimee winked at Sandra, then leaned close to the base of Craig's cock and wrapped her mouth around the side of his shaft, then began to glide along his length. Sandra glanced at James, then back to the hard cock in front of her, heat spiraling through her as she watched Aimee's mouth move on it. Sandra leaned forward and wrapped her lips around the other side of Craig's cock, then mirrored Aimee's movement.

Up and down they moved, warming Craig's shaft with their mouths. He felt incredibly hard beneath Sandra's lips. As their mouths moved toward his cockhead, she tucked her hand under his balls. Aimee followed suit and Sandra shifted her hand so they each cradled one ball. When they reached his cockhead, they continued upward, Sandra following Aimee's movements, then their lips met. Aimee's hand cupped Sandra's head and she drew her closer, pressing her lips to Sandra's. Sandra had never felt a woman's lips on hers before. They were so soft and delicate.

Craig's cock twitched in her hand. Aimee giggled as she released Sandra's mouth.

"It gets a guy every time. They *love* watching women kiss."

"Among other things," Craig responded, his voice tight.

"Yeah, yeah, we know, sweetie." Aimee swallowed Craig's cockhead and her cheeks hollowed.

She guided Sandra's hand to his balls and Sandra gently massaged them as Aimee glided down on Craig's cock, swallowing him whole, despite his generous length. Fascinated, Sandra watched Aimee glide up and down, taking him deep into her mouth. As Sandra stroked Craig's tightened balls with one hand, her other stroked over his hard tight ass.

Craig groaned and spasms shuddered through his body. His hard butt cheeks clenched under her touch. Finally he relaxed and Aimee glided away, releasing his cock from her mouth. She smiled, then winked at James.

"Sandra, I think James might be ready for some action, but Craig will need a little help." Aimee's fingers curled around Sandra's arms and she drew her forward. "Willing to encourage him?" Aimee tucked her fingers under the hem of Sandra's tank top and started rolling it up.

"Um . . . I don't know." Goose bumps flashed across

Sandra's skin as Aimee's fingers glided along her bared rib cage, then brushed underneath her breast.

Aimee pushed the top above Sandra's breasts and ran her hands over them. Then she reached around behind Sandra and released the bra hooks. Seconds later, Sandra sucked in a breath at the feel of Aimee's fingers gliding over her puckering nipples.

A woman's touch was so different from a man's. Light and delicate. Aimee leaned forward and brushed her lips over Sandra's nipple, then sucked it into her mouth while probing with her tongue. Heat rushed through Sandra. She tugged the tank top over her head and tossed away the bra, then leaned back on the couch. She couldn't believe Aimee's touch could excite her this much, not to mention the hot gazes of both men watching them with steamy intensity.

Aimee sucked deeply and Sandra cried out in delight. Aimee's hands stroked down her ribs, sending tremors through her . . . past her navel . . . then paused at the waistband of her jeans. Would she really go that far to excite the men? Would Sandra let her?

Aimee sat up and grinned at Sandra, then dropped back against the couch. Sitting there with her naked breasts peering at Sandra, Aimee winked.

Sandra stared at Aimee's round, firm breasts. She knew exactly what Aimee wanted. For Sandra to continue the show. Glancing at Craig's now semirigid cock, she could see the plan was working like a charm.

She stroked Aimee's shoulder-length, layered blonde hair behind her ear, then allowed her hand to glide down

Aimee's chest. Pausing beside her breast, Sandra gazed at the dusky pink puckered nipple, then ran her finger over it. Aimee drew in a breath, then arched her chest forward.

What would it feel like in her mouth? She ran her fingers over the hard nub, then leaned forward and kissed the white flesh around the aureole. She ran the tip of her tongue over the pebbled flesh, then around the hard bead in the center. She licked it and sucked a little. Aimee drew in a deep breath and her hand curled around Sandra's head, her fingers forking through her long hair. Sandra moved to Aimee's other nipple and stroked it with her tongue, then sucked.

"Damn, you two are so fucking hot," Craig said, his voice strung taut.

Aimee grasped Sandra's face and drew it toward her own. Her mouth locked on Sandra's in a passionate kiss. Aimee sat up and pressed her tongue into Sandra's mouth, swirling it deep. Then Sandra pulled Aimee to her feet. Aimee unbuttoned her jeans and pushed them down. Her thong went next. She was totally shaven.

Sandra glanced at Craig, his hand around his fully erect cock, then at James, also sporting a huge erection. She smiled, then shed her own jeans and undies. Aimee sat on the couch and tugged Sandra down beside her.

"How about we switch partners?" Aimee suggested, staring straight at James.

Sandra glanced at Craig and he smiled broadly. Sandra nodded, wanting to feel that big cock inside her again. Craig dropped to his knees in front of her and stroked her breasts as James shed his clothes and strode toward the couch. Sandra stroked a finger along the sexy tiger tattoo on Craig's bicep.

"Beautiful." Craig lifted her breasts in his hands, then leaned forward and captured her nipple in his mouth.

She clutched his head to her breast, enjoying the feel of his tongue lapping over her sensitive bud. Beside her, James gave similar attention to Aimee's breasts. Heat pulsed through her at the combination of visual and tactile stimulation.

Aimee cried out. Sandra glanced across to see James' head moving over her groin. Craig's mouth moved downward, then his tongue lapped at her clit and she gasped. His fingers parted her wet folds and slid inside her as his tongue probed her sensitive nub. She clung to his head, his hair coiled around her fingers, as pleasure swelled inside her.

Then he stopped.

Her eyelids popped open and she stared at his grinning face. Then his fingers moved inside her again, and his tongue teased her clit. The pleasure built again, bringing her close to the abyss . . . then he stopped again.

Leaning against the back of the couch, sucking in air, she longed for completion.

Aimee gasped, then clutched James' head, stopping him. "Wait."

James stared at her with a questioning look.

"I want to watch you and Craig both fuck Sandra." Aimee smiled at James. "Just keep a little for me afterward, okay?"

James smiled and glanced at Sandra. She turned her gaze to Aimee.

"I don't know . . ."

"Look, not full-on or anything." Aimee winked. "If they did that, James wouldn't be able to hold back."

Sandra glanced at Craig, his big cock pointing straight at her, then at James, his cock, even longer, but not as thick.

Oh, God, both of them. That would be . . . sensational.

Sandra took a deep breath, then nodded.

Craig smiled, then pressed his cock against her slick opening. He dragged his cockhead over it, then pushed forward. Slowly, the corona pushed inside her, stretching her. She grasped his shoulders and he glided all the way inside. She groaned at the exquisite feel of his big hard shaft deep inside her.

"Oh, doll, you are so hot around me." Craig drew back and surged forward again.

Sandra clung to his shoulders as pleasure swelled through her. He stroked again and she arched forward to meet him.

Then he withdrew. Her eyes widened.

Craig moved back and James positioned himself in front of her. He stroked her wet slit with his fingers, then pressed his cock against her. He surged forward in an immediate deep thrust. She lifted her hips, meeting him head-on. He thrust several times, then pulled out. Craig returned, his cock driving deep again.

Pleasure built, then eased . . . built, then eased . . . as the two men shared her. Driving their cocks into her time and time again. Beside her, Aimee stroked her own breast with one hand, and with her other she pushed fingers inside herself.

Craig pushed into Sandra again. As he pumped his cock into her, the pleasure increased in intensity. He pulled out and

James pressed against her. At his second thrust, she knew she wouldn't last much longer no matter what they decided to do to delay her. She sucked in air as intense sensations flared. James pulled out and she feared she'd come on the spot, with no hard cock to squeeze on. Then Craig pushed inside. She grabbed his shoulders and pulled him tight to her body.

"Fuck me hard," she demanded.

He chuckled and thrust faster. When he slowed, she wrapped her legs around him and arched forward.

"Make me come. Now!"

He leaned in and kissed her. "You bet."

He thrust. Deep. Hard.

Fast.

She gasped as pleasure pummeled her insides. It swelled to a cacophonous crescendo, then burst through every cell in her body, exploding in pure ecstasy. Craig groaned, then she felt him stiffen and erupt inside her.

Sandra fell back against the couch cushions, and Craig fell into her arms. She held him close as James pushed into Aimee beside her. He thrust and Aimee moaned. Both climaxed within moments.

As Sandra slumped there, Craig resting against her, her arms around his massive shoulders, Aimee and James gasping for breath beside them, she sighed. What an incredible experience.

The only problem was, she still didn't know for sure which man was her Fantasy Stranger.

Ten

Sandra took Craig's hand and he drew her to her feet and into a solid hug.

He smiled broadly. "That was something else."

He gave her another kiss before he released her. James kissed Aimee, then took Sandra in his arms and kissed her soundly.

Sandra picked up her clothes and dropped them on the couch, then pulled on her panties and her jeans. She sat down and gazed at Craig, who was giving Aimee a passionate kiss, then at James.

One of these two men was her Fantasy Stranger.

Before she'd made love with James on the picnic table, she'd been sure he was the Fantasy Stranger. His touch had been sweet and tender like her Fantasy Stranger's, but different. Of course the circumstances were different and maybe he'd purposefully acted different, so she wouldn't figure it out. But she didn't think he was quite as large as her Fantasy Stranger, either. Maybe with the blindfold, or because of her long celibacy, she had simply imagined the Fantasy Stranger to be bigger than he really was, but . . . she wasn't convinced James was the stranger.

She picked up her bra and pushed the straps over her shoulders and fastened the hooks, then adjusted the lacy cups.

Now that she'd had sex with Craig, too, she should be convinced he was her Fantasy Stranger, but the size of his erection wasn't enough to confirm it. Craig's touch was even more different. And with the fast and furious flurry of thrusts, one man to the other . . . She drew in a deep breath. She just couldn't be sure.

She pulled on her tank top and realized she felt a little numb. Everything around her felt distant somehow.

"You ready to go?" Aimee asked.

Sandra nodded.

"We'll walk you back," James said.

"Uh, you know what? We'll be fine. Thanks." Aimee picked up Sandra's bag and handed it to her, then led her to the door.

"See you tomorrow," Craig said as Aimee opened the sliding door.

"Sure thing," Aimee said.

As soon as Sandra stepped into the clear night air, the sound of the crickets chirping in the background and moonlight casting a soft glow on the trees and grass, she suddenly realized what she'd just done.

Aimee closed the door behind them.

Oh, God. I just had wild sex with two men.

Aimee drew her down the deck steps and toward the path through the trees. They walked in silence for a few moments.

"That was pretty exciting, eh?" Aimee said, sending a sidelong glance at Sandra.

"Yeah." Sandra couldn't round up any other words.

"The guys had a really good time."

"Uh-huh." Sandra prayed Aimee wouldn't ask her the question. Wouldn't ask her if—

"You had a good time, right?"

"Um . . . sure."

Aimee stopped. "Oh, come on, honey. Don't tell me you didn't enjoy that."

Sandra stopped walking and turned to face her friend, then her gaze dropped to her sandal-clad foot and she tapped the surface of a rock embedded in the ground. She'd be lying if she said that.

"It's not that I didn't enjoy it, it's just that . . ." She sighed and glanced at Aimee, then back to her foot. "Come on, Aimee. I just had sex with two guys at the same time. Guys I hardly know."

"Aw, sweetie." Aimee took Sandra's hand and squeezed it. "What are you worried about? I'm not going to tell anyone about this. The guys won't tell anyone. It was just a good time shared by consenting adults. There's *nothing* wrong with that."

Sandra nodded but without conviction.

"Honey, look at me."

Sandra's gaze returned to Aimee.

"Listen, do you think any less of me because of what just happened?"

Sandra's brow furrowed. She considered Aimee a close friend and thought she knew the woman pretty well, but Sandra would never have suspected that Aimee would get involved in such casual wild sex. Yet did that mean she thought less of her?

Actually, she kind of admired the way Aimee took it all in stride. Aimee knew both Craig and James . . . had had sex with both of them before. When she and Craig had made love on the raft in front of Sandra and James, it hadn't felt dirty or wrong. It had felt like Aimee was being playful. Simply having fun. And with an openness toward sex that Sandra wished she could share. Sandra didn't believe for a moment that Aimee would grab the first sexy stranger who passed by and have sex with him in public. What she'd done had been an exciting escapade among friends. Friends who trusted and respected one another.

"No." Sandra squeezed Aimee's hand. "I don't think less of you. I think you're kind of quirky. And a little crazy. But I think you're a great person who really knows how to have fun."

Aimee smiled. "Thank you. So if you think that about me, then allow yourself the same courtesy. You enjoyed sex with two incredibly good-looking, sexy guys. Any woman would love to be in your shoes. So relax. Okay?"

Sandra nodded. "Okay."

They continued to the cottage, where Sandra headed straight to bed. As she lay there with her arm tossed across her forehead, staring at the moonlight washing across her bedspread, she replayed the conversation with Aimee.

You enjoyed sex with two incredibly good-looking, sexy guys. Any woman would love to be in your shoes.

That might be true, but most women would just fantasize about it. Not many would actually do it.

Sandra sighed, confusion swirling through her.

The only thing she knew for sure was that the memory of those hard cocks driving into her was going to haunt her memories, and her dreams, for a long time to come.

The next morning, Sandra didn't wake up until ten thirty. She climbed out of bed and pulled on her red bikini and a pair of shorts. As she trod into the kitchen she could smell fresh coffee. Aimee must be up. She glanced at the fridge and noticed that item four had been ticked off the list.

She sighed and poured herself a mug of coffee and peered out the patio door to see Aimee sunning herself on the deck. Sandra slid open the door and stepped outside.

"Good morning." Sandra sat on the chair beside Aimee.

"Hi there." Aimee closed the magazine she'd been reading and tossed it on the table beside her, then picked up her mug and took a sip. "When I'm finished with this I'm going for a swim. Want to join me?"

Join her? And probably run into Craig. Maybe James, too.

"No, thanks."

"You sure? It's not because of last night, is it? You're not avoiding the guys?"

Sandra shrugged. "We had a great time last night. Let's just leave it at that."

"You think it'll be weird, right?"

"Maybe a little."

Aimee finished her coffee and stood up. "Okay, well, I'll be gone about an hour or so. What are you going to do?"

"I'm going to lie in the sun and finish my book. I'm dying to see how it ends."

Aimee slid open the door. "Hmm, turning down two hot guys for a book." She grinned and shrugged. "Whatever turns you on, baby." She went inside and closed the door. A few minutes later, she returned wearing her orange floral bikini and a towel wrapped around her hips. "If you change your mind, you know where to find us."

Sandra watched her go, then went inside and fetched her book from her bedside table. She returned to the deck, kicked off her shorts, and sat down, staring wistfully at the place between the trees where the path disappeared.

Maybe she should go and join them. Two sexy guys and a wild time awaited her. But feelings of uncertainty—about last night, about the desires she felt now—gnawed at her insides.

Aimee had done a good job convincing her that last night had been okay. *A good time shared by consenting adults*. After more than a year of abstinence, Sandra deserved to let loose. To live out a fantasy or two. But to go off with Aimee now again, to join her and the two men in another sexual romp—the fact that she so desperately *wanted* to—scared her a little.

It felt almost like an addiction. She wanted it too much.

No, she'd had her fun last night. And the day before. That was enough. She'd actually ticked off half the items on the list.

Today she would return home. Back to reality. And these kinds of sexual antics had no place in her regular world.

Aimee returned around one and they had lunch together, then began packing their stuff. Once the cooler was filled with leftovers and they had wiped out the fridge, they carried everything to the back door.

"Hey, there."

Sandra glanced up to see Craig smiling at her through the screen door. James stood behind him.

"Want a hand with those?" Craig asked.

"Uh . . . sure. Thanks." Sandra opened the door and Craig grabbed the cooler while James picked up her suitcase.

"Great. Reinforcements." Aimee returned from her final walk around the cottage to ensure everything was turned off and all the doors and windows were secured.

Sandra walked along the path following behind the wheeled cooler Craig pulled, James by her side.

"I missed you this morning. Did you finish your book?"

"Oh, uh . . . not quite." How could she? She'd been daydreaming about swimming naked with James . . . and Craig. And climbing up on the swim raft and then feeling their hands on her naked skin. Their hot bodies pressed against her. Their hard cocks pushing into her.

"That's too bad," James said.

They arrived at the dock and Craig hefted the cooler into Aimee's boat, then climbed aboard. James handed him Sandra's suitcase and Craig set it down beside the cooler at the back of the boat.

Then James turned to Sandra and smiled. "I'd really love to see you again."

The panic she felt must have flashed across her eyes because a tiny frown crossed his sexy lips. He tucked his hand under her chin and drew it up, then captured her lips. The heat of his mouth on hers burned through her and despite her better judgment, she returned the kiss. His arms wrapped around her and he drew her close. Their bodies pressed tight together, and her heart pounded in her chest.

Oh, God, why hadn't she gone to the beach with Aimee this morning? She already longed for James' hot naked body to be pressed against hers. To feel him slide inside her and take her to heaven again.

He released her lips and smiled. "Aimee has my number. Call me anytime."

She nodded, dazed. She turned around, and came face-to-face with Craig.

"That goes for me, too." Craig tugged her close and captured her lips in a mildly aggressive and oh-so-sexy kiss.

Once he released her lips, she sucked in air. Oh, God, she wanted to strip right here and beg them to fuck her.

"Thanks. I . . . uh . . . better go now." She stepped over the side of the boat, settling one foot inside, and wobbled a little as the boat swayed on the water.

Craig caught her hips to steady her, then held on with a firm grip as she stepped all the way on board.

"Thanks." She smiled at him, then settled on the front passenger seat. The sun beat down on her bare arms and shoulders as she watched Aimee kiss James, then Craig.

Aimee hopped into the boat and climbed behind the wheel. "All ready to head home?" Aimee asked.

Sandra nodded, but in fact, she wasn't at all sure she was.

Sandra put down her cup of Hawaiian blend decaf coffee on the side table and flopped onto the couch in her living room. The day at work had been unbearable. Her boss had come back with a huge list of changes she wanted on Sandra's proposed design for the new Web site, most of them impractical, especially from a maintenance perspective, but that wasn't the worst. The problem was she couldn't drag her mind away from the weekend at the cottage.

She picked up her coffee and breathed in the rich aroma, then took a sip.

A deep craving to see James and Craig again and to have another torrid sexual adventure kept her mind gyrating and her body vibrating with need.

A knock sounded at the door. She sighed and stood up, then walked to the door and opened it.

Devlin stood smiling at her. "Hey there, stranger. May I come in?"

Eleven

Sandra smiled and stepped back. "Yes, of course."

The sight of his handsome face, the closeness of his body as he stepped inside, sent her insides trembling. She'd been attracted to Devlin before, but now that her sexual appetite had been awakened to a whole new level this past weekend, she could barely stand next to him without wanting to throw her arms around him and devour his lips in a passionate kiss.

Once inside the entrance, he stepped out of his shoes. She walked toward the living room and he followed her.

Oh, God. Having Devlin here kicked her already stark craving up several notches. Here he was, a real live man, within reach. A man who sent her insides sparking.

Except he'd already turned her down once. At least Aimee's suggestion of going away for the weekend had worked. Sandra no longer felt the keen sting of embarrassment.

"Would you like some coffee? I've got a pot of decaf on."

"Sure."

He followed her into the kitchen and she poured some coffee into a mug and handed it to him, then watched as he added sugar.

"I hope you don't mind my stopping by without calling."

Sandra shrugged. "We're friends. You can do that."

He nodded. "That's the reason I came by. To ensure nothing gets in the way of that friendship."

Her stomach clenched. Had Aimee told him about what had happened at the cottage? Had he decided he couldn't have a friend who would behave that way?

Oh, God, now I'm being completely paranoid.

Aimee had said she wouldn't tell anyone and, even if she had, Devlin wouldn't care.

Devlin stared at her wide eyes and knew she wasn't thinking about the same thing he was.

"I'm talking about the night you kissed me. I'm pretty sure you've been avoiding me since then, and I wanted to make sure we're okay. That what happened won't impact our friendship."

"Oh . . . no, of course not. I was a little embarrassed afterward, but it doesn't affect how I feel about you."

And how did she feel about him? That kiss told him she wanted to be more than friends, and that was great. Just not yet. He'd promised himself he'd wait six months.

But right now he had to do damage control.

"Good." He picked up his coffee and headed for the living room. "So we're still on for dinner on Saturday?"

"Right. It's my turn to cook this time. I'm going to try

a new dessert recipe I found online. Chocolate cake with a chocolate-and-orange-liqueur filling."

Devlin had taken a gourmet cooking course with her six months ago—they'd invited Aimee but she had no interest in cooking—and now they alternated cooking for each other once a month to keep their skills honed. Aimee liked eating, though, so she joined them, too.

"Sounds good." He always looked forward to their cooking nights. He liked sharing his creations with Sandra, and he loved the artistic flair of her presentation.

He sat on the easy chair while Sandra settled on the couch, then picked up her coffee and sipped.

"So how was the weekend?"

"Uh . . . good."

He sipped his coffee, enjoying the new blend she'd chosen. "Aimee told me James and Craig were at the other cottage."

Sandra stared inside her cup. "You know James and Craig?"

"Yeah, I met them at Aimee's cottage a few years ago. Aimee told me you knew James back in college."

Sandra nodded, swirling the liquid in her cup.

James had told Devlin a little about his history with Sandra, and Devlin got the impression James had been quite attracted to her, which made Devlin a bit nervous. The past link between James and Sandra had come as a complete surprise. And a disturbing complication. Aimee had assured Devlin it was nothing to worry about, though, so he decided to stick with the plan.

"So with you and Aimee alone on an island with two available guys . . ." He grinned. "Did you check anything off your list?"

Sandra nearly choked on her coffee, then coughed.

"What did Aimee tell you?"

"Nothing." He raised his eyebrows and his grin broadened. "But from your reaction, I assume I'm spot-on."

Looking at her pale face, he felt a little mean goading her like this, but he wanted her to open up about it and didn't know how else to broach the subject. Aimee had told him Sandra was a bit reticent about her experiences with the men—and with her Fantasy Stranger—but Devlin wanted her to talk about it so he could encourage her. And so it would bring them to another level of intimacy in their friendship.

"Sandra, if something did happen . . . you know I wouldn't think badly of you. In fact, quite the opposite. I'd think it was great that you'd gone after what you wanted. Embraced excitement and adventure."

She raised her gaze to meet his. "Really?"

Her small voice and wide eyes, so begging for approval, tore at his heart.

He stood up and walked toward the couch, then settled down beside her. "Of course." He tucked his arm around her and drew her close to his side. "There's nothing wrong with going after what you want. What's the point in having a dream if you never go after it?"

"Well, I wouldn't say the items on that list were my dream."

He raised an eyebrow and grinned. "Really? You don't daydream about hot guys making wild and passionate love to you?"

Her cheeks blazed an amazing shade of red, and he laughed.

"Look, whatever you did this weekend, I salute you. In fact, I think you should do more of the same. You deserve to have a great time and don't allow anyone to judge you."

A slow smile spread across her face and she nodded. "You know, you're right. There's nothing wrong with being a bit wild every now and again. I mean, Aimee already told me that, and I thought I'd accepted it, but the thought of doing it again . . . I thought maybe once was okay, but more than that meant . . . you know, that I was . . ." She shrugged.

"Kinky?"

She shook her head.

"A little sex-starved?"

"Actually, more like a sex maniac."

"Well, there's nothing wrong with a little maniacal sex once in a while."

She batted his arm and he laughed.

"There's nothing wrong with having a healthy sex drive," he said. "And that's exactly what you have. A *healthy* sex drive."

"So you don't think there's anything wrong with me having sex with two guys?"

"At the same time?"

Her eyes glinted with defiance. "Yes. At the same time."

He leaned back and swirled the coffee in his mug, dragging out the time, letting her think he was carefully considering his answer.

"Well, I only have one thing to say about that."

"What's that?" As much as she tried to appear defiant, she looked more like a kitten trying to stare down a gigantic dog.

He grinned. "Can I watch next time?"

As Sandra closed the door behind Devlin, she smiled. He really was a sensational guy. And such a supportive friend. He was right. Having a healthy sexual appetite was perfectly fine, and putting it that way made her feel so much better. In fact, having Devlin's approval meant a lot to her because she trusted his judgment.

She picked up the cups from the coffee table and carried them into the kitchen, then put them in the dishwasher and turned it on. She yawned and stretched. Early to bed would be a good idea after the active weekend she'd had, and the fact that she hadn't slept at all well last night, deeply craving even more sexual excitement. She wandered to the bathroom, did her nighttime routine, then pulled on her pajamas and climbed into bed.

Maybe she hadn't turned into a sex maniac, but some maniacal sex, as Devlin had called it, would go great right about now. She turned out the light and, with thoughts of Devlin in her mind, drifted off to sleep.

His arms were around her and Sandra leaned back against his hard body. His hands cupped her breasts and she arched forward. Her nipples ached and her body burned with need.

"I want you," a male voice rumbled.

She turned in his arms to see his face, but she couldn't make out his features in the dim light. She couldn't see her Fantasy Stranger.

She leaned forward and kissed him. His lips caressed hers with a gentle persuasion, stoking her need.

"I want you, too." She stroked his cheek, then down his chest.

Hard muscles rippled beneath her fingertips. She continued over his navel, then lower. Until she brushed against the tip of his cock. She grinned at him, then kissed down his chest.

She wrapped her fingers around his thick cock—as long and hard as she remembered—and kissed the tip, then took the head in her mouth like a lollipop. She licked around and around until she heard him groan. She glided down and easily took him all the way in, despite his size. His fingers stroked through her hair as she alternated between sucking and licking. He tensed and groaned. Her mouth filled with hot liquid.

She rolled on her back and stretched out beside him. She stroked over her breasts and toyed with her nipples. He smiled and leaned toward her, then captured one hard nub in his mouth. She sighed at the incredible heat of his mouth around her. He stroked over her other nipple as his tongue swirled over the first. She sighed, then gasped as he sucked. Hard and deep.

Then he released it and kissed up her chest, then nuzzled her neck. Tingles danced along her skin and shivers raced down her back. He stroked her breasts, teasing both nipples. Heat flared inside her. She reached for his cock, needing it inside her. She stroked it. Supple skin gliding over hard rock.

"I need you. Make love to me," she said.

He chuckled, then prowled over her, pinning her between his knees. He leaned down and captured her lips, spiraling his tongue inside her mouth. Her tongue joined with his and they undulated together. He dove deep, mastering her mouth with his bold, swirling strokes, then drew back, leaving her gasping.

He smiled down at her, then lifted himself onto his knees. His hand curled around his rigid shaft and he stroked it. She leaned forward and licked it, savoring the hard flesh under her tongue. He pushed forward and her mouth engulfed him. She ran her tongue around his cockhead, unable to get enough of him.

He drew back, caressed her breasts, then stroked down her belly and between her legs. She arched against his hand. He glided his finger along her slickness. His cockhead brushed her thigh, then the tip pressed against her wet folds. She held her breath as he glided along her moist opening, then he pushed inside . . . just a little. She groaned, wanting more. He pushed until his cockhead was nestled inside her. She raised her hips, trying to force him in deeper, but he placed his hand on her stomach and held her still.

Then he drove forward. She groaned at the exquisite feel of his cock filling her. Thick. Hard. *Hot.* Branding her insides with excruciating pleasure. He drew back slowly, the ridge of his cockhead dragging along her passage, stimulating it. Then he drove into her again. She squeezed him, trying to pull him in even deeper. But still he drew back, stroking her insides, filling her with mind-boggling pleasure.

He drove into her a third time, and she trembled at the staggering pleasure. Buried deep inside her, he leaned down and licked her nipple, then sucked. Her fingers tangled in his hair and curled through it. Long hair.

Like Devlin's. Her gaze shot to his face. He sat up and moonlight streaming in the window cast his features alight. He smiled.

It was Devlin. Shock filled her as he drew back and plunged forward again. Then again. As he continued to thrust into her, searing her insides, her shock faded away. Devlin was making love to her.

Wonderful, sweet Devlin.

Pleasure blazed through her, singeing every nerve ending. An orgasm quivered, then flared through her as she squeezed his cock tight inside her. The pleasure intensified as she tightened around his thick shaft. Squeezing. Just as she reached the pinnacle, his hard cock seemed to disappear. As her body trembled on the edge of ecstasy, her eyes opened.

She was alone.

Devlin hadn't been there at all, but the pleasure still shuddering through her was vividly real. And she wanted more of it. So bad it made her ache.

Sandra glanced out the window of the bus as it moved down the busy city street, her cell phone against her ear.

"Listen, Aimee, do you think you could bow out Saturday night?" Sandra shifted a little to make room for a lady to sit beside her.

"But I love the gourmet dinners you cook," Aimee said.

"I know, but I promise I'll make it up to you. I'll come to your house and cook up the lobster bisque you like so much."

"And a crème brûlée for dessert?"

"You've got it."

Sandra's stop was coming up, so she stood up and moved toward the door.

"All right then," Aimee said. "You've got a deal. But why do you want me to cancel?"

"I want to have some time alone with Devlin. To talk."

"Hmm. Imagine. Only last week you were totally avoiding him. But I thought you sorted things out when he dropped by your place last Tuesday."

Sandra's eyebrows drew together. "How did you know about that?" Sandra hadn't mentioned it to Aimee.

The bus came to a stop and Sandra stepped off the bus into the warm sunshine outside.

"Oh, Devlin told me he was concerned and had dropped by to talk to you. He's a great guy, you know."

Sandra's stomach quivered and a deep yearning seared her soul as she thought about Devlin. "Yeah, I do. That's why I want to make sure everything's solid between us."

Saturday evening, Devlin knocked on Sandra's door, a bottle of wine in his hand. A moment later, she opened the door and smiled at him, setting her face aglow. His heart did a little hippety-hop at the sight.

"Come on in. I hope you're hungry."

His gaze caressed her curvy form as she stepped back to let him in. He was hungry all right, but with a hunger he would not satisfy yet. If only she would return to the cottage so he could be her Fantasy Stranger again and allow him to satisfy, for a short time, the yearning for her that burned through him constantly.

He stepped inside and shed his shoes, then followed her into the kitchen. Sandra lifted the lid from one of the steaming pots on the stove and dipped a spoon inside, then tasted.

"Mmm. Smells delicious." Devlin placed the bottle on the counter.

"I'm making fusilli pasta with artichokes." She measured out a teaspoon and a half of butter and added it to the sauce, then stirred. "Would you pour the pasta into the water?"

He lifted the lid from the pot beside the sauce, then grabbed the large measuring cup full of dry spiral-shaped pasta and poured it in. Sandra set the timer on the stove.

"Should I open the wine now?" he asked.

She opened the cupboard and brought out two stemmed wineglasses. "Sure."

He'd intended to let it breathe, but as soon as he pulled the cork free, she held out her glass. He poured some into hers, then into his. She sniffed it, then took a sip.

"Mmm. Nice. You always bring the best wine."

"Where's Aimee?" He sipped his wine.

Usually she was already there when he arrived.

"She couldn't make it tonight."

He raised an eyebrow. "Really? She never misses our dinners."

"There's always a first time for everything."

One part of him was delighted to be here with just Sandra—almost like a date—but another part quivered with nerves.

Sandra tossed a salad, then divided it into two wooden bowls and carried them out to the dining room. She returned just as the kitchen timer dinged and she drained the pasta and spooned it onto two dinner plates. Devlin ladled sauce on top, then they carried their plates and glasses into the dining room and sat down to eat.

Relaxing music played in the background and candles set the table alight with a soft glow.

"How's that project you're involved in at work?" she asked. "It has something to do with helping big companies monitor their energy usage, doesn't it?"

"That's right. My team finished the software last month and we have one client beta testing it."

As they ate, they talked about his project for a bit, then

discussed some upcoming movies they both wanted to see. Once they were done, she stood up and gathered their plates, then headed for the kitchen. He finished clearing the table while she put on coffee. Soon an unfamiliar coffee aroma wafted through the small kitchen. A new blend, no doubt. Sandra definitely had a passion for coffee.

He set her fancy stemmed glass mugs on the counter and she filled them. As he added sugar to his, she opened the fridge and set a cheesecake on the counter.

"It's chocolate amaretto." She sliced two pieces and set each on a dessert plate.

"Oh? What happened to the chocolate cake with orange-chocolate-liqueur filling?"

Her face scrunched up. "Don't ask."

He laughed as she handed him a plate. He picked up his mug and accompanied her to the living room, settling on the chair across from the couch where she sat. He glided his fork into the cheesecake then took a bite. It melted in his mouth.

"Well, this is absolutely delicious."

She smiled. "Thank you."

When he'd finished his dessert, he set his plate on the coffee table. Once she was done, she set her plate on top of his and pushed them away. She took a sip of her coffee.

"I wanted to thank you for coming over the other night." She gazed at him over her mug. "You know, to make sure things are okay between us."

He smiled. "Things were awkward and I didn't want it to stay that way. Our friendship is really important to me."

She nodded. "It is to me, too." She set down her cup. "I really appreciated your encouragement that night. About trying new and different things. About not judging myself." Her gaze locked with his. "You made me feel a lot better."

"I'm glad."

"In fact, it made me rethink other things I've done and wonder if I judged myself too harshly. For instance, what happened between you and me that Friday."

Uh-oh. He didn't know where this was going, but alarm bells clanged inside his head.

She leaned forward. "May I ask you something?"

"Of course."

"When you turned me down that night, was it because I'd had too much to drink? Or was it because you aren't attracted to me?"

Damn it.

He stared at his hands as he rubbed his palms together. "You had had quite a few drinks that night. There's no way I would take advantage of you."

"So, what would have happened if I hadn't been drinking?"

He shrugged. "Well, then, it wouldn't have happened."

"But if it had?"

He frowned. "Sandra, you're really putting me on the spot."

"Devlin, I practically threw myself at you. Sure, I'd had a few drinks, but I would never do that unless I was attracted to a man. I'm sure you know that."

He sighed. Of course he did, and to tell her otherwise would only hurt her self-esteem. He nodded.

"So my feelings for you are already out there. I'd just like to know if those feeling are reciprocated."

"Sandra, I think the world of you. I—"

She held out the flat of her palm. "Whoa. I get it. You aren't attracted to me, but you care about me as a friend." She stood up. "It's okay. I understand."

The look of hurt in her eyes tore at his heart. He stood up and followed her into the kitchen.

"Sandra, wait. That's not it."

She set her empty cup on the counter and turned to him.

"Devlin, it's okay. I'm a big girl. You're not into me. I get it. And that's all right. As long as I haven't freaked you out, we can continue being friends."

He took her hand, and the feel of her soft skin nearly unraveled his resolve not to tug her against him and consume her in a deeply passionate kiss. He steeled his control and simply stroked the back of her hand with his thumb.

"In fact, I do find you attractive."

Twelve

Sandra heart pounded as she gazed deeply into Devlin's blue eyes sprinkled with golden specks.

"Very attractive," he continued.

Her heart pounded loudly in her chest. It was true. She could see it shimmering in his eyes. Hear it in the slight tremor of his voice.

"So can we—?"

His finger covered her lips.

"No. We can't." He stepped closer and rested his hands on her shoulders as he stared deeply into her eyes.

The heat of his body close to hers and the intensity of his gaze unnerved her.

"There's nothing I'd like better than to . . ."

She held her breath at his pause, waiting for the words.

His gaze faltered, and he drew in a deep breath. "Sandra, believe me. There's nothing I'd like more. But you've just ended a very long marriage and are single for . . . pretty much the first time in your entire adult life. I think you need to date a little and find yourself before you settle into something serious again. Otherwise, we'd be starting a new relationship on very shaky ground, and if it didn't work out, we could ruin what we have. And your friendship is very important to me."

She didn't doubt that, but what she'd seen in his eyes was more than a desire for friendship. Sure, she could understand fighting a slight attraction that might burn out after a few months in order to retain a longer-term friendship, but what she'd seen in his eyes was . . . passion. The intensity of his desire had shone brightly.

She moved closer and rested her hand flat on his chest and enjoyed the feel of strong, rugged muscles beneath her palm.

In a low, sultry voice, she said, "What if we don't jump into a full-on relationship just yet? We could be friends *with benefits*."

She was sure she could feel his heartbeat race beneath her palm. He placed his hand over hers as if to remove it from his chest, but he hesitated.

"No. It wouldn't work. If we're meant to be together, a few more months isn't going to hurt us."

She stroked her other hand up his chest and along the side of his neck, then across his raspy jaw. She kissed the tip of his chin.

"But why wait? Why postpone the inevitable?" she insisted, desperately wanting to feel his arms around her. She lightly brushed his lips with hers.

Devlin found himself spellbound by her touch, loving the feel of her hands on his chest, her lips on his skin. Then her mouth brushed his and panic welled up in him. Any second now his hormones would take over and he would have her naked and on the floor, driving into her with all the passion searing through him.

He had to do something to deter her. And fast.

The first thought that flared through his brain was to scare her. Be something she would be afraid to tackle.

He grabbed her wrists and pressed them behind her, which pushed her breasts forward enticingly. He tried to ignore the heat blazing through his groin as he pulled her forward and captured her lips. His tongue drove into her mouth and he savored the sweetness of her. He drew his tongue back and she gasped as he sucked her tongue into his mouth, drawing it deep. He backed her against the wall and lifted her wrists, then pinned them beside her head. He drove his tongue into her mouth again and explored.

Her breasts heaved against his chest as he consumed her with his kiss. Then he released her mouth and pressed his lips to her neck, kissed the hollow, and nibbled along the side. Then he sucked deeply. When he drew away, a dark red mark colored her skin.

If this worked, his biggest problem would be how to turn it around once the time was right for him to actually start a relationship with her. But he'd figure that out later. Right now, he needed to stop her from trying to coax him into an intimate relationship that very second.

His gaze locked with hers. Shock glazed her olive green eyes.

A feral grin curled his lips. "You see, my tastes run a little to the wild side. I like a woman who is willing to submit." His grin widened. "Totally."

There was no way an independent woman like Sandra would go for that kind of thing.

"Really?" With wide eyes, she drew in a deep breath and then to his total surprise smiled. "How exciting!"

Sandra threw on her pajamas and slumped into bed. The memory of Devlin's strong hands holding her pressed against the wall, his mouth searing hers with the heat of his passion, along with his tongue driving into her mouth, mastering her, filled her with an inexhaustible craving. Oh, God, it had been so exciting.

She tossed and turned all night, flipping between sleepless bouts of longing for his hands on her body and dreams of being naked and bound while he made passionate love to her.

At lunch the next day, she sat with Aimee in a restaurant overlooking the canal. They both ordered the soup and salad special.

As soon as the waitress left, Sandra leaned toward Aimee.

"What do you think about Devlin and I getting involved?" Sandra asked.

Aimee placed her napkin on her lap and smoothed it with her hand.

Usually Aimee had an opinion about this kind of thing and was happy to express it. The fact that she wasn't jumping right in meant she and Devlin had probably already talked about it.

Sandra raised an eyebrow. "You *know* something. Have you talked to Devlin about this?"

"Devlin and I are friends," Aimee said. "We talk about a lot of things."

Sandra leaned forward. "You and I are friends, too."

"I know, honey, but it wouldn't be fair to Devlin."

"Look, I'm really into Devlin and I think we would be good together. And I'm sure he's attracted to me, too. But it's like he's fighting it and I don't know why."

"Have you talked to him about it?" Aimee asked.

"Yeah. Last night, when we had dinner, I asked him outright if he was attracted to me."

Aimee's deep blue eyes widened. "What did he say?"

"He said he is."

"Really?"

"But then when I suggested we move to the next level—"

"You mean dating?"

"Okay, the level after that. Anyway, he launched into some lame excuse about the fact it might ruin our friendship. That I needed some time to date before we could even consider getting together."

Aimee patted her hand. "It's not lame, honey. If you have an intimate relationship with him, then later break it off . . . Things get awkward."

Sandra nibbled her lower lip. Of course, there was sense to that argument. "I don't think that'll happen to us."

"Everyone thinks that at first."

"Okay, maybe, but when I pushed him a little harder, he changed stories again. This time he told me he was . . . into kinkier stuff."

Aimee's lips curled in a smile. "Oh, yeah. Like what?"

"Like dominance. Requiring the woman to be totally submissive. Then he pushed me against the wall and kissed me. I almost felt like he was trying to"—she drummed her fingers on the table—"I don't know. Frighten me off or something."

"And did he?"

"Are you kidding? It was totally hot." She grabbed a breadstick from the basket and nibbled the end.

Aimee laughed. "Poor Devlin. I assume you told him that."

"Absolutely. I desperately wanted to drag him off to bed right then and there. But he mumbled something about me not really getting it, which was total gibberish, then he practically fled the apartment." She gazed at Aimee. "I'm very confused. If you can shed any light on this, please do."

"Well, Devlin's always been a straight shooter. If he says he's attracted to you, but he's resisting acting on it, that's all there is to it."

"But why would he change stories? Do you think he doesn't want to have sex with me, but he's afraid he'll hurt my feelings?"

Aimee toyed with her spoon. "No, I don't think that's the case."

An unsettling thought set Sandra frowning. "Damn, does that mean he's not really into domination?"

She couldn't believe how turned on the idea of being dominated by Devlin made her feel. She'd never even considered the idea before; now she seemed almost obsessed with it.

Aimee laughed. "Well, I don't know about that."

Sandra sipped her water. "You know, ever since the weekend at your cottage, I keep having really hot dreams."

"About James and Craig?"

"Well, really about the Fantasy Stranger." Sandra shrugged. "But one of them is the Fantasy Stranger, right?"

Aimee stroked the tip of her finger down the side of her water glass, following a drop of condensation. "That's classified information."

Sandra narrowed her eyes. Why did it seem Aimee was suddenly being cagey? Almost as if the Fantasy Stranger was someone entirely different. Heat blazed through her at the thought. Could it be she'd actually been with three different men at the cottage that weekend? Had her Fantasy Stranger really been a total stranger she'd never even met?

Oh, God. Should she really find that thought so amazingly erotic?

Aimee glanced up at her again. "Maybe it's time to go back to the cottage again. I'm pretty sure I could arrange it this weekend? What do you say?"

"With both Craig and James?"

Aimee nodded as she chewed her lettuce, then swallowed. "And you could experience a little of item two."

Bondage.

Sandra pointed her breadstick at her friend. "You seem to have that list memorized."

Aimee grinned. "And you don't?"

Sandra laughed. "I guess I do." How could she not? Thoughts of doing those things with her new lovers—and with Devlin—occupied her mind, and her dreams, constantly.

Her insides ached with need. There was only one thing that occupied her thoughts more.

She licked her lips.

"And do you think maybe . . . could you arrange a visit from my Fantasy Stranger again?"

Aimee laughed. "Of course."

Devlin reached into his pocket for his vibrating cell phone. "Hello."

"You're driving the woman nuts."

Devlin smiled. Aimee. "Any particular woman?"

He put down his book on the table beside his mug of coffee, stretched out his legs, and slumped back on the upholstered chair in the cozy coffee shop by the river.

"You know exactly which woman. You are driving Sandra nuts."

"Why do you say that?"

"We met for lunch today and she told me about last night. By the way, a woman must *totally submit* to you?"

He chuckled as he remembered how Sandra's eyes had widened, then her pupils had dilated in sexual excitement. Or so it had seemed from her following comments. Of course, he hadn't found it at all funny last night. In fact, he'd sped out of there as fast as he could. If he hadn't, he would have woken up in her bed this morning, his plan totally tossed out the window.

"I thought that would scare her off." He took a sip of his coffee.

"What? Turning her on with your dominating masculinity?"

"I had to think of something." He'd had no idea it would have that effect on her. Who knew threatening to dominate a woman like Sandra would act as an aphrodisiac?

"Slick move."

He grinned. "So is that how you see me?"

"What do you mean?"

"Do you see me as dominating and masculine?"

"Nooo. But clearly Sandra does. In fact, right now, that seems to be all she can think about."

The thought that Sandra was thinking about him that way—as strong and sexy, dominating her in the bedroom—set his groin aching.

"So why did she talk to you about it?" he asked.

"Because she didn't understand why you wouldn't act on your attraction for her."

He tapped his finger on the handle of his mug. "But I told her the truth."

"Followed by a crazy excuse. All you did was confuse her."

He groaned.

"No, it's okay. It's all good. I just don't think you should wait too long."

"Because of her history with James? Do you think it might lead to a serious relationship after all?"

"I think it made it easier for her to get involved sexually," Aimee said, "but she told me she doesn't want to get caught up in anything serious just yet."

Relief flooded through him.

"But . . . I don't know," Aimee continued. "Sandra strikes me as the type of woman who wants to be in a relationship. Having sex with both Craig and James will certainly keep her distracted for a while, but at some point she's going to want to settle into a relationship. With their unrequited lust from the past, James has an edge. Since she wants to be with you now, why don't you—"

"Aimee, I've got to stick to the plan. I don't want to be part of a crowd. When she's with me, I want it to be special."

"Sweetie, if you two are right for each other, then being together will be special no matter who else is around, or what you're doing together. That's what love is all about."

He stared out the window at the ducks swimming along the glittering river, letting the words sink in.

He absolutely believed that was true. And he knew he loved Sandra.

But . . . what if she didn't love him back?

"Devlin, I know you want a chance at forever after with her, but you know, no one can guarantee that at the start of any relationship. Sometimes you've just got to take a risk."

A risk? He'd moved too fast before. Been too confident. And lost the girl. Not this time.

"The plan will work." He had to believe that. "It will be good for Sandra to enjoy more erotic adventures."

"Okay. There are at least four more things on the list." He could hear the smile in her voice.

"Can you clear Saturday for another gig as her Fantasy Stranger?"

"Of course." Memories of Sandra lying on the air mattress below him, her face contorted in ecstasy, set his cock throbbing.

His role as Fantasy Stranger kept him as part of Sandra's erotic adventures. And it gave him a chance to compete with James. Sandra might not know the Fantasy Stranger was Devlin, but his feelings for her worked in his favor, because he was sure she could feel the love in his touch.

Wednesday night, Sandra went to sleep frustrated and anxious for Friday to arrive. The next morning, she woke up still shuddering from ecstatic pleasure. She squeezed her thighs together, riding the end of the orgasm, but without the hardness of a man inside her it faded fast. She sighed and lay sprawled on the bed, damp sheets tangled around her legs and her top pulled up, leaving her breasts bare.

Oh, God, she wanted a real man. Not these chaotic, confusing dreams. Always featuring her Fantasy Stranger. This time when he'd come out of the shadows, he'd had James' face. Which made no sense, because she was pretty sure the stranger was Craig.

But not totally sure. Maybe she'd been wrong when she'd ruled out James. It had been so long since she'd been with a man. She didn't know what to think anymore.

Right now, all she knew for sure was that she was dying to get to the cottage again. To be with both men. To feel them making love to her. Their hard cocks giving her pleasure. Even the thought sent tingles scurrying along her spine, and made her insides spasm with need.

She glanced at the clock. Seven thirty-five. She kicked the sheet away and hopped out of bed, then raced into the bathroom for her shower. Fifteen minutes later, she went into the kitchen, her nose twitching at the earthy aroma of the Asian blend she'd set up in the coffeemaker last night. She placed some bread in the toaster, then poured a cup and took a sip, appreciating the powerful, big body enhanced by its herbal nuances and soft cinnamon flavor. She hadn't packed this one for the cottage because she knew Aimee wouldn't care for it.

Once the toast popped up, she buttered it, then ate at the counter, thinking about the work she had to get done by the end of the week. On the bus, she reviewed the report detailing the requirements for the complex Web form she had to develop. That was the biggest task she had to complete by Friday. She arrived at work about ten minutes early, cleared up some of the smaller tasks, then set about work on the form.

After about two hours, she glared at the HTML code in front of her, wondering why the Web page wouldn't do what she wanted. She tapped her pen on the desk as she tried to fathom what was wrong with the code.

"Hey, what's up?" Aimee sat down in Sandra's royal blue guest chair.

"Having trouble getting this input form to work properly."

Aimee stood up and glanced over Sandra's shoulder. Aimee leaned in and pointed at the screen. "You didn't close your table column."

Sandra stared at the code where Aimee pointed. "Damn, you're right. I've been staring at this for fifteen minutes. Why the heck didn't I see that?"

"Well, I can think of two really good reasons."

At the amused curl of Aimee's lips, Sandra knew she referred to James and Craig. And she was absolutely right.

Aimee sat down again. "And about that. I hate to tell you this, but I can't go on Friday."

Thirteen

Sandra felt the color drain from her face. "You mean we're not going this weekend?"

Aimee laughed. "I wouldn't do that to you."

She reached forward and plucked the pen from Sandra's fingers. Sandra realized she'd been gripping it so tightly it was surprising it hadn't snapped in two.

"If you had to wait another week," Aimee continued, "you'd be a basket case. I can't go Friday, but I can go up on Saturday."

"So we're just delaying a day." *Oh, thank God.*

"No. I mean, I'll delay, but I don't see any reason you can't go up on Friday. The guys will be there."

"How will I get to the island? I don't know how to drive a boat. And I'm not sure I can find the island." Out on the water, all the treed coastline looked the same to her, and there were several islands on the lake.

"No problem. You can meet the guys at the marina and they'll take you on their boat. Is that okay?"

A whole Friday night on the island, just her and the two incredibly sexy men. Her insides quivered.

"Oh, yeah. That's just fine."

All day at work on Friday, Sandra could barely concentrate on what she was doing. Thoughts of seeing James and Craig again kept her insides simmering. Somehow she finished the Web form and handed it off to her boss for comments. Any changes would be handled next week.

Finally, five o'clock arrived. She gathered her stuff and stopped by Aimee's desk.

"On your way?" Aimee asked.

"Yeah. You still have to work?" Sandra asked.

"Well, you know, I was thinking about that. I could probably finish this up in the next two hours or so, then you and I could grab a late dinner and be at the cottage by eleven or so."

Sandra's stomach twisted. "Oh, uh . . . yeah, sure."

Aimee laughed and waved her hand back and forth. "Don't worry. I'm just kidding. I wouldn't do that to you. For one, I think you'd burst if you had to wait another hour let alone four. And"—she winked—"I assume you're looking forward to some alone time with the guys."

Sandra sighed. "You know it's not that I don't want you there, I just—"

Aimee laughed again. "Just go!"

Sandra grinned and turned around, then hurried toward the elevator. Someone held the door for her and she scooted in, then pressed P2. She'd driven her car today so she could head straight out. Her suitcase and a cooler of groceries were already packed in the trunk.

She hopped in the car and drove through the underground parking garage, then out into the bright sunshine. She negotiated her way through the thick downtown rush-hour traffic, smiling all the way. About an hour later, she pulled into the small marina and parked her car.

She opened the trunk and pulled out the wheeled cooler Aimee had lent her. It was the kind that claimed to keep ice frozen for up to five days, which was great since she'd had to leave it in the car all day. She'd packed enough food for both her and Aimee for the weekend. She tugged out her small suitcase and set it on top of the cooler, then locked up the car. Pulling the cooler along behind her, she headed to the dock that housed Aimee's boat. Aimee had told her Craig's boat slip was five down from Aimee's.

"Hey, gorgeous. There you are." Craig waved at her from farther down the dock.

The sight of him standing there with no shirt, the tiger tattoo prowling up his arm and his extremely well-defined muscles bulging, took her breath away.

My, God, what does that man do to work out?

Oh, man, she wanted to run her hands all over him. To feel the hardness of that totally ripped, extremely masculine body. To feel those strong arms around her and totally melt against him. Be consumed by his erotically aggressive kisses.

She tore her gaze away, shifting to James, who stood in the boat. He smiled. He wore a light cotton shirt, the front draped open revealing his rigid, well-sculpted muscles. Not as bulky as Craig's, but exceptional nonetheless.

Craig walked toward her, then took the cooler handle from her and drew it toward the boat. He lifted the cooler, suitcase and all, and handed it to James, who hefted it to the floor of the boat next to their cooler. James took her hand and helped her into the rocking boat. The warmth of his fingers enveloping hers sent goose bumps skittering along her arm.

Sandra glanced around, a little nervous the guys would show some expression of affection.

If one of them were to hug her right now, with her hormones racing, she might get carried away.

"Have a good drive from the city?" James asked.

She nodded and made small talk about traffic and her workweek, perched on one of the seats facing the back of the boat. Craig sat in the driver's seat, which put her back-to-back with him. She could feel the heat of his body only inches behind her.

James unfastened the ropes tying them to the dock, then sat in the front passenger seat. The engine revved and the boat moved away from the dock. In a few moments, they were on open water and the boat surged forward as it picked up speed. Her heart thumped in anticipation as the small craft bumped up and down on the water, then settled to a smooth ride.

They would be at the island very soon. The wind whipped her hair around as she watched the white crests of the wake behind them. She glanced along the shore and noticed several barbecues smoking as outdoor chefs cooked the evening meal. Quite a few families, or groups of friends, were already sitting around picnic tables, eating.

Sandra's stomach grumbled, but hunger for food was not her topmost priority right now.

The boat slowed and she glanced around to see they were heading toward shore. She recognized the familiar neon orange buoys scattered around to mark rocks. Craig pulled up beside the wooden dock and the boat bumped against it lightly. James stood up and stepped onto the dock, grabbed the ropes attached to the wood, and looped the ends around the cleats on the boat.

He offered his hand to Sandra and she took it to steady herself as she stepped onto the dock. Then he pulled her forward and wrapped his arms around her. His lips captured hers, his tongue delving into her mouth. She stroked her hands over his shoulders, then around his neck as she tangled her tongue with his. Craig moved close behind her, then his hand stroked over her right buttock and squeezed.

James released her lips and Craig turned her around.

"Oh, baby, I have been looking forward to this." Craig's arms encircled her and his lips engulfed hers. His tongue seared the inside of her mouth.

James' hands curled around her hips, then glided up her sides, stopping just below her breasts. He drew her back, easing her body away from Craig's a little, then James' hands glided over her breasts, enveloping them in his warm palms. Craig stroked her ass and he pulled her pelvis tight to his. A large bulge greeted her, sending heat thrumming through her and causing a tremendous ache in her groin. James arched forward, pressing his impressive bulge against her backside.

Oh, God, she could hardly breathe. With all the heat rushing through her, she was surprised steam didn't spout from her ears. She dragged her hands down Craig's chest, loving the feel of hard sculpted muscles under her fingertips. He released her lips and she gasped for air. She stroked down his belly, then over his bulge, already bigger and harder than it had been moments ago. She unzipped and slid inside, anxious to feel him in her hand. She wrapped her fingers around his hot flesh and squeezed, then stroked him up and down.

One of James' hands slid down her midriff, past her navel. She sucked in a breath as his fingers pushed under the waistband of her shorts and glided across the band of her panties. Then he slid underneath and down.

She squeezed Craig's big cock as James' hand glided over her curls, then along her very wet slit. She gasped as he pushed two fingers inside her. His other hand slid down to her hips and he drew her tight against him, the length of his erection settling between her buttocks. So hard and long.

She continued stroking Craig's big cock as Craig nuzzled her neck, then found the hem of her tank top. His big hands glided underneath and found her breasts, then cupped them. James' fingers swirled inside her. Craig lifted her top and gazed at her lace-clad breasts with admiration, then he tugged one cup underneath and he leaned forward to take her nipple in his mouth. Her fingers slipped from his hard shaft.

The sensations of his hot mouth on her sensitive nub and James' fingers inside her wet opening, stroking her, overwhelmed her with pleasure. Then Craig sucked and James found her clit. She sucked in air and clung to Craig's shoulder, then gasped as an orgasm washed over her. She fell back against James and moaned in pleasure.

As she floated back to earth, still collapsed against James, the guys chuckled. Craig kissed her.

"I think you missed us," Craig said.

Still catching her breath, she gazed at him with wide eyes. "You bet I did."

She pulled her tank top over her head and tossed it into the boat, then walked toward the shore. She kicked off her sandals, then shed her shorts as she strode toward the bushes leading into the woods, then moved to a large rock that was just the right height to sit on. Or lie on. She turned around and unfastened her bra, then dropped it to the ground. Both men watched hungrily as she tucked her thumbs under the band of her panties and pushed them down, then kicked them aside.

She stood before them totally naked, her nipples hard and distended. She stroked them, then cupped her hands under her breasts and lifted.

"See anything you like?" She felt wicked and totally wanton.

Both men surged forward and each took a nipple in his mouth. Sinking down on the cold rock, she reveled in the pleasure of their hot mouths sucking on her. Craig stroked down her stomach, then glided his fingertips over her wet slit. As she opened her legs wider, he slipped his fingers inside her.

She stroked her hand over James' head, gliding her fingers through his dark brown waves, and he lifted his head and smiled, then kissed her lips. She reached for his belt buckle and tugged him forward, then pulled down his zipper and reached inside for his cock. She drew it out, then lovingly glided her fingers over it.

"Mmm." She leaned forward and licked his bulbous cockhead, then swirled her tongue around the tip.

Craig knelt in front of her and licked her slit. She tossed her head back and murmured a soft sound of approval as she squeezed James' shaft. She stroked Craig's short sandy brown hair, then tugged a little until he raised his head.

"I want your cock," she said.

He grinned and stood up. "I can't argue with that." He unzipped and drew out his enormous erection.

She grabbed it in her other hand and kissed it. Now she stared at two big cocks, one in each hand. She licked Craig, then James again. Wrapping her lips around James' cockhead, she squeezed and sucked, then released him and captured Craig's even bigger cockhead in her mouth. She licked the end with her tongue, then swirled around the top.

She released him, then pressed the two cocks together and licked them both. Base to tip, again and again, swirling her tongue back and forth as she dragged it upward. She eased them toward her and stared at the cockheads, squeezed together, then licked across the tips. She captured Craig in her mouth, then opened wider and squeezed James in, too.

Both cockheads in her mouth. She sucked and both men groaned. She wrapped a hand around each of them and stroked up and down. Sucking. Stroking. She cupped their balls, and caressed, then stroked their shafts again. She took them a little deeper, filling her mouth impossibly full, then sucked again. Harder.

Craig's hand cupped her head. "Oh, yeah, doll. That's great."

She found their balls again and fondled them as her tongue swirled over their tips. Then she stroked behind their balls, and sucked long and hard.

James erupted first, then Craig right behind him. They filled her mouth with hot liquid.

She stroked them, then drew them free and smiled.

James grinned. "Is it time to go get the stuff from the boat?"

She tightened her hands around their cocks. "Not on your life."

She stood up and grabbed Craig around the waist, then positioned him in front of the rock. She unfastened his belt and pushed his pants down. He kicked off his jeans, then his forest green boxers. She pressed her hand on his chest until he sat down, then she climbed on his lap, her calves tucked beside his thighs. As much as she wanted him to fuck her, his wilted cock wouldn't do her any good right now, so she stroked her body against his, dragging her breasts up his solid sculpted chest. Her hard nipples pressed into him as she hugged him tight, locking her lips on his and thrusting her tongue inside his mouth. His tongue undulated against hers, then drove into her mouth, setting her senses on fire.

She felt his cock rise beneath her. She wrapped her hand

around it and squeezed, then pressed the head of his semierect shaft against her dripping opening. She stroked it along her slit, back and forth. Soon his cock was as solid as a rock.

She centered it against her opening, then slowly sank down on him. Her breath caught as his huge erection pushed deep inside, stretching her. Her arms wrapped around his muscular shoulders and she snuggled against him, enjoying the feeling of being impaled by his impressive cock.

James chuckled. "Would you two like to be alone?"

Sandra smiled. "There's no way I would waste a second man."

She pressed her hand on Craig's chest and eased him back. Once he was lying down, she pushed herself up on her knees, enjoying the feel of his cockhead stroking her vagina as she lifted her body. He fell free and she leaned forward, presenting her backside to James in invitation. His hand stroked over her ass, then she felt hard flesh press against her slit. He glided inside her vagina, pushing in deep. He pivoted in and out a couple of times, then drew out. She grabbed Craig's cock and sank down on it again.

James' hot slick cockhead pressed against her back opening and he eased forward slowly. Soon his cockhead was fully immersed inside her. He stopped, giving her time to relax. She drew in a deep breath as he started forward again. After a few long, erotic moments, his entire shaft was inside her.

Oh, God, she felt so full. Two big cocks inside her. She squeezed her muscles.

"Doll, I am so close," Craig said.

"Oh, man, me, too." James stroked her ass.

She leaned her hands on the rock, then rocked her pelvis forward. Craig's finger found her clit. Sharp pleasure seared through her. She rocked back and forth. The men began to move, pushing into her, then back, then deep again. James cupped her breasts and squeezed gently as he penetrated again. Pleasure welled up, then erupted through her as an orgasm blasted through every cell of her body. She wailed at the incredible sensations pulsing through her and exploded in ecstasy.

She gasped for air, both men holding her tight between them. Then she sighed.

"That was . . ." She pushed her long black hair back from her face. "Oh, man, you guys are . . ." She shook her head. "I mean . . . just wow!"

James chuckled as he pulled free. Craig stood up, lifting her to her feet with him, then kissed her.

"I think you could use a rest after that." Craig lifted her and tossed her over his shoulder, then grasped her thighs and started to walk toward the path. The ground bounced beneath her as she flopped on his shoulder, enjoying the ride. His free hand stroked over her bare ass, and even in her sated state, she could feel erotic stirrings again.

It was going to be a long and incredibly exciting weekend!

"What is all this stuff?" Sandra peered at the red cloth shopping bag Aimee had set on the bed in front of her.

"I brought these for you to wear tonight," Aimee said.

Sandra lifted one of the leather straps, a thick black band with a metal ring attached.

"That's for your wrist. There's another there, too." Aimee picked up a narrow leather strap. As she lifted it, Sandra noticed there were other straps attached to it. "This is the body harness you'll be wearing."

Sandra raised an eyebrow. "Really?"

"You wanted to try some bondage, right?"

"Doesn't that just mean the guys tie me up or put on handcuffs or something?"

"Sure, you could do that, but why not do the whole shebang?"

Sandra plucked the harness from Aimee's fingers and stared at it. "I'm not even sure how to put it on."

"Don't worry about that. I'll help."

Sandra pursed her lips as she removed her clothes. Once she stood in only her bra and panties, she glanced toward Aimee.

"Keep going," Aimee said.

Sandra glanced down at her powder blue bra and panties. Not exactly what she would choose to wear with black leather. She riffled in the bag to see if Aimee had brought something appropriate, but she couldn't find any bra or panties, leather or otherwise, in the bag.

"I didn't bring a black bra." Sandra did have black panties, though.

"No need. You wear this alone. Nothing else. Nada. Got it?"

"Oh."

Sandra reached behind herself and unclasped her bra, then dropped her panties to the floor and stepped out of them.

"Here, put this over your head."

Sandra ducked her head under the leather strap Aimee held up and she positioned the harness over Sandra's breasts, the straps forming a triangle around each one. Aimee walked behind Sandra and drew a strap around her waist, then fastened the small buckle. A pair of straps still dangled free in front of her.

"Okay, I have to feed the other straps between your legs and fasten them back here," Aimee said.

Feeling a little strange about this, Sandra widened her stance. She and Aimee had changed together plenty of times, but this was . . . different.

Aimee reached between Sandra's thighs to grasp the straps, then she fastened them to the waist strap. She stood up and turned Sandra to face the mirror.

"Check it out. You look gorgeous. The guys will be enthralled."

Sandra glanced in the mirror and smiled. The harness was actually quite attractive. The angles of the straps surrounding her breasts emphasized their soft round shape. The diamond formed by the straps pulling off to each side by the waist strap, then downward between her legs emphasized her flat stomach and drew attention to her . . . uh, pussy.

"That little heart is really cute." Aimee grinned. "Maybe I should do that with my pubes." She pursed her lips together. "But I'd have to grow it back first, and that's a pain."

"I'm sure what you have now is . . . fine." Sandra wasn't used to talking about pubic hair trimming with Aimee, but then, the nature of their relationship seemed to be changing.

"Now we'll just put the straps on your ankles and wrists."

"Ankles, too?" Sandra asked.

Aimee laughed. "Yeah. How else could they lay you out spread-eagled?"

The thought sent heat flooding through Sandra's system. For the first time since Aimee had presented her with the red bag of goodies, Sandra started thinking about the fact the guys would be seeing her in this outfit that covered nothing, and would be doing things like . . . well, bondage things.

Aimee stood up and began removing her own clothes. "You don't mind helping me with mine, right?"

"Oh, uh . . . sure."

Aimee glanced at her. "You don't mind me taking part tonight, do you?"

"No, of course not. I told you that already."

Aimee had asked her a couple of days ago if she could take part in the bondage session and Sandra had agreed. After all, it didn't seem fair for Sandra to hog all the guys! Especially since Aimee provided not only the guys but the island, too.

"I know, but you look like you're having second thoughts."

Sandra shook her head. She'd watched Craig and Aimee having sex on the swim raft the first morning they'd been on the island, then they'd had a foursome the next day. There was no reason she should be shy about Aimee joining them tonight.

"I'm totally okay with it. Now let's get you ready so we can start having some fun."

Aimee laughed. "Okay, then."

Ten minutes later, Aimee stood before Sandra wearing a similar harness. They both pulled on satin robes and stepped into their sandals, then set out for the other cottage.

They walked through the woods along the dirt path. Sandra heard a snap through the thick of the trees to her left, as though someone, or something, were walking there.

"Aimee, are there bears on the island?"

"Bears? No, why do you—"

The sound of a bush rustling stopped Aimee's words. Sandra sped up, Aimee following close behind her.

Suddenly, Aimee shrieked.

Fourteen

Before Sandra could glance around behind her, something grabbed her. She sucked in air as a big arm slid around her waist and tugged her backward . . . against a solid body.

A raspy cheek rubbed against hers and she noticed a tiger tattooed on the arm surrounding her.

"Hey, there," Craig's voice murmured in her ear.

She exhaled, slumping against him. He spun her around, then backed her against a tree. Holding her arms pinned above her head, his solid body pressing her tight against the bark, his mouth meshed with hers and his tongue thrust into her mouth. He devoured her with a hungry, passionate kiss, leaving her breathless. She pushed against the strong grip of his hands, adrenaline rushing through her. He chuckled and grazed her neck with his lips, then licked that intensely sensitive spot at the base, right at the shoulder. Tingles danced down her spine and she wanted to melt against him. Instead, she arched her body as if trying to escape.

He pressed his body tighter against her, pinning her

against the narrow tree trunk, her breasts crushed against his solid chest. He glided his hands down her hips. His big hands cupped her ass through the silk and he pulled her tight against his pelvis. A very large bulge pressed into her. She squirmed against him, suddenly anxious to see that big cock of his. To hold it. To stroke it. To feel it glide into her.

Oh, God, her insides ached for him.

He drew his mouth away and his intense gaze pierced through her. "Don't try to escape."

She had to concentrate on breathing. Excitement quivered through her. This big, muscular, *masculine* man held her pinned against a tree, his body crushing hers, telling her she was his prisoner. The insinuation that he intended to overpower her. She drew in a deep breath. To dominate her. She exhaled.

To have his way with her.

"What will . . ." Her voice came out a croak, so she cleared it and began again. "What will you do with me?"

He chuckled, a devilish twinkle in his eye. He pressed his lips to her ear and murmured, "You know exactly what I'll do." He grinned and nudged his head toward James, who was fastening a leather collar around Aimee's neck. "And my partner, too. We'll both enjoy our time with you and your friend."

He eased back and she nearly stumbled forward. He steadied her, then turned her around and grasped both arms. He tugged them behind her and held her wrists together with one hand. She felt him fumble in his pocket, then heard the sound of metal on metal. He released her wrists, but she could not pull them forward. She glanced at Aimee and James off to her right and noticed that James had joined Aimee's wrists together by attaching a carabiner clip to the ring on each cuff, making them like handcuffs.

Craig stepped in front of her, pulled a black leather collar from his hip pocket, slid it around her neck, and buckled it. Next to them, James clipped a leather leash to the ring on Aimee's collar, while Craig drew a black cloth from his pocket, slid it over Sandra's eyes, and tied it behind her head.

It was strange standing in the woods with her eyes covered. In total blackness.

Like the night with her Fantasy Stranger.

Was Craig her Fantasy Stranger? Would she relive that wonderful experience again with him?

But this time he intended to overpower her. Take her by force. *Oh, God, how exciting!*

It wouldn't be the same as that other night. That time had been intense but ultimately tender and loving. Tonight promised to be intense, too, but in a way that was tumultuous and breathtaking.

She was almost afraid to discover that Craig was her Fantasy Stranger. Or even James. Because that would change it forever.

Maybe her perfect memory of that night was just a manifestation of her long year without any man, of her building up the memory of what making love with a man could be. Whoever had played that part had given her something so perfect, so precious, that she was afraid of ruining it forever.

She felt Craig's finger glide over the front of her collar,

then slide through the ring. He tugged her forward. He walked close to her—so close, their thighs brushed together as they moved.

"Step up," Craig said.

She nudged her toe forward and felt a vertical surface. She dragged her foot upward. Straight. A step. She lifted her foot until she felt a bump. The top of the step. She placed her foot on top, then carefully moved her other foot onto the next step. Craig guided her up two more steps. Onto the deck of his cottage.

She heard a door slide open and he pressed her forward. A moment later, the door slid closed. They continued walking, then turned. Into a bedroom?

Craig walked her forward, then held her shoulders firm, keeping her in place.

Sandra heard a clink, then James said, "Take off your robe."

She heard the rustling of cloth. He must have freed Aimee's hands.

One of the men whistled. "Well, now. There's a sexy sight." James' voice.

There was silence for a few moments and she didn't know what was going on, then she heard Aimee's soft moan and she got a rough idea.

"Now, take off her robe."

A second later, Sandra felt a soft touch against her wrists, then the tension between them loosened. She dropped her hands to her sides. Someone pulled on Sandra's belt, jostling a little, then it released. Soft fingers brushed along her neck, then under the collar of her robe. Down the lapel. Easing the fabric apart. Slowly.

She sucked in a breath as cool air washed along her chest. Her nipples puckered as the robe slowly eased down her shoulders, then her arms. Finally it fell to the floor and goose bumps danced across her skin.

"Hells bells, those are a sensational pair of tits," Craig said.

Her cheeks flushed and she became intensely aware of her breathing, especially how each inward breath lifted her breasts. Both men would be staring at them, watching her distended nipples hardening,

"Touch them," James said.

Sandra didn't know if he was talking to her or Aimee, but Aimee's soft hands covered Sandra's breasts. She massaged a little, then stroked underneath.

"I'd like to see those nipples a little harder," James said.

Aimee stroked Sandra's nipple gently. It throbbed and hardened even more. Then a soft warm mouth covered her other nipple. Aimee's tongue played over Sandra's nub lightly. Teasing. Then she sucked softly, triggering intense tingles through her breast. Sandra's vagina ached with need.

"Very nice," James said. "Now kiss her."

Aimee's hands cupped Sandra's cheeks, then soft lips caressed Sandra's. Aimee's tongue dipped inside Sandra's mouth. It was such a sweet, gentle touch, Sandra found herself returning it.

"Oh, yeah, baby." Craig chuckled. "That's what I like to see."

Aimee deepened the kiss, gliding her arms around Sandra and drawing her against her body. Their breasts crushed against each other like warm erotic cushions. Aimee's hard nipples pressed against Sandra, making her own nipples harder still.

"Okay, that's enough." James' voice sounded hoarse.

Sandra could imagine his big cock was pressing so hard against his pants it must be painful. She almost giggled as Aimee's lips released hers. Two strong wrists grasped her arms and raised them, drawing them far apart, then she heard the now-familiar metal on metal as they attached her wrists to something over her head.

A moment later, she felt her arms pulled upward. Soon she found herself standing on her toes. Then pressure strained against her wrists as her toes left the ground. Her legs dangled free beneath her.

No sight. No stable floor beneath her feet. She felt so . . . vulnerable.

She heard a chain clank and she realized she wasn't moving anymore. The men grasped her thighs and lifted them. She felt something glide under each thigh, the sound of chains clinking. When the men released her legs, they stayed suspended, some kind of wide strap holding them up.

She now hung in the air, her wrists above her head, wide apart, her legs suspended in front of her, also wide apart.

Her arms open . . . her legs spread wide . . . her body basically naked. Everything was open to them. She couldn't cover herself or fend off these pretend captors in any way. It felt incredibly sexy.

Fingers moved along the back of her head, then her blindfold came free. Aimee, the nakedness of her body emphasized by the black straps of her harness, stood in front of her. James stood beside her, the blindfold in his hand. He tossed it aside. She glanced up and saw that her wrists were attached to each end of a metal bar and her legs were held up by black leather slings hanging from chains also attached to the bar.

Craig unhooked a chain from the wall, and Sandra watched the tiger tattoo on his arm as she felt herself being lowered. When her hips were about waist height, the movement stopped and Craig reattached the chain. James stepped behind Aimee and positioned her straight in front of Sandra. His hands cupped the undersides of Aimee's breasts and he lifted them.

"These are so beautiful. I'd like you to lick them." James eased Aimee forward, holding one breast toward Sandra.

The dusky pink nipple stood firm and proud. Sandra pushed out her tongue and lapped it across the pebbly surface of the aureole, then over the hard nub. She twirled her tongue over the nipple several times. Aimee's eyes closed and she murmured an appreciative sound. James offered the other nipple to Sandra and she licked it.

"Now take it in your mouth and suck," James instructed.

Sandra opened her mouth and took it inside. She swirled her tongue over it again, then sucked lightly. Craig, who stood behind Aimee now, stroked over Aimee's bare behind while he watched Sandra.

"Harder now." James' blue-gray eyes glinted.

She sucked harder and Aimee moaned. James licked

Aimee's other nipple, then latched on. As the two of them sucked, Aimee's moans grew louder.

Finally, James drew away. "That's enough."

Sandra released Aimee's hard nipple, wishing someone would do something to her achy nipples. She got her wish as Craig leaned in and began to suck one nipple. James led Aimee to the wall and attached her leash to a hook, then returned to suck on Sandra's other nipple.

Pleasure thrummed through her at the feel of two hot man-mouths on her. James' hand stroked up and down her thigh, coming close, but not close enough, to her aching vagina. Craig's hand stroked her other thigh, lightly, in small circles. Every time he moved up her thigh, he came closer to her slit. She could feel the melting heat fill her opening. James' finger stroked over one of the harness straps between her legs, then outlined the little heart formed by her trimmed curls. Craig's fingers found her folds. He glided along them, then dipped between, lightly caressing her opening. She drew in a breath.

"Very wet." Craig grinned. "She likes this."

"Well, maybe she'll like this, too." James unfastened his jeans and dropped them to the floor, then stepped behind her.

He adjusted the chains holding up her wrists so that her shoulders lowered until her back was horizontal. He dropped his boxers to the floor and his hard cock bobbed forward. He stepped closer and pressed his cockhead to her cheek. She turned and opened her mouth, anxious to feel that wonderful cock in her mouth. He pressed it against her lips and she licked it, then he pressed it deeper, until it filled her mouth.

Craig's fingers, which had stopped moving while he watched James, stroked the length of her wet slit again. Then one finger slid inside. James pushed his cock deeper into her mouth. Craig stroked her inside, then slid in another finger. As Craig stroked, heat flared through her. She sucked on James' thick, hard cock.

Craig's fingers disappeared, then she felt his lips on her inner thigh. She trembled as his mouth moved over her folds. He licked her slit and she drew in a deep breath, then sucked harder on James. James groaned as Craig's tongue found her clitoris. He licked and stroked the tender nub, sending rockets through her insides.

James pushed in deep and Sandra relaxed her throat and opened to accommodate him. He drew back and she released him, then licked his shaft. He moved closer and she licked his firm, shaven balls. Craig sucked on her clit and she gasped.

"You're going to make her come," James said.

Immediately, Craig stopped. "I wouldn't want that to happen too soon."

Craig stood up and dropped his shorts to the floor, then tossed away his boxers. He wrapped his hand around his huge cock and stepped beside her face, opposite James. He offered his cock to her and she licked it, then took it in her mouth and stroked the cockhead with her tongue. After a moment, he pushed in deeper, then pulsed in and out while she squeezed him inside her mouth.

He pulled free and she turned her head back to James. He glided into her mouth, then pulsed. She sucked and squeezed. James pulled free, then positioned himself between her legs and licked her slit. She moaned then swallowed Craig again, sucking hard as James licked her. He found her clit and teased mercilessly. She sucked hard on Craig's cock, then released it and moaned as intense sensations swelled through her.

Waves of pleasure rose within her and she knew, any moment now, her first orgasm would arrive.

Then James drew away. "This captive is a little too willing. I'd like some resistance."

Her insides clenched as tiny spasms erupted. So damn close!

Craig grinned. "You're right."

Craig walked to Aimee and released her leash from the wall. He linked her wrists together behind her again, then led her across the room.

James adjusted the chains on Sandra's wrists, pulling her up to a sitting position. Then he walked to the closet and grabbed another bar like the one Sandra was suspended from. He placed it on the floor beside Aimee and attached one of Aimee's ankles to one end while Craig attached the other ankle to the other end. This essentially forced Aimee's legs wide-open. James stood up and moved close behind her and cupped her breasts. She squirmed as if trying to resist. Craig stroked down her hips, then knelt down and licked her navel. Then downward. With her legs held wide, Aimee couldn't resist.

Sandra watched in fascination as Craig's tongue lapped over her slit, then found her clit. Her own clitoris ached for more attention.

James squeezed and fondled Aimee's breasts while Craig feasted on her clit.

Aimee gasped and he pulled back. He stood up and pressed his cock to her opening. Then his long rigid cock slid into her. Sandra's vagina clenched, need burning through her. Aimee moaned softly as that huge cock filled her to the base. Then he pulled out. His shaft glistened with Aimee's moisture. James moved around and he pressed her to the wall, then placed his hard cock to her opening and pushed inside.

Sandra watched James' cock sink into Aimee. Oh, God, she wanted to feel that right now.

James glided in and out several times, then stepped aside. Craig took his place and pushed his cock into her, thrusting slowly a couple of times. Then James again. When he pulled out, Craig grinned and glanced at James.

"I feel like a sandwich. What about you?" Craig asked.

"Definitely."

Craig grabbed Aimee's shoulders and drew her forward. She hobbled toward him, trying to keep her balance with her legs spread wide by the bar. When they reached the dresser, Craig stopped, then grasped her hips and impaled himself deep inside her. Then he leaned back against the dresser as James moved forward.

Sandra licked her lips as James, still slick from Aimee's moisture, pushed his cockhead against her back opening and eased forward. Slowly, his long cock disappeared into her ass. Sandra's breathing increased as she watched her friend standing there with two big cocks inside her. Aimee's cheeks were flushed red and her breathing was loud and erratic.

The men began to move and Aimee moaned. Yearning thrummed through Sandra at the spectacle. The men increased their thrusts, pounding into Aimee as her moans increased.

"Oh, God . . . oh, yes!" Aimee groaned, then wailed as an orgasm claimed her.

The men thrust, faster and faster. Craig groaned. Then James. They both collapsed against her, sandwiching her between their hard bodies.

Sandra wanted to weep in desperation.

Finally the men pulled out of Aimee. Craig released her ankles and James unfastened her wrists. She walked to the easy chair near the bed and slumped into it, curling up like a cat in front of the fire, a satisfied smile on her face.

Sandra's gaze fell to Craig's wilted cock, then James'.

Damn, she wanted them now, but she needed them hard. Remembering that they wanted resistance, she arched her body.

"Let me free." She raised her hips, then dropped them, then her breasts, undulating up and down as if trying to pull free of the chains.

They watched her, grinning. Craig's cock twitched a little.

"Aimee, you've got to help me."

Aimee smiled.

"Oh, honey, you don't know what you're missing. Those big cocks stuffed inside me. Fucking me so hard." She glanced toward the men. "But those cocks won't do you much good in their current state." She winked. "So, of course, I'll help you."

Aimee stood up and walked toward Sandra. She stroked along Sandra's waist, then over her breasts. Sandra sucked in air at the sweet sensation. Aimee continued to stroke Sandra's body. Up and down. Over her breasts, down her belly, across her hips. She moved between Sandra's legs and stroked below her navel then . . . farther down. As Aimee's delicate fingers stroked over her wet flesh, Sandra moaned, then sucked in air as Aimee's tongue lapped along her slit. Her fingers slipped inside and Sandra clenched around them.

"Oh, honey. You really do need these men to fuck you." She smiled. "And from the look of things, they'll be ready very soon."

Sandra glanced around to see both men stroking their semirigid cocks.

Aimee licked along Sandra's slit again, then found her clit. Sandra cried out in pleasure.

"Whoa there." Craig grasped Aimee's shoulders and drew her away. "It's our turn now."

James' hands cupped her breasts and he pulled her tight against him. She arched against his hands, her nipples digging into his hot palms. He nuzzled her neck, sending tingles dancing through her. Craig stood in front of her, grasped her knees, and pushed them apart. Shivers galloped along her nerve endings at his abruptness. He stepped forward and pressed his iron-hard cock to her wetness.

James tightened his grip on her breasts, then fondled them. Craig thrust forward. She gasped as he impaled her, his huge cock stretching her. He swirled his hips, spiraling his shaft inside her. She groaned at the exquisite sensations. It went on and on, making her dizzy with delight.

James released her breasts, then moved in front of her. Craig drew out. Slowly. His wide cockhead stroking her passage. When he fell free, she wanted to weep with disappointment. Then James stepped up. His cock drove forward, penetrating her deeply. She squeezed him hard, wanting to pull him in as deep as she could. He tipped his pelvis forward and back in a rocking motion, sending ripples of sensation blossoming inside her as his cock massaged her passage.

He pulled out, then stepped behind her again. She felt his slick cockhead press against her back opening, then pressure. Her opening stretched as he pushed forward, widening around the corona. Once his cockhead was inside, he paused.

Craig pressed his cock to her slit and he eased forward, filling her slowly. Before he was all the way in, James eased forward again, too. Both of them pressing into her at the same time. Two long hard shafts. Pushing deeper. She held her breath at the intense sensations.

Then they stopped, both fully immersed. Neither of them moved. They simply held her locked between them. Both men pressed tight against her, front and back. Hard, muscular chests. Big broad shoulders. Long hard shafts inside her.

Finally, she exhaled and sucked in a breath. She began to squirm, needing more.

Craig chuckled and began to draw back. Then he eased forward again. Then both men began to move. Pushing into her. Drawing back. Forward again. They found a rhythm that set her senses on fire. Pulsing deep. Thrusting. Stretching her. Her insides ached with pleasure washing through every cell, growing with every surge forward. Her hands balled into fists. She wanted to cling to Craig's broad shoulders, but her wrists were suspended above her.

She sucked in air faster and faster as they picked up the pace. Their cocks plunged into her. Pleasure blazed through her body, catapulting her to an explosion of pure joy. She let out a soulful wail, then switched to an ear-piercing shriek as they continued to pound into her, launching her into ecstasy.

James grunted, followed immediately by Craig. She felt heat inside her as both climaxed.

They stopped moving, collapsing against her. James nuzzled behind her ear and Craig cupped the back of her head and kissed her. A sweet, gentle kiss.

Reminiscent of her Fantasy Stranger.

Her gaze pivoted to his face.

Was Craig her Fantasy Stranger?

Fifteen

Sandra sat on the grass in front of James, his arm around her waist as she leaned back against him. His cheek rested against her hair. After the sensational bondage session, the four of them had cuddled for a while in bed, then the guys had cooked some steaks on the barbecue. After dinner, they all settled on the grass under the stars with a bottle of wine and stared out over the glistening water as they talked.

Sandra sipped her wine, then sighed, enjoying being right here, right now. A soft breeze lifted a lock of her hair and it danced against her face. James stroked it behind her ear.

"Are you cold?" he asked. "I could grab a blanket from inside."

Although the thought of snuggling under a blanket with James had a definite appeal, Sandra smiled and shook her head. "No, I'm fine, thanks."

She did not want to move from this spot.

She glanced toward Aimee, who looked quite cozy

settled against Craig's side, his arm around her hip. Sandra's gaze wandered to the tiger tattoo prowling up his arm and over his shoulder.

"I really like that tattoo of yours, Craig," Sandra said. "Is there some significance to the tiger?"

Craig smiled and rotated his shoulder, flexing the muscles in his arm. "In Eastern mythology, a tiger represents power. In fact, it's on a par with the dragon. A lot of people get dragon tattoos, though. I wanted to do something a little different."

Aimee laughed. "Yeah? That's not what your sister told me."

Craig's eyes narrowed. "Cindy told you about my tattoo?"

"That's right, big fella. You want to give us the whole story, or should I spill it?"

He chuckled. "Okay. I'm fifteen years older than Cindy, and when she was about four, I had a favorite shirt, with stripes, that I liked to wear. One time when I was wearing it, Cindy said I was striped like a tiger. I roared and we horsed around a little. She started calling me "Tiger" after that. The nickname stuck and, when she was in her teens, she dared me to get a tattoo of a tiger."

"So that's when you went out and got it?" Sandra asked, imagining Craig roughhousing with a little four-year-old. What an endearing image.

"Not exactly. If I did everything she dared me to do, I'd be covered in tattoos and piercings, with green hair, living in Bora Bora. Or Alaska." He stroked Aimee's hair.

"When she was in her last year of high school, she struggled with her marks and I told her if she made the honor roll, I'd get the tattoo." He glanced around at their watching eyes. "Hey, I didn't think she'd actually make it, but that girl studied with a vengeance."

Aimee nudged his chest. "Yeah, and she told me you helped her every step of the way." Aimee glanced at Sandra. "He's just a big softy."

"Softy?" Craig tightened his arms around Aimee's waist and pulled her tight to him. "I might be *big,* but I'm not *soft.*"

Aimee's eyes widened and her lips turned up in a big grin. "Oh, you're right."

She turned toward him and stroked his cheek with one finger, then leaned in and kissed him. He flipped her onto his lap, then his mouth meshed with hers again and he gave her a long, lingering kiss. When he released her, she gazed up at him with glittering eyes, her cheeks flushed and her breathing accelerated.

James nuzzled the back of Sandra's neck and tingles danced down her spine. His hand stroked upward, then covered her breast. He caressed her as they watched Craig kiss Aimee again.

Would James suggest they go into the cottage and give Craig and Aimee some privacy? Or would he just start something right here on the grass?

She smiled at the thought. That was the beauty of this little island. They could be free and open, not worried about people from neighboring cottages passing by. They had total privacy.

She liked the idea of being out in the open, the stars over their heads, the trees around them. Making love in the moonlight. So romantic. And sexy.

And not worrying about Craig and Aimee right next to them. In fact, hoping they would join in. It had been exhilarating earlier, being touched by Aimee. Touching Aimee. Knowing how excited it made the men. Remembering how excited it had made her.

Craig's hand glided underneath Aimee's robe and Sandra could see his hand moving under the fabric, stroking Aimee's breast. The nipple on Aimee's other breast peaked, the taut outline visible through the silk fabric.

Sandra's own nipples surged forward. James cupped her other breast and he caressed both of them.

Heat simmered through her. She wanted him again. His big hard cock. Craig's big hard cock, too. She wanted both men to lie on the ground, their naked erections facing the stars while Aimee and Sandra both licked them like tall lollipops, then climbed aboard and rode them to heaven.

"Um . . ." Aimee glanced at her watch.

Aimee sat up and the fabric of her robe pushed sideways because of Craig's hand underneath, revealing the side of her naked breast.

"Sandra, we should get going."

Sandra tipped her head in surprise. "Really? But it's still early." Sandra had no idea what time it was. She just knew she didn't want the night to end yet.

Craig drew his hands from Aimee's chest. A little of her dusky nipple peeked out before she tugged the robe closed.

James stood up, easing Sandra to her feet, too. "We'll walk you back."

Sandra's eyebrows furrowed. "Okay."

It wasn't like Aimee to cut an evening short like this, but maybe she was really tired. She had had to work late last night and had probably left early this morning to drive up here.

James held Sandra's hand as they walked along the path through the woods.

Once they arrived at the cottage, Aimee stopped.

"You know, it's a beautiful night. It's a shame to go inside." Aimee smiled at Sandra. "I think you should sleep outside."

Sandra frowned. "Are you nuts?"

Aimee laughed. "No, really. The hammock is really comfortable, and the night air is . . . exhilarating."

"Really?"

Clearly, Aimee had something in mind. And, judging from the wild experiences Sandra had enjoyed since following Aimee's lead, Sandra knew she'd be smart to go along.

"Yeah. And you don't have to worry about any *strangers* in the woods. You'll be perfectly safe."

A shiver danced up Sandra's spine. Her Fantasy Stranger. That's what Aimee was hinting at.

"Okay. I'll sleep in the hammock." She'd sleep on the ground if that's what Aimee told her to do to be with her Fantasy Stranger.

Sandra stepped toward the cloth hammock, which hung between two sturdy trees.

"Wait." Aimee walked toward her. "You can't sleep in your robe."

"I can't?"

Aimee shook her head. Sandra untied the belt and glanced at the men, watching her. Ah well, they'd both seen her naked so being shy now made no sense. She opened the robe and dropped it to the ground. Having shed the harness before dinner, she now stood totally naked before them, enjoying the heat of the men's gazes.

The hammock had been hung fairly high, but she noticed a step stool beside it, so she climbed up and sat down on the hammock.

"I think you should lie sideways," Aimee suggested.

The hammock was very wide. Sandra lay down as Aimee had suggested, with the trees on either side of her.

"It's pretty bright, with the moonlight and all, so here's a night mask to block the light." Aimee pulled a black satin mask from the large pocket of her robe and handed it to Sandra. Sandra placed it over her eyes and tugged the elastic straps around her head. The mask sat comfortably in place.

"Oh, and just so you won't fall off during the night, we're going to tie you to the hammock."

She felt straps attached to her wrists, then hands drew her arms to either side of her and attached them to the hammock.

"Good night," Aimee said.

Sandra heard footsteps on the deck stairs, then the sounds of the door sliding open and closed. She lay out in the open, with the crickets chirping, wondering if she really wanted to stay out here alone for long. But surely her Fantasy Stranger would come along soon. In fact, whichever man it was had probably stayed outside while the other had accompanied Aimee inside. Or possibly the other man had stayed outside to watch.

But as she lay there, the warmth of the wine still heating her insides, the soft rustling of the leaves high above her, she found herself relaxing. Tiredness washed over her and she dozed off.

Slowly, she resurfaced to consciousness as she felt something petal-soft brush against her cheek, then her nose. The sweet scent of a rose filled her nostrils.

Then lips brushed the side of her neck. Goose bumps flashed across her skin. His hands stroked over her breasts, caressing softly. Her nipples peaked, longing for his touch. She arched against him, sighing softly. His hand slipped away.

A moment later, he stroked her calves, then her thighs. She opened, wanting to feel his touch against her slick folds, but he grasped her ankles and she felt herself pulled down the hammock until her legs dangled over the edge, her knees supported by the cloth. The hammock tipped, putting her in a sitting position.

He drew her legs wide and she felt his muscular legs between her thighs. Then his hands cupped her face. Their lips joined and his tongue swirled into her mouth. She sighed, accepting him. So sweet. So tender. His arms came around her and he drew her against him. Her breasts pressed against his hard naked chest. So solid and firm. She could feel his long cock pressing against her stomach. Hard and ready for her.

"Oh, I want you." She couldn't wrap her arms around him because they were pulled above her head, still fastened to the hammock.

He slipped away from her, then his lips found her nipple and she sighed. His other hand caressed her other breast. She arched as he licked her hard nub. Then he sucked and she moaned.

"Yes, touch me. I want to feel your hands on me." She couldn't see him or hear him, other than his breathing, so she wanted to break the silence between them.

He caressed her breasts, teasing one nipple with his fingers while he sucked on the other, driving her wild.

"Oh, yes. That's so good."

He kissed down her stomach, then over her curls. His tongue traced a path around the heart they formed. His fingers stroked over her folds, then slipped inside her. She clenched around him. Ready and wanting. Desperate to feel him inside her.

Devlin's cock was so hard he thought it would burst. He'd arrived at the cottage at eight o'clock, as planned with Aimee, and waited in the bushes until Aimee had brought Sandra and the others back to the cottage. Thoughts of making love to Sandra again had his cock swollen, especially knowing what Aimee had planned for Sandra earlier this evening—Sandra bound and suspended, used as the men's plaything. When he'd seen the four of them step out of the woods, jealousy had flooded through him, but it had fled at the sight of Sandra's naked body once she'd dropped her robe to the ground. Then he'd found it exciting seeing the men watch her with hunger in their eyes.

Now she lay in the hammock before him, her legs sprawled over the edge, open wide, ready for him. She wanted him to touch her. Her hot inner passage squeezed his fingers. She was dripping wet and ready for him.

He drew his fingers from her heat, then stroked over her clit. He leaned forward and licked it, then pressed the tip of his tongue against the button. She squirmed, then moaned softly as he lapped harder. Then he sucked on her and her moan increased.

She was so hot and wet. His cock throbbed with need.

"I want you inside me." Her throaty words drove him wild.

He stood up and pressed his cockhead to her slick opening. Oh, man, she was so wet and hot. He pushed forward, allowing his cockhead to slip inside.

Sandra squeezed the big cockhead inside her. He swirled a little but wouldn't give her any more. She wanted that big cock all the way in.

"Please, fuck me." She gasped as he drove into her in one deep thrust.

He held her tight against his pelvis. She wrapped her legs around him, sucking in air at the intensely full sensation.

Then he drew back and drove deep again. She was so close already. His thrusts increased, sending the hammock rocking.

Magical sensations quivered through her, then ricocheted along her nerve endings. His big cock plunged into her again and again. Pleasure thrummed through her body, then bliss erupted inside her as she skyrocketed into a glorious orgasm.

He pumped a few more times, then stiffened against her as he filled her with heat.

She sighed and collapsed against the hammock. He drew away, then she felt him adjust the hammock under her legs again. He freed one of her hands, then drew it toward her other hand and fastened them together. A moment later, he climbed into the hammock behind her and snuggled up in a spoon position. She fell asleep in the warmth of his arms, his lips nuzzling her neck with incredible tenderness.

Sandra awoke the next morning with the sun shining on her face and a soft blanket over her. She brushed her hair from her face and realized her wrists were no longer attached to the hammock.

She pulled off the eye mask and glanced behind her, but she already knew her Fantasy Stranger was gone. She'd known it the moment she'd woken up.

Being in his arms last night had been sensational. His tenderness . . . the loving way he touched her . . . the way her heart fluttered when he was near . . . All these things made her time with him extraordinary. Far beyond what she felt with James and Craig. Even though her Fantasy Stranger was one of them.

It was like there was some deeper truth they shared when they were together. As if by blindfolding her, he could show his true self. Show how much he felt for her. And she sensed he had very deep feelings for her. Maybe even . . . love.

But that was ridiculous. She didn't want any man falling in love with her right now. And *she* sure didn't want to fall in love. Not yet. Eric had been the only man she'd ever been with before coming to the cottage with Aimee. Devlin had been right. She needed to take this time to experience different men. To be a little wild.

To be free.

She rolled on her back and stared up at the trees as birds twittered in the branches. Her insides quivered with yearning to be with her Fantasy Stranger again.

Ah, damn. Maybe if she could figure out once and for all if he was James or Craig . . . but no. That wouldn't help. Knowing would probably make it even harder. At least now, when she was with them without the pretense of the Fantasy Stranger persona, they all had a good time but with no emotional attachment. If she knew which one it was, it might throw off the balance and complicate everything.

"Hey, sleepyhead." Aimee walked toward the hammock carrying a big blue beach towel. "I brought you a towel. Let's go for a swim."

Sandra pushed her feet over the edge of the hammock and

stood up. Aimee handed her the towel and Sandra wrapped it around her body, then followed Aimee, similarly clad in only a beach towel, toward the path.

"By the way, I ticked off items one and two on the list. Being held captive and bondage." Aimee grinned. "That means only two to go."

Sixteen

Sandra laughed. "Too bad we don't have more time here so we could finish them off."

She couldn't believe she'd actually done most of the items on the list. Over the course of two short weeks, she'd become a wild woman. And she loved it!

"Don't worry. There are still plenty of weekends left this summer."

Moments later, they stepped onto the beach where they'd gone skinny-dipping that first morning on the island. Craig waved at them from the raft, where he stood totally naked, then dove into the water. James lay on his back on the raft, also naked.

Aimee laughed and shed her towel, then ran into the water. Sandra tossed aside her towel and followed. She swam straight to the raft and climbed onto it, then stood in front of James, blocking the sun. He opened his eyes and smiled up at her.

"Good morning."

"It is," she agreed, then she knelt over his thighs and wrapped her hands around his cock. It had been lying quietly on his legs, but at her touch, it bounced to life. She stroked and it swelled and hardened in her hand. An amazing thing, really.

With her free hand, she stroked her breast, the nipples already hard from the cool water. He covered her other breast with his hot hand and stroked. She wanted him. Now. She tweaked her nipple, then stroked down her stomach to her opening, then stroked herself, feeling the slickness. She pressed his cock to her slit and eased herself down on him.

"Oh, God that feels good," he said. "I take it you missed me."

"Oh, yeah." She squeezed him inside her, then rose up and glided down again.

She rode up and down, filling her passage with his hard shaft, driving pleasure through her. It welled up and blasted through her as she wailed in release. He groaned and filled her with hot liquid.

She rolled on her back and glanced around. Craig and Aimee sat on the side of the raft watching her, Craig stroking his own huge cock. Her gaze shifted to the tiger tattoo on his bicep. So sexy.

She opened her arms to him. "Craig. How about it?"

Craig glanced toward Aimee, and she smiled and nodded. He prowled over her and pressed his huge cock to her opening. She gasped as he thrust straight in. She wrapped her arms around his big broad shoulders.

"Fuck me. Hard."

He grinned and kissed her nose. Then he drew back and thrust again. And again. He pounded into her, catapulting her to another orgasm. She clung to his shoulders as she moaned, waves of pleasure washing through her. He tensed and groaned.

Craig rolled to her side and lay beside her. As her breathing returned to normal, she heard moaning and glanced around. James' cock thrust in and out of Aimee on the other side of the swim raft.

She felt no jealousy watching James fucking Aimee.

But what if she knew he was her Fantasy Stranger. Would she feel jealous then? What if she knew it was Craig?

What if Aimee suggested putting on a mask to be with Sandra's Fantasy Stranger? The very thought sent jealousy surging through her.

Sandra watched the shore whipping past as the boat raced across the water.

"Are you asking me to tell you who the Fantasy Stranger is?" Aimee asked.

Sandra pursed her lips. "No, that's not it. I just . . . I don't understand why I'm feeling this way. If I know who it is, will I stop obsessing over him? Or will it only make it worse?"

"What if these feelings you have for the Fantasy Stranger are real?"

"But that doesn't make any sense. If they were real, why wouldn't I feel them when I'm with the man without the mask?"

Aimee shrugged. "I don't know. Maybe the Fantasy Stranger isn't either James or Craig."

Sandra raised an eyebrow. "Are you telling me you brought a third man to the island?"

"Well, why not?" Aimee grinned. "You liked the two you saw. Would it have been wrong of me to have a spare tucked away for a special occasion?"

"Yes, it would be wrong." Sandra leaned back in her seat.

Aimee glanced toward her. "Why?"

"Well, because I'd never met him."

Aimee turned the boat in a wide curve, and Sandra saw the marina ahead.

"You'd never met Craig before and I thought you hadn't met James."

"But I did meet them before I had sex with them."

"Well, that's exactly the point, honey." Aimee slowed the boat as they approached the dock. "You had met them. So neither of them fit the sex with a *stranger* role."

"Are you saying the Fantasy Stranger isn't James or Craig?"

"I'm not really saying anything. You said you didn't want to know who he was. You'll just have to trust me on this."

Aimee pulled the boat into the slip and turned off the engine, then hopped onto the dock and tossed a loop over the cleat. Sandra stood up and handed the luggage to her.

Sandra wasn't sure if Aimee was just playing with her or seriously trying to tell her that the Fantasy Stranger was a third man. She didn't really believe that, though, because he just felt too . . . familiar. Even the first time, it had been as if her body knew him, though since it was the first time she'd made love in more than a year, her reeling senses had been in too tumultuous a state to really know what was real and imagined.

She hopped out of the boat and followed Aimee as she dragged the cooler, with the luggage atop, to the car.

But that familiarity, that sense of knowing him, had her pretty convinced it was James, even though when he was her Fantasy Stranger, his cock seemed bigger. More like Craig's. But that really could be a trick of her mind.

Sandra tossed and turned that night, thoughts of her Fantasy Stranger filling her mind.

All the fantastic sex she'd had with James and Craig—being captured by Craig, overpowered by him, sandwiched between both men—should have given her enough fantasies to fill her mind with wonder. But her thoughts kept wandering back to being in the arms of her Fantasy Stranger. She longed to feel the tenderness of his touch again. To feel his lips brush against her neck. To feel his arms around her, holding her tight to his solid body.

She *ached* for him.

Finally, she fell asleep, and dreamed of him. Hot . . . steamy . . . intense dreams. He touched her with a gentle passion that stirred her soul. His body joined with hers, filling her with intense desire. He made her feel cherished and . . . *loved.*

As he moved inside her, heat built within her . . . then exploded in exultant waves of bliss. She awoke in the throes of a powerful orgasm that washed through her body as she shuddered in ecstasy.

As she lay gasping on the bed, memories of his body pressed tight to hers still quivering through her brain, she realized she had to get over this fantasy.

She needed to stay grounded in reality. The whole problem with her marriage had been that she'd gotten lost in the fantasy of love and happily-ever-after. It's not that she didn't believe in those things, but they should be based on fact. On real feelings, for a real man.

And her Fantasy Stranger wasn't real. These strong feelings she had were probably just a result of the mask heightening her other senses, making things feel more intimate. The feelings she had for the Fantasy Stranger were no more real than the love she'd thought she'd felt for her ex-husband.

As long as she kept that in perspective, everything would be fine.

And the best way to do that would be to focus on a real man.

Sandra glanced at Aimee over her sandwich. "Remember our conversation about Devlin last week? How he's resisting starting up something with me?"

"You mean, how he's resisting your feminine wiles and how you'd really like to *totally submit* to him?" Aimee grinned. "Yeah, I remember."

"Okay, well . . . Do you think I'd be a really bad person if I . . . you know, sort of seduced him into it?"

Aimee's gaze locked with hers and she smiled broadly. "Not at all. I think it would be brilliant."

"Even though he told me he didn't want to endanger our friendship?"

Aimee shrugged. "Look, you have one opinion about this, he has another. There's nothing wrong with trying to convince a person to change his mind, right?"

Sandra smiled. "That's what I was thinking." She sipped her drink. "I'd need your help."

"You've got it. What do you have in mind?"

"Well, first . . . You have a key to Devlin's apartment, right?"

On Friday evening, as the setting sun cast the clouds a deep orange against the backdrop of a rich blue sky, Devlin walked toward the front door of his apartment building. His cell phone rang and he pulled it from his pocket.

"Hello?"

"Hi, it's Aimee."

"Hey, there. What's up?"

"Are you on your way home?"

He turned his key in the lock and pushed open the front door, then stepped from the warm outside air into the air-conditioned lobby.

"Yeah, I just stepped inside. Why?" He strode to the elevator and pushed the call button. The elevator on the right opened immediately and he stepped inside.

"Well, I left a surprise in your apartment. I wanted to make sure you found it."

He and Aimee had exchanged keys quite a while ago, for emergencies and to take care of each other's places when one of them went on vacations or business trips. Plants, mail, that kind of thing.

"A surprise? But it's not my birthday. What's up?" He stepped off the elevator and headed toward his apartment.

"You'll see. Just make sure you go right up. Okay?"

"Sure. Do you want me to call you after I find out what it is?" He stopped outside his door and reached into his pocket for his keys.

Aimee giggled. "Um . . . no, that's okay. Later will be fine." Then she hung up.

Devlin had no idea what that was all about.

Curious, he opened the door and glanced around. He didn't see anything in the living room or dining room. He went into the kitchen, but there was no surprise there. Then he spotted a note on the fridge held by a round blue magnet.

Look in the bedroom.

Devlin walked down the hall and stopped outside his bedroom. The door was closed. He hadn't left it that way. He turned the knob and pushed open the door, then peered inside.

His gaze darted immediately to the bed.

Sandra.

His heart raced.

Naked.

He sucked in a lungful of air.

And tied up.

Seventeen

Devlin grabbed the doorjamb and concentrated on breathing, his gaze locked on the intensely erotic sight of Sandra with her arms spread out wide above her head, her wrists bound to the headboard, and her legs spread open and bound to the footboard. A leather collar was around her neck.

"I know I'm your prisoner," she said. "You can do anything you want to me and I can't stop you. There's no point in me resisting."

His cock twitched in his pants, fully engorged.

Resisting? But he had to resist. He couldn't make love to her. No matter how much he wanted to. No matter how much she wanted him to.

His gaze glided over her full, perfectly formed breasts, the tight nipples thrusting straight up, then down to her pussy with the neatly trimmed heart shape, and his hormones ricocheted through him. Intense heat settled in his groin and his cock ached desperately.

All resistance ebbed from him. He had no choice. He *had* to have her.

He grabbed the knot of his tie and pulled it downward as he stepped toward her, then tugged it over his head and tossed it aside. He unfastened the top couple of buttons of his shirt, making it easier to breath, then tugged off his shirt and dropped it to the floor.

As he unfastened his belt, he hesitated. What if she recognized him as her Fantasy Stranger? His cock inside her. The way he touched her. Surely she'd know.

She arched her naked body in a slow-motion surge against the bonds. His cock strained harder against the cloth binding it. He flung open his belt, unzipped his pants, and dropped them to the floor.

He'd act differently. He wouldn't *let* her know he was the same man. As her Fantasy Stranger, he'd been gentle and loving. A tender lover. Now she wanted a captor. Someone to ravage her. He would play her fantasy to the hilt.

He thrust his gray boxers to the floor and tossed aside his socks, then stepped beside her.

Her eyes widened as her gaze took in his erection.

"Oh, my God. It's so big."

His cock twitched at the admiration in her voice.

"The better to fuck you with, my dear." He pressed his cockhead to her mouth and she licked the end. Then he pushed between her lips. The feel of her hot moist mouth surrounding him made him groan. He wrapped his hand around her head and curled his fingers in her long black hair, then pulled her forward, filling her with his cock. She gagged a little and he drew back, then glided forward slowly. She relaxed and he pushed half his shaft into her mouth, then stopped. She squeezed him and he groaned.

Still cupping her head, he drew back a little.

"Now suck it."

She obeyed and heat surged through him. He had to stop himself from thrusting deep, to feel her heat all around him. His balls tightened as she sucked, excitement speeding through every cell. Then he erupted into her, intense pleasure ripping through his body.

He drew back, his deflated cock dropping from her mouth. She ran her tongue around her lips and gazed up at him, hunger in her eyes.

Oh, God, he wanted her.

He wanted to dive on top of her right now, knowing his cock would surge to full height at the first touch of her body against his. Even now, it swelled.

But it would be over too fast. He wanted more.

"You are very complacent, and I like a little fight in my women." He unfastened the cord attaching her wrist straps to the headboard, then moved to the foot of the bed and unfastened her ankles from the footboard. He hooked his finger through the ring of her collar and drew her forward. "Maybe a little punishment will enliven your spirit."

He led her into the kitchen, then leaned her over the wooden table. He drew her arms over the other side of the table and used the rope to attach her wrists to the table legs, holding her in place. Walking around behind her, he gazed at her delicious ass on display in front of him. He leaned down and eased her legs apart, then bound them to the table, too.

He stood up and his blood flooded to his groin at seeing her legs wide apart, her round, firm ass parted slightly to reveal her moist folds. He wanted to run his fingers over them, then thrust inside her silky opening. Then he wanted to press his cock to her and drive into her . . . straight to heaven.

But he held back.

He placed his hands on the small of her back, then ran them up to her shoulder blades and around until he brushed the sides of her breasts. He pushed under her, between the soft flesh of her mounds and the cool wood of the table, finding her nipples. They were hard and distended.

"You like the cold, hard table against your breasts, don't you?"

When she didn't answer, he gently grasped her hair and coiled it around his hand, then drew her head back a little. He kissed her arched neck.

"You like the table against your breasts, don't you?" he repeated.

"Yes," she murmured.

With his free hand, he stroked under her breast, then cupped it and squeezed.

"You like me touching your breast . . . squeezing it. Don't you?"

"Yes." Her word came out deep and throaty.

He stroked around her hips and over her round ass.

"You like me touching you here?" he asked.

"Yes."

"And here?" He stroked between her cheeks and over her slit. Slick moisture coated his fingertips.

"Oh, God, yes."

He drew his hand away, then smacked lightly across her buttock. She gasped.

"Do you like that?"

"Um . . . I . . ."

He smacked again, a little harder this time. Then he stroked over her rosy cheek, then he smacked the other cheek.

"I think you like it."

His fingers trailed over her slit again, and she moaned.

He smacked her bottom again, then stroked. Smacked, then stroked.

"Do you like it?" He slid his fingers inside her slit.

"Yes."

He pushed deeper.

"Oh, yes."

He drew his fingers out, then grabbed a chair, and sat down. He leaned forward and drew her cheeks apart, then licked along her slit. She moaned.

"Oh, please fuck me."

He stood up and smacked her bottom, a little harder this time. The rosiness turned deeper pink.

"No demands. You're my prisoner, remember?"

He stood up and left the room.

Sandra groaned as she heard him leave. The hunger inside her demanded to be satisfied, but she could do nothing with her arms and legs bound. If she could she would have chased after him, demand that he satisfy her. Or see to it herself. But she could do neither. The ache burned within her.

A few moments later, she heard him enter the room again. His hand glided over her ass in a gentle caress, so different from the firm slaps he'd administered earlier. The sensations had been sharp and stinging . . . and incredibly erotic.

She considered goading him into slapping her ass again, but the idea of letting him lead won out.

He stepped in front of her, his massive cock in his hand. He brought it to her lips and she opened for him. His cockhead slid inside and she took it.

"Suck," he commanded.

She obeyed, squeezing the mushroom-shaped flesh inside her mouth, then sucking hard. After a moment, he pulled free.

"Good." He walked around behind her, then his hand stroked over her ass again.

Then *smack*. Her cheek burned and heat flushed through her. She arched her ass toward him. He smacked again and she groaned. His fingers stroked over her slit, then glided into her. He leaned in and licked her again as his finger found her clit and stroked lightly.

"Oh, yes." It felt erotic and intense.

His fingers pulled free, then glided between her cheeks to her back opening. He pushed one slick fingertip into her. Slowly. Then a second. After a couple of moments, he swirled his fingers around, then pushed deeper. He pulled them away, then something bigger pressed against her. Thicker than a finger, and hard. But not as thick as his cock. It pushed inside a little, then stopped. Then it pushed a little deeper.

"Relax," he urged.

She drew in a deep breath and let the tension ease from her. Whatever it was pushed in deeper, then stopped. He swirled it around in her ass. It felt sexy and wicked. And incredibly good.

His fingers stroked over her slit and dipped inside her. The combination of sensations flooded her with wild longing. Her breathing increased as the pleasure increased. As she moaned, his fingers slipped free. She moaned in frustration.

He left the room again, leaving the thing still embedded in her ass.

Devlin waited in the other room for what felt like forever, but his watch showed it as five minutes. He stepped into the kitchen again, his gaze resting on her curved ass, the vivid purple circle resting flat on her ass cheeks the only evidence of the butt plug inside her. At the thought of that silicone cone inside her tight opening, his cock twitched.

He walked up behind her and sat down on the chair, her ass parted in front of him. He grasped the base of the butt plug and swirled it in a spiral. She moaned. He leaned forward and licked her slit, tasting her sweet, slick nectar. God, he loved feeling her under his tongue. Loved the whimpers of pleasure she made.

He leaned back and stroked her slit, then dragged his damp fingers over his cock, glazing it in her moisture. He didn't touch her at all, just stared at her. She squirmed, clearly feeling his hot gaze boring into her.

He stroked over her round ass, then smacked several times, enjoying the rosy blush of her flesh. Unable to stand the intense burn inside himself any longer, he stood up and pressed his cock to her opening, then drove forward. His cock plunged into her, deep and hard. She gasped and moaned. He grasped her hips, then drew back and thrust again. Her passage massaged his aching cock as he surged forward. She squeezed around him and he moaned.

His balls tightened and he knew it was time. He began to thrust steadily. Deep. Fast. Hard.

She gasped, then wailed. As she arched against him, crying out in ecstasy, he exploded inside her in an intense, truly mind-blowing release, the pleasure surging beyond anything he'd ever experienced.

After a few moments, once they'd both caught their breath, he released her wrists from the rope wrapped around the table legs, then her ankles. He helped her to stand up, then she stepped into his arms and kissed him. As her naked body pressed against his, he felt stirrings in his groin again. God, even though she'd just fully satisfied him, he wanted her again. And he knew he would never stop wanting her.

Their lips parted and she gazed up at him, her olive green eyes glowing.

"You're not mad at me?" she asked.

"Mad?" The question dumbfounded him.

"Well, you had been resisting taking this step and I sort of forced you."

He grinned. "Yes. You did, didn't you?" His hands stroked over her ass and he pulled her tight against his pelvis, his semi-rigid cock pressing against her. "Maybe I'll just have to punish you again."

He smacked her ass. She wrapped her hand around his cock and pumped, driving him to distraction as blood rushed to her touch.

"Bring it on," she challenged.

He pulled her tight against him as he backed her against the wall. He pressed his now fully erect cock to her opening and drove inside her hot, welcoming slit. He plunged deep, driving her against the wall. She gasped, her eyes dark with hunger.

He thrust into her, again and again, watching her face. Her cheeks flushed and her eyes glimmered. She clung to his shoulders, then threw her head back and gasped. As she moaned in orgasm, he groaned, elated at his ability to bring her such pleasure.

After a moment she smiled, then stroked his cheek. "Hey, stud. You're pretty incredible."

He kissed her, then smiled. "That's Master Stud to you."

She giggled and he took her hand and led her to the bedroom. They curled up in his bed and he drew her snug against his body. She stroked his cheek, then released his hair from its binding and ran her fingers through it as she snuggled against his shoulder.

God, he loved this woman. He desperately wanted her to be a permanent part of his life.

Somehow he had to convince her that he was the right man for her.

Devlin opened his eyes to the early morning light, totally aware of the sleeping woman pressed close to his body. His cock responded in the most natural way, swelling at the depth of longing in him. He turned his head toward her. Sandra's eyes were closed and her breathing even. His heart accelerated at the sight of her. She looked like a sleeping goddess. He wanted to stroke her soft cheek, then capture her slightly parted lips and kiss her to wakefulness.

Last night, he'd done his best to behave differently from when he played her Fantasy Stranger, not wanting her to figure out he and the Fantasy Stranger were one and the same. He didn't want to ruin things now. As much as he'd like to wake her with a kiss, then make slow, passionate love to her all morning, he didn't want to take the chance of ruining his plan.

Of course, his plan seemed totally off the rails right now, but he could get it back on track. Right now, that meant continuing to play the part he'd designed for himself.

Eighteen

Slowly, Devlin drew his arm from under Sandra. She murmured, then sighed and rolled away. He sat up and pushed his hair behind his ear, then picked up the covered elastic from the bedside table.

He showered and shaved, then sat in the upholstered chair in his bedroom with the printed report he'd brought home from work, and began to read.

"Hey, there."

Sandra's sleepy voice drew his attention from the words on the page. He glanced toward the bed. His heart tightened in his chest at the sight of her angelic face, her eyes only partly open, a soft smile on her lips. She seemed to glow in the early morning light.

She pushed back strands of the long black hair that wisped across her face, then patted the mattress beside her.

"Why don't you come back to bed?"

Everything inside him demanded he leap up and fly

into the bed with her again. To feel her warm body against him. To devour the sweetness of her lips.

He smiled. "I would, but I have some work I need to get done." It wasn't a lie. He had to read the report, but not until Wednesday. If he climbed back into bed with her, though . . . if he allowed himself to spend too much time with her . . . he was afraid she'd see his need for her. His love.

And that would ruin everything.

With the sheet pressed to her chest, she pushed herself onto her knees and smiled. The curl of her lips turned impish. Then she dropped the sheet. His gaze dropped to her naked breasts. Her dark pink nipples pointed straight toward him as though tempting him to return to them. To take each one in turn into his mouth to feel the pebbly texture. To taste the salty-sweetness of the tips.

His gaze glided lower, fixing on her heart-shaped curls, then lower still, to the place his now rock-hard cock wanted so desperately to be.

But he held his ground.

Unperturbed, she shifted on her knees, then pushed herself from the bed and walked toward him with a sexy sway that sent his hormones surging. She curled her fingers around his report and drew it from his fingers. She sat down on his lap, sliding her arms around his neck.

"Are you sure I can't change your mind?" She pressed her lips against his, and her tongue pressed into his mouth.

Somehow he kept his breathing even, despite the fact he

was a hair from flipping her onto the floor and grinding into her until he made her scream in ecstasy.

He flicked his tongue against hers, then withdrew his mouth.

"Very tempting, but I do need to read this."

The instant the words were out of his mouth, he realized he'd gone too far. The hurt look in her eyes confirmed it. This was the first time—at least as himself—that he'd made love to Sandra. He'd turned her down twice before this, and she'd finally had to seduce him. He didn't want her to think he really didn't want her.

"I tell you what. If you're willing to be a good little submissive slave and do exactly as I tell you, then maybe we can spend the day together."

She seemed to tremble a little and her lips joined with his in a quick, breathtaking kiss. A broad smile claimed her lips. "Yes, Master Stud."

His cock twitched at the word *Master.* Damn, he liked the sound of it. Maybe too much.

"Uh . . . okay. Let's forget the . . . Stud." He'd been going to say *Master,* but couldn't bring himself to give it up.

"Yes, *Master.*"

His cock hardened even more.

Oh, God. This is going to be a very long—and exciting—day.

Devlin sat at his computer, reading his e-mail. He had commanded Sandra to make coffee, then breakfast. He could already smell the coffee brewing.

A knock sounded against the open door.

"Come in," he said.

In his peripheral vision, he could see her moving into the room, but he resisted looking up, retaining a masterful distance.

"I brought you some coffee." She paused, then followed with "Master."

A quiver raced through him. Sandra. His own personal sex slave. Oh, man, how could he just sit here, ignoring her? But if he didn't, how could he hide his feelings?

He had to look at her.

His gaze swiveled to her, and his breath caught. She stood beside him wearing only an apron. Her breasts bare, the nipples at full attention. Her black curls vaguely visible through the thin white fabric of the lacy apron she kept at his place for their cooking nights.

She set the coffee down on the desk beside him, then dropped the spoon on the floor. With a little force, it seemed. She turned around, placing her deliciously round ass in front of him, then leaned over to pick up the errant spoon. His cock swelled. As attractive as the curve of her delightful ass was displayed in front of him, his gaze locked on the intimate folds framed between those cheeks. He wanted to lean forward and lick that intimate flesh.

She stood up and turned toward him again, holding the spoon in front of him.

"Look what you've done," he said as he took the stainless steel handle from her fingers. "Now it's dirty." He trailed the spoon over her breast, then across her hard nipple. "Just like you."

"I'm sorry, Master. I should be punished." She turned around and bent over, offering her sweet ass for punishment.

He tossed the spoon aside, then stroked her round cheeks. He smacked one cheek, then the other, but the sight of her swollen lips and the glistening flesh between was too much to resist. He smacked one more time, enjoying the rosy flush on her soft flesh, then dragged his finger along her damp folds. At the slick feel of her, his cock twitched. He slid a finger inside her, then another. Oh, God, she felt so good.

"Turn around," he said as he slipped his fingers free.

She faced him again. Moisture glistened on his fingers. Her feminine scent wafted to his nostrils and they flared. His gaze drifted to her breast and he glided his damp fingers over her tight, hard nipple.

He drew her close to him and pressed his mouth to her slick nipple, then swirled his tongue over it. At the taste of her sweet femininity, he began to suck. She gasped. Her fingers curled in his hair. Her nipple swelled inside his mouth as he drew it deep. She pulled his head tighter against her.

He released her nipple and immediately clamped over the other one. The aureole pebbled against his tongue as he sucked hard. He pushed in the keyboard tray as he turned her to lean against his desk. She perched on the edge of the wooden surface as her fingers tangled in his hair. He drew back and released his hair from the elastic, knowing she liked it free, then his gaze fell to her heart-shaped curls.

"I'm hungry."

"Yes, Master."

She didn't offer to get breakfast. Smart girl.

He reached around behind her and untied the apron, then grasped her knees and lifted, planting her feet on the arms of his chair. Then he leaned forward and nuzzled her furry heart. The musky aroma of her filled his nostrils, sending his hormones skyrocketing. He stroked his finger over her curls, then placed a thumb on each side of her folds and drew them apart. A little button of flesh peered back at him. He leaned forward and dabbed his tongue on her clitoris and she moaned. He licked it and she quivered beneath him.

He could barely stand it. Knowing the effect he had on her. How he could simply touch her there and make her climax. He licked again, then sucked. She moaned and arched back. His monitor toppled backward. He grabbed her, stopping her from toppling, too, then set the monitor straight again.

As much as he wanted to go back to giving her pleasure, this didn't seem like it would work. She stood up and pushed his chair back, then knelt in front of him.

"Master, I have been bad again and distracted you from your work." She stroked her hand over his rampant bulge. "Please allow me to set matters right."

He grinned. "Of course."

She unfastened the button on his jeans, then pulled down the zipper. A second later, his hard cock stood at full height in front of her.

"Master, your cock is so very big." She wrapped both hands around it, one above the other, then squeezed and stroked.

She leaned forward and her tongue danced over the tip of him. Her tongue glided all over his cockhead, then swirled under the ridge of the corona. All the while her hands squeezed his hard shaft.

His breaths came quickly as heat boiled through his groin. She smiled at him, then captured his whole cockhead in her mouth. She sucked and he groaned at the exquisite sensation. Then she squeezed him in her mouth.

He could stand it no longer. His cock needed to be deep inside her. He grasped her shoulders and dragged her from his twitching member, then he stood up and backed her to the wall. His cock found her opening and he grabbed it and guided it as he thrust inside her.

God, why did he keep taking her against the wall?

Sandra gasped as his big cock pushed into her, her insides aching with need. He grabbed her wrists and pushed them above her head, then he thrust into her again, and groaned.

This morning, when he'd seemed distant, almost as if he'd wanted to get rid of her, she'd been worried this had been a big mistake. She now understood his concern about a relationship causing problems with their friendship, because if he had turned her away, she wasn't sure she would have been able to overcome the feelings of rejection that would have left her with.

Now, seeing the look of intense desire on his face, she knew it had not been a mistake. In fact, it had probably been one of the best decisions of her life.

He drew back and thrust again. She moaned at the feel

of his huge shaft driving into her, stretching her. She pushed against the hold of his hands on her wrists, loving the feeling of vulnerability it gave her being overpowered by his strength.

He nuzzled her neck, sending tingles dancing along her back. She quivered, then moaned as he thrust again. Pleasure swelled through her like ocean waves cresting in a mighty storm. Building. Surging. Until finally it erupted through her in a powerful surge of ecstasy, blinding in its intensity.

He drew her hands to his shoulders as he thrust and she clung to him, riding the torrent as bliss filled her entire being. He groaned and a gush of heat filled her, sending her pleasure skyrocketing again.

Finally, she collapsed against the wall and sighed. His mouth captured her lips and he kissed her with so much passion it took her breath away. She dropped her head to his shoulder and sighed again.

This was as close to heaven as she'd ever felt in a man's arms.

Even closer than she'd felt to her Fantasy Stranger.

Devlin sat across the table eating the delicious herb omelet Sandra had made, along with toast and honey. It was difficult concentrating on the food with Sandra sitting across from him naked, the sunshine from the summer sun caressing her round breasts. He longed to reach out and stroke her soft mounds.

Finally, he finished the last bite and set down his fork and knife. Sandra stood and picked up his plate, then stacked the other dishes on top and carried them to the kitchen. He watched her naked ass sway as she left the room. A moment later, she reappeared.

"I know you need to read your report," she said. "If you want to do that in your bedroom, I could just lie down next to you while you read."

He chuckled. "Did I get you up too early?"

She smiled. "I wouldn't mind some downtime."

He nodded. "Okay, let's go."

She followed him into the bedroom and he picked up the report from the table beside the chair where she'd placed it earlier. As he walked toward the bed, she moved the pillow a foot or so down. He glanced at her questioningly.

She smiled and walked toward him. "I think you'll be more comfortable with fewer clothes on."

She pushed his unbuttoned shirt from his shoulders, then tugged his T-shirt over his head. Her hand stroked over his chest, then down his stomach, sending heat to his groin. She released his belt, then the button on his jeans, and unzipped them. They dropped to the floor. His cock twitched as she slid her fingers under the elastic of his boxers, then she drew them down, freeing his semierect cock.

"There. Now you can relax."

Is she kidding?

He lay down and rested his head on the pillow. He had to bend his knees so his feet didn't hang over the edge.

"Why don't you lie on your side?" she suggested.

Not a bad idea. That way his cock wouldn't be a flagpole signaling his desire for her.

He rolled over and curled his legs. She sat on the bed, then lay down, but not the way he'd expected. Instead of lying facing him, she lay with her legs at the top of the bed, bent like his. Placing her delightful pussy with the fuzzy heart right in front of him. And his cock right in front of her face.

Her delicate fingertips traced the length of his cock.

"If you keep touching me, I won't get any reading done."

"Are you saying you don't want me to touch you, Master?"

Master. He'd never tire of hearing her call him that. Thus, he should act masterfully.

"That's right. Don't touch me." He couldn't believe he'd just told her that.

"Yes, Master." She drew her hands away from his cock and took a deep breath. "Master?"

"Yes?" He was already regretting that decision and wondering how to get her to touch him again.

"You meant with my hands, right?"

Nineteen

Devlin's cock twitched. "Uh . . . yes, that's right. Don't touch me with your hands."

"Okay." Sandra sighed again and linked her hands behind her back as if bound.

He held the report in front of his face, trying to focus on the words, which seemed impossible with this intense longing surging through him. She seemed very well behaved right now. Finally he calmed enough that the words in front of him started to make sense. He began to read. After a few paragraphs, she shifted a little. He read a little more.

He stopped at the feel of something warm and moist touching the tip of his cock. Her tongue. She licked him, then nuzzled her face against him. His now-raging erection twitched. She nuzzled again, her soft cheek stroking his cock while her lips teased his balls.

He kept trying to read. Her tongue flicked over his balls. He lowered the report, seeing her furry little heart in front of him. He could just lean forward and . . .

No, he was going to read. It was a challenge now.

She licked his shaft, just a delicate brush of her tongue. He drew in a breath, then let it out slowly.

"I'm a little sleepy," she said. "I think I'll have a nap."

"Okay," he said.

But her tongue returned to his cock, then her mouth covered his cockhead. His heart thundered in his chest.

"I thought you were going to sleep."

She nodded, which caused her mouth to glide over his cockhead, driving him bonkers. She released him.

"Uh-huh. I just find it calming to have something in my mouth."

She captured him again, his whole cockhead warm and cozy inside her mouth. She licked a little, then sucked softly. Everything inside him wanted to thrust forward, filling her throat with his shaft. He held himself still with great effort.

The sucking stopped, but her mouth still enveloped him. After a few quiet moments, he glanced down. Her eyes were closed and she seemed to be sleeping. With his erection protruding from her mouth.

He lifted his report and tried to read. Which was totally impossible with his cock so warm and cozy.

She sucked again, then stopped. He glanced down but her eyes remained closed.

Ah, she was definitely pretending.

He lowered his report and gazed at her lovely pussy. If she could play, so could he. He reached forward and outlined the upside-down heart with his fingertip, then he leaned forward and nuzzled the fur. He licked over the curls, which had been trimmed short. He eased back, then stroked the curls with his finger again, then higher, toward her thighs. He slid over her opening, then dipped inside. Oh, man, she was so wet.

That's it. He tipped her onto her back and prowled over her. His cock fell free from her mouth.

"Now you can use your hands," he said.

She giggled. Her soft hands wrapped around him as he pushed his tongue into her soft folds.

Sandra gasped as his tongue found her clit. She stroked his hard cock, then swallowed it as deep as she could and began to suck. He licked her and teased her clit. His fingers slipped inside her while she sucked him. He sucked on her and stroked inside her. She pumped him.

The orgasm swept through her fast and furious, sending shudders through her entire body, quivering out the ends of her toes. She lay back, gasping. But she'd released his cock. She grabbed it, ready to take it in her mouth again, but he rolled onto his back.

"Climb on top of me," he commanded.

She pushed onto her knees, but when she started to turn toward him, he caught her arm and urged her in the other direction.

"No, face that way."

She climbed over him, then settled on her knees facing the foot of the bed. His cock glided into her, filling her so full, and at a different angle.

"Make me come," he commanded.

"Yes, Master."

She lifted herself and lowered again. His hands slipped around her and stroked her breasts. Her nipples peaked, and delightful sensations quivered through her. She rose and fell again, his cock stroking her inside passage.

"Oh, yeah, sweetheart. That's incredible."

She rode him faster, driving his huge cock deep into her, propelling her closer to nirvana once again. His raspy breathing told her he was close. Heat swept through her as his cock surged into her again and again. Then she sucked in air and wailed as yet another orgasm blasted through her. He groaned, then released heat inside her. She squeezed him, tugging him deeper. He swirled, sending her higher, into a state of total abandon. She wailed in pure ecstasy.

Finally she collapsed on the bed. He curled around and snuggled up behind her. She dozed off in the warmth of his embrace.

When she awoke an hour later, he was in the chair again. She decided she really must let him finish his work without distraction. She showered and dressed, then made them both a sandwich for lunch.

She glanced across the kitchen table and smiled, totally convinced he was just as happy as she was about this change in their relationship.

She took a final sip of coffee, then gathered the plates and carried them to the sink.

"Well, I'm going to head home now."

He walked beside her and pulled her into his arms. "You sick of me already?"

"Of course not." She kissed him, loving the feel of his masculine lips on hers. "I just feel guilty about keeping you from your work. If I don't go now, my Master will have to punish me for being really, *really* bad." She grinned, then curled her hand around his neck and kissed him again.

He stroked her ass and pulled her tight to him. Then he smacked her butt. "But you love punishment."

"Well, it has its moments." She grinned and nuzzled his neck. "Maybe you'll have to show me the advantages again. How about Wednesday?"

"Unfortunately, I'll be working late most of the week, so let's make it Friday."

"It's a date."

He kissed her again. She stroked her fingers along his solid chest and sighed, then reluctantly drew herself away. He followed her to the door. She picked up her purse and opened the door. He grabbed her and pulled her into his arms again, kissing her so passionately she almost dropped her purse and dragged him off to bed again.

But she didn't.

"Good-bye," she murmured once he released her lips.

"Friday."

She smiled and nodded. She walked down the hallway, then waved at him just before she turned the corner. He waved back. She continued walking, wondering how she'd possibly survive five whole days without seeing him.

The warm glow from the morning with Devlin followed Sandra through the rest of the day as she ran errands, caught a movie with Aimee, then returned home. When she climbed into bed, she stared at the ceiling, wondering what Devlin was doing right now. Was he in bed, too? Was he thinking of her?

She wished he was here, holding her in his arms. Loving her.

Shock rocketed through her at the thought. Loving her? Did she want more from Devlin than sex?

Ah, damn, what did she expect? She and Devlin were more than casual acquaintances, or even new lovers. She'd known Devlin for almost a year. They spent a lot of time together . . . as friends, sure, but she always knew he was more to her than just a friend. She was attracted to him, but she also felt a deep connection to him.

She had to be very careful not to get trapped again. For the first time in her life, she was following her heart and living fearlessly. As for commitment, she'd already been there, done that. She'd thought it would make her happy, but it had done just the opposite.

The bottom line was that both she and her ex, Eric, had been afraid to be alone. His parents had gone through a divorce, and his mother had never remarried. Sandra's mom had been a single parent right from the start. Sandra hadn't wanted to go through life alone. She'd been thrilled when Eric had wanted to get engaged and make a lifetime commitment.

She thought she'd never be alone.

But then she'd found the emptiness of a loveless marriage was worse than being alone.

She rolled over and patted her pillow. Her fingers clung to the sheets as she stared out the window at the clear night sky. Now she was making the same mistake again, convincing herself she was in love with Devlin. Their friendship had turned to an intimate relationship. That's all. It didn't mean love.

And her longing for him now was simply that. A longing. For sex. If James or Craig were here, she could alleviate that need by being with them.

Being with Devlin was no different from being with James or Craig. It was the mix of friendship and intimacy that confused her.

She needed to keep things in perspective.

She was not falling in love with Devlin.

"Aimee's invited me to the cottage again this weekend." Holding the phone to her ear, Sandra tapped her pen on the kitchen counter.

"Okay," Devlin replied, "so I guess we can change our plans to the following weekend."

"So you're okay with me going? Even though Craig and James will be there?"

"Sure, why wouldn't I be?"

She was pleased he wasn't being possessive, but at the same time, a part of her felt a little let down.

"Okay, good." She doodled small curlicues on the pad of paper sitting on the countertop. "Actually, I asked Aimee if you could come along, too. What do you think?"

He hesitated. "Are the other guys okay with me coming along?"

"Aimee says she's sure they won't have a problem with it. You all know each other anyway, right?"

"True, but we haven't . . . um . . . been in this kind of situation before."

She put the pen down and leaned back on the tall stool. "Will you be uncomfortable?"

"No, of course not. What about you? Will you be uncomfortable with all of us . . . mixing?"

She smiled. "Me and three men? Are you kidding? That's a dream come true."

"Okay, then. Count me in."

As soon as Devlin hung up the phone, he sucked in a deep breath. His heart ached. As much as he believed in his plan, now that they'd shared passionately intimate moments together, he had hoped she would think of him as special. Inviting him to the cottage while the other two guys were there, however, clearly showed she simply thought of him as one of the crowd.

Devlin watched the shore approach as Aimee negotiated the boat past the neon orange buoys, then pulled along the side of the dock. She hopped from the boat to the dock, grabbed the rope, and looped it over the cleat on the front hull. The boat bobbed against the side and Devlin grabbed Sandra's hips to steady her, then helped her from the boat. He grabbed the cooler and hefted it over the side to the dock, then retrieved each of the bags and set them beside it.

He glanced around at the rumble of another boat engine approaching the dock.

"Hey, guys," Craig called from behind the wheel, James beside him.

Their boat pulled up on the other side of the dock and Devlin hooked a line on their boat. The guys hopped out and the first thing Craig did was grab hold of Sandra's hand and pull her into a deep embrace, his lips claiming hers. James grabbed Aimee and dipped her back in a comical yet passionate kiss.

Once they released the women, Craig grinned at Devlin and held out his hand. "Sorry, buddy. All you get's a handshake."

"Aw, really?" Aimee grinned. "I could really get into you three mixing it up a little." She winked and hooked her arm around Sandra's shoulder. "If Sandra and I were to kiss, would two of you?"

"Okay, the natives are definitely getting restless." Craig tugged Aimee into his arms and kissed her. "You just want to make trouble."

"Oh, I'll give you trouble all right." She stroked over his crotch.

Twenty

Devlin's groin tightened at the sight. He knew the four of them had gotten involved in some adventurous sex while on the island, but he hadn't realized how free and open they'd become. It would take a little getting used to.

He glanced toward Sandra and realized James was kissing her now. Devlin's chest constricted, knowing the history between them. Damn, maybe he shouldn't have come this weekend. It was one thing knowing what Sandra was doing with these guys; it was another seeing it right in front of him.

James released Sandra and her gaze strayed to Devlin. He glanced toward the guys' boat so she wouldn't see the jealousy in his eyes.

"Let me give you a hand with your gear." He climbed aboard their boat and within moments, the three of them had the bags and cooler on the dock beside the others.

"Why don't you ladies go ahead up and we'll bring your stuff?" James suggested.

Aimee smiled. "Sounds good to me. We'll go fire up the barbecue."

"Great idea." Craig grinned. "You've already got us fired up."

Sandra glanced at Devlin. He smiled and nodded. She turned and accompanied Aimee along the path toward their cottage.

Craig opened their cooler and pulled out a bottle of beer, opened it, and handed it to Devlin, then retrieved one for James and himself, too. They all took a swig.

"You going to be okay with this?" James asked Devlin.

"Yeah, sure. Why not?"

"Because we all know you're in love with Sandra. It must be strange seeing her kissing other men, let alone . . . what we'll be doing later."

So the men had purposely pushed his buttons.

"Yeah. No worries."

"Okay. Look," James said, "if you're worried about me and Sandra, because of our history, don't be. Aimee filled us in, and it's pretty clear I don't stand a chance. And I'm fine with that." He patted Devlin's shoulder. "You've got nothing to worry about. To Sandra, Craig and I are just a distraction."

Devlin nodded, glad of the encouragement. He took another swig of his beer as James stacked the bags on top of the wheeled cooler. Devlin picked up the lone bag that didn't fit and carried it as the other two men pulled the coolers along the dock and onto the path.

Sandra stretched her legs out on the lounge chair as she gazed over the water, which was as still as glass. She took a sip of her hard lemonade.

After finishing up dinner, they'd gone outside to sit on the deck and relax, enjoying the haunting call of the loons across the calm lake.

Aimee stood up and leaned back against the deck railing. "Sandra, come over here for a minute."

Sandra put down her bottle and stood up, then strolled to Aimee's side.

"I just thought I saw something on your top." Aimee peered closely at Sandra's cotton blouse, then stroked her hand along the top of Sandra's breast.

Sandra knew there was nothing on her clean white blouse. This was Aimee's way of getting things started. Aimee stroked again, then cupped Sandra's breast.

"I think you should take it off."

"You're right." Sandra smiled as she gazed at the three eager male faces watching. Even Devlin. She knew he'd been tense about coming up here, but dinner and a few beers seemed to have relaxed him. She was glad about that.

"I'll help you." Aimee winked impishly, then released the buttons on Sandra's blouse.

As her blouse opened, revealing her lacy pink bra beneath, the heat of the male gazes on her intensified. Finally, her blouse draped open and she shrugged it from her shoulders.

"Oh, honey, whatever was on your top went right through." Aimee reached around Sandra's body and released the bra clasp, then dropped the straps from her shoulders.

Sandra slipped her arms from the straps but held the bra cups in place for a moment, suddenly shy to be half naked in front of all three men. This was the first time Devlin would see her in this sort of situation, with the other men seeing her body, touching her, in front of him. She was a little nervous about it. But she sucked in a breath, keeping her gaze anywhere but on Devlin, and dropped the lace garment to the ground.

Aimee stroked over Sandra's breasts and her nipples peaked. She was becoming more relaxed with her body responding to Aimee. It was fun and exciting sharing with her friend like this.

"You have such pretty breasts," Aimee said as she stroked. She cupped Sandra's cheek, then kissed her.

Aimee's soft tongue slipped into her mouth and Sandra opened to receive it, then stroked Aimee's tongue with her own. So sweet and delicate. Then Aimee drew back and leaned down to Sandra's breast. As Aimee took Sandra's nipple into her mouth, Sandra sucked in a breath at the warm sensation.

"You know, it's such a lovely warm evening, I think all of us should go topless." Sandra glanced to the men. Devlin's gaze was locked on Aimee's hand still stroking Sandra's breast.

Craig tugged his shirt over his head and tossed it aside,

revealing his tiger tattoo. James and Devlin immediately followed suit. Then all of them stared at Aimee.

She laughed. "Okay." She grabbed the hem of her tank top and pulled it over her head. She then released the clasp of her front-opening red bra and peeled it back, revealing her large round breasts with the dusky nipples already hard and ready.

Sandra reached out and caressed one of Aimee's round breasts, glided her fingers over the pebbly aureole, then stroked the beadlike nipple between her thumb and finger. She pulled Aimee against her body, their breasts crushing together, then licked Aimee's lips. Aimee's tongue peeked out and their tongue tips danced together, visible to the men.

Sandra drew back and gazed at their audience. "Gee, the men look like their jeans are too tight."

"It was a big dinner," Aimee said.

"Maybe they should unzip them," Sandra suggested.

"Or take them off entirely." Aimee grinned.

"We will, if you will." Craig's wide smile gleamed.

Aimee smiled at Sandra and reached for the button on her cutoffs. Sandra unfastened her own denim shorts and they both dropped them to the deck. Now they both wore only their thongs, Sandra's black lace and Aimee's red satin.

Three clunks sounded as the men dropped their jeans and stepped out of them. Now they stood before Aimee and Sandra in only their boxers.

"You know, I think I'll just be over there if you need any

help, honey." Aimee crossed to a lounge chair and stretched out, clearly indicating that this was Sandra's party.

"You all look so sexy." Sandra gazed at the three solid, muscular chests in front of her, then glided over the boxers.

Craig's cock extended out the front of his boxers. James stroked his, still inside the soft cloth. Devlin did the same. She walked to Craig and kissed him, her hand stroking over the taut muscles of his abs to the waistband of his boxers, but no lower. Then she kissed James, stroking his tight abs, too.

When she kissed Devlin, he tightened his hold on her and cupped his hand around her head, his fingers spiking through her hair, and kissed her fiercely.

Devlin didn't want to be the third man Sandra kissed. He wanted to be the *only* man. But he couldn't back out now. For one, he was too damned turned on. Also, he needed to show her he could give her this freedom.

And a part of him wanted to see the other men touch her.

The only way he could accept his two opposite desires—to keep her to himself and to share her—was to be in total control.

"Remember I told you a woman must totally submit to me," he murmured quietly in her ear.

She gazed up at him with wide eyes. "Yes."

"That goes for right now, too."

Twenty-one

Sandra stared at Devlin, his blue eyes glittering with authority. "Yes, Master."

The other men grinned at her words.

"Gentlemen, this woman is my love slave, and I am willing to share her with you tonight."

"Sounds good to me," James said.

Craig grinned expectantly.

"Go to the railing," Devlin commanded.

Sandra walked to the wooden railing and faced the men.

"Now hang on to the railing."

She reached behind herself and grasped the top of the railing, which caused her breasts to thrust forward. The men stared at her peaking nipples.

"Stand just like that until I come back." Devlin disappeared into the house, then returned a moment later with a zippered bag. He drew out two wrist cuffs and strapped them around her wrists. He attached a carabiner clip to the ring on each cuff, then brought out some rope which he fed through the clip on one band, coiled it through the vertical bars of the railing, then fed it through the clip on the other band. He pulled the rope, pulling her wrists tight behind her, then tied it.

"Very good." He stood in front of her and stroked her breasts gently, then down her belly. When he reached her black panties, he slipped his finger under the hem, dipping enough to stroke the top of the heart, then glided sideways to her hip. He slid a finger under the hem at her other hip and he drew the panties down her legs, then off.

Now she stood in front of the men, her hands tied behind her, totally naked.

"Open your legs," Devlin commanded.

Sandra moved her feet wider apart, exposing her opening, heat thrumming through her.

Devlin stared at her. Could he really continue with this? Share her with the other men?

Aimee stood up, dropped her panties to the ground, and stood beside Sandra, then placed her hands on the railing behind her, thrusting her breasts forward.

"I can be quite submissive, too."

Devlin had never thought of Aimee sexually, but she was a beautiful woman, and with her standing there, with her breasts thrust forward and her totally shaven pussy exposed, his hormones raced through him even faster. If Sandra could enjoy other men in front of him, why shouldn't he indulge, too?

"Can you now?" He stroked over her soft breasts. His

cock swelled harder. He pulled her into his arms and claimed her mouth, then thrust his tongue inside. She gasped, then melted against him.

He released her and glanced at Sandra. She smiled, her olive green eyes dark with interest. Time to give her a show.

He drew Aimee across the deck with him until he stood beside one of the lounge chairs. He pushed off his boxers. Aimee's gaze locked on his cock and her eyes widened. He smiled and wrapped his hand around it.

"Okay, slave, show me what you can do with this."

Aimee sat down on the end of the chair and reached for his cock. Her mouth wrapped around his cockhead and she licked it. Then she glided forward and . . . Oh, God, she took him deeper than he'd ever been in a woman's mouth. She glided back and took him deep again. Then she drew back and sucked and licked.

He glanced at Sandra, who watched Aimee sucking him. Sandra's cheeks flushed. He couldn't tell if she was turned on by watching Aimee or jealous.

"Enough." Damn, with much more of that, he'd come, and he didn't want to do that yet.

Aimee released him and he sat on the chair.

"Sit in front of me," he instructed.

She sat facing Sandra and he drew her back against him, his erection nestled against her ass.

"James and Craig, go and touch Sandra's breasts."

Sandra watched as the two men, who had also shed their boxers, walked toward her, their cocks bobbing up and down.

James stroked one breast while Craig squeezed the other. James ran his fingertips over her hard nipple. Craig took her other nipple between his fingertips and squeezed. Hard.

"Oh." The sharp sensation spiked through her.

James leaned down and licked her nipple, then sucked it into his mouth. Craig followed suit, and she had two men pulling on her nipples with their hot mouths. Wild sensations flooded through her.

She glanced at Devlin and he had one hand on each of Aimee's breasts, stroking them.

"I want one of you to lick her pussy," Devlin said.

Craig dropped to his knees in front of her and stroked her hips, then cupped her ass and pulled her toward him. When she felt his tongue stroke over her folds, she sucked in a deep breath.

"Good. Now let James lick her."

Craig moved aside and James slipped between her legs. His tongue stroked over her folds and she murmured softly.

"Find her clit and lick it."

James found the button of flesh and he pushed the tip of his tongue against it, then twirled. She sucked in air. He sucked on her clit and she gasped.

"Now Craig."

James moved aside and Craig slipped into position. He pressed his thumbs on either side of her folds and drew them apart, then licked her. His tongue found her clit and he teased it with light pressure, then sucked. She gasped and moaned as an orgasm washed through her.

"Now stroke her breasts."

The men stood and each cupped one of her breasts in his warm hand.

"Aimee, stand up," Devlin said.

Aimee stood up and Sandra's gaze locked on Devlin's huge, erect cock.

"What would you like to do now, Aimee?" Devlin asked.

Aimee gazed at Sandra, nipping her lower lip with her teeth. Sandra knew exactly what Aimee wanted to do right now—the same thing she'd like to do if Devlin's big cock were pushing against her. Clearly, Aimee wanted Sandra's approval. And why shouldn't she give it? The niggling feeling of jealousy made no sense, given the situation. She smiled and gave a slight nod to her friend.

"I'd like to enjoy that huge cock of yours."

Devlin smiled. His cock ached in need. Watching Sandra orgasm while Craig had sucked on her clit had almost sent him over the edge.

"Well, enjoy all you want."

Aimee knelt beside him and took his cock in her mouth, then licked around the corona. He twitched in her mouth. She sucked a little, then released him, stood up again, and dropped her panties to the ground. She arched her leg over him and positioned his cock against her slick opening, then lowered herself onto him. His cock glided along her slick passage, filling her. She raised herself and glided down on him again. He stroked her breast, then glided down her stomach to her pussy. As she lifted her body again, he found her clit and stroked it. She dropped down, sucking in air.

She rode him up and down, stroking his aching cock with her wet heat. He teased her clit. Her breathing accelerated, along with the speed of her pumping on him. He grabbed her hips and guided her up and down, feeling the tension in his groin increase. A soft moan escaped from Aimee's lips, then she threw her head back and wailed. Heat rocketed through him and he joined her in orgasm.

Sandra watched Aimee and Devlin climax together, and her insides ached for a man. She arched against the hands on her breasts, barely aware of the other two men who also watched Devlin and Aimee.

Finally, Aimee collapsed on Devlin and sighed in his arms. That's where Sandra wanted to be right now. In Devlin's arms, with his cock deep inside her.

But she wanted it hard. Ready to fuck her.

Aimee stood up and Devlin's wilted cock fell against his stomach. Sandra's insides quivered. Somehow, she'd believed he would stride over and take her right now.

"Oh, God, Master, I need to be fucked," she said.

His gaze locked on her and he grinned..

"James and Craig. You heard the slave. Fuck her."

James stepped in front of Sandra and pressed his cock to her opening, then sank it deep inside her.

"Ohhhh, yes."

He pulled back and Craig sank his bigger cock inside her.

She moaned.

James thrust into her twice, then Craig did the same. The cocks felt glorious inside her, gliding into her depths, but with the break between the strokes, it wasn't enough.

Her gaze fell on Devlin. His cock had swelled to full height. She longed to feel it deep inside her. He smiled, then stood up. Was he going to push inside her? Would she feel his big cock sliding into her?

Craig's cock pushed in, stroked twice, then drew out.

"Wait, guys." Devlin reached behind her and freed one wrist, then the other.

"Turn around," he instructed.

She turned around and faced the lake. Devlin guided her forward until she leaned over the railing, then reattached her wrists.

A cockhead pressed against her opening, then pushed inside. Big. Was it Devlin?

It glided into her several times, then pulled out. A cock pressed against her back opening, then eased inside. That was James. He pushed in deep, stroked a few times, then pulled out. Another cock slipped into her vagina. Bigger. Stroking deep. Then gone.

James pressed into her ass again and stroked.

Pleasure built within her. Hands grasped her hips and cocks entered her, alternating between her two openings.

"Oh, please . . . make me come," she pleaded.

Finally one cock thrust into her hard, then started stroking. Deep. Filling her full and hard.

"Oh, yes. Oh, please keep fucking me."

It rammed into her again and again. Pleasure spiraled through her and she wailed as an ecstatic orgasm washed through her. She leaned against the railing, gasping for air.

Had it been Craig or Devlin who had fucked her to orgasm?

Hands reached around her and released her wrists. Someone turned her around and she found herself facing Devlin. Behind him, she saw Craig fucking Aimee against the cottage wall. Devlin pulled her into his arms and kissed her, then he backed her along the deck toward the corner. She felt hands grasp her hips from behind and a cock press to her opening. James. Behind her. His cock glided into her ass as his hands stroked over her breasts.

Devlin stepped forward and pressed his cock to her slit, and she gasped as he drove in deep, pressing her hard against James' solid body behind her. Devlin's hands curled around her hair, and he tugged her head back and sucked on her neck. Then he nuzzled her ear.

"You like two big cocks inside you, don't you?"

She nodded, wanting to feel those cocks moving, driving her pleasure higher.

He captured her lips and drove his tongue deep.

Both men began to move, their cocks gliding deep into her, stroking her insides.

Aimee moaned in orgasm behind Devlin. Craig groaned.

Wild sensations spiraled through Sandra as the hard shafts pulsed into her. Sparks danced along her nerve endings as James squeezed her breasts. Devlin's cock spiraled inside her. She gasped. Intense pleasure swelled through her, then catapulted her to a place of pure bliss. Devlin thrust deep again and she clung to his shoulders as she wailed in pure ecstasy. He groaned and filled her with liquid heat. James groaned behind her, pulling her tight against him.

She slumped between them, spent. James kissed her neck and stepped back. Devlin captured her lips again and his cock twitched inside her. Her vagina clenched around him automatically. He cupped her ass and pulled her tight against him again.

"You want more?" he murmured against her ear.

"Oh, yes."

He pivoted forward, driving deep again. He drew back, then walked her to the railing, leaned her against it, and thrust hard. He drove into her several times and she tensed, then pleasure burst through her again. Her body seemed to shatter, exploding into the cosmos. She quivered in complete rapture.

She dropped against him, her head resting on his shoulder.

Devlin was so special. And she felt special in his arms.

As much as she loved being with James and Craig, she felt more with Devlin. And her heart knew being with Devlin meant much more to her than just the sensational sex. She wrapped her arms around his waist and hung on tightly, despite the intense fear rushing through her at that thought.

Sandra woke up to a hand stroking her breast and a hard erection between her thighs from behind. She opened her eyes to see blonde hair in front of her. Aimee. Sandra's breasts pushed into Aimee's back, but there was a male hand between them toying with her nipple. She peered over Aimee's shoulders to see James staring back at her. He winked and squeezed her nipple again, then kissed Aimee's neck.

Sandra noticed the tiger tattoo on the arm around her and glanced over her shoulder to see Craig behind her. It was his big erection gliding between her legs. She reached down and stroked his cockhead as it pulsed forward.

But where was Devlin?

Aimee rolled on top of James, pushing him onto his back. James' hand slipped away from Sandra's breast. Aimee took James' cock and slid it inside, then moved on top of him. Craig tugged on Sandra's shoulder until she rolled toward him. She glanced around and saw Devlin sitting in the armchair by the window.

Devlin smiled. "Good morning."

Craig pulled her on top of him and his big cock glided into her. She was already slick and ready for him, but she sucked in air as he penetrated deep.

Devlin stood up and approached the bed. "Do you like that big cock of Craig's deep inside you?"

Craig pushed a little deeper for emphasis and she gasped, then nodded, her gaze on Devlin's. Devlin stood beside the bed and reached for a tube on the bedside table. He squeezed some gel onto his fingers, then stroked his erect cock, slathering it until it glistened.

"I'm going to fuck you at the same time as Craig."

She sucked in air at the thought. Both Craig and Devlin

were big. Very big. She stared at Devlin's glazed cock. In fact, Devlin's was longer by about an inch, and wider around.

"I don't know if I can. I mean, taking you . . . back there."

"You can, and you will. Remember. Total submission."

"Yes, Master."

Devlin climbed on the bed behind her, straddling his knees over Craig's but between hers, forcing her legs wider, and cupped her breasts. Craig drew her forward until she lay on him, her breasts crushed against his bulging, muscular chest. She felt Devlin's hand stroke between her cheeks, then his fingers found her back opening. One finger slid inside, followed by another. He twirled his fingers, gently prodding and stretching. He drew them free, and his cockhead pressed against her.

She sucked in a breath as it pressed forward. She stretched around him, more and more.

"Relax," he murmured against her ear.

Aimee's gasps increased beside her and Sandra squeezed Craig inside her. She drew in a deep breath and concentrated on relaxing. Devlin pressed forward again, stretching her even more. She breathed deeply, allowing his cock to push inside until, finally, his whole cockhead was inside her.

Craig pushed in a little, then drew back, sending sparks of sensation through her. Devlin glided deeper, then Craig pulsed inside her. She clung to his shoulders. Finally, Devlin was deep inside her, and so was Craig.

Beside her Aimee's breathing came in gasps and the bed bounced with James' thrusts. Devlin drew back a little, sending quivers through Sandra. Aimee moaned in orgasm and Devlin pushed in again.

"Oh, God, yes. Yes!" Aimee wailed again, and James groaned.

Craig and Devlin began to move inside Sandra, and she couldn't believe how incredibly full she was. The cocks pulled out a little, then pushed in deep. They moved in rhythm, stretching, then drawing back. Filling her, then withdrawing. Their big cockheads glided along her insides, and she felt faint at the intensity of it. Potent pleasure washed through her and she grasped Craig's shoulders, riding the incessant waves of pleasure. She sucked in air, then gasped as conscious thought left her. She felt only movement. And pleasure. Incredible quivers of excitement as the hard shafts filled her, then pulled free, then filled her again.

Her eyes closed and her insides clenched as shudders thrummed through her body. She sucked in air, then wailed as ecstasy encompassed her whole body, blasting through her being in a mind-shattering orgasm. She gasped again, then blackness surrounded her.

Twenty-two

Devlin had never seen a woman faint during orgasm before. And right as both he and Craig groaned with their own release.

Devlin drew his cock from her tight opening. Craig rolled her onto her side, his cock still inside her.

Sandra opened her eyes in a daze. "Oh, man." She glanced over Craig's shoulder at Devlin. "That was incredible. Thank you."

"You're welcome," Devlin said at the same time as Craig. What the heck? It had been a team effort.

"How about James and I get breakfast while you three rest," Aimee suggested. She grinned as she hopped out of bed and took James' hand, then led him out of the room.

Devlin climbed into bed behind Sandra. She kissed Craig, then rolled over and kissed Devlin. She snuggled into his arms and fell asleep again. He held her close, wishing he could do this every night of his life.

After breakfast, Sandra helped Devlin and Craig clean up the dishes, since Aimee and James had cooked. Afterward, she and Aimee pulled on their bikinis and they all strolled to the quiet bay with the swim raft. Devlin spread a blanket on the sand and flopped down, then patted the space beside him. Sandra sat next to him and they watched the others run into the water and swim to the rock.

"Are you enjoying the weekend?" Sandra asked, wondering what Devlin thought of it all now that he was here.

"Are you kidding? It's incredible." He drew her onto his lap facing him, then kissed her. "It's amazing watching you with the other guys." He stroked her black hair behind her ear, sending shivers through her at the light touch. "Enjoying yourself." His gaze rested on her face, and he smiled. "You're so sexy when you're with them. When they're touching you."

He caressed her cheek, then kissed her again. She wrapped her hand around his head and stroked her tongue inside his mouth.

Aimee laughed in the background, then a chorus of splashes broke out.

Devlin lay back and pulled Sandra on top of his body. His bulge pressed into her. He wrapped his arms around her, then rolled her onto her side and held her. She could hear Aimee and the guys in the water, but all she could think of was Devlin and the solid strength of his body pressed tight to hers.

"Aimee seems to be having a lot of fun. Do you want to go join her?"

"No. I'm happy right where I am." She snuggled her cheek against his bare chest.

The sound of splashing diminished and she wondered if Aimee and the guys were turning to more erotic activities. It felt so strange lying here with Devlin and knowing if she glanced up, she might see Aimee having sex with two men right in front of them . . . and that it wouldn't faze Sandra in the least. Nor Devlin.

She ran her hand across his solid chest. "Devlin, have you ever done this kind of thing before?"

"Shared a woman with another guy? Or guys?" He stroked her hair. "No, this is a first for me."

"What about two women sharing *you*? That's every man's fantasy, right?"

He laughed. "I guess that's true. But it's tough enough to find one special woman to be with, let alone two."

She glanced up at him. "Sure, but they don't have to be special as in long-term commitment. You said yourself it's okay to have casual sex." But pleasure wafted through her that he considered her special.

"That's true for a while. But you get to a point where casual sex just doesn't satisfy anymore."

The warmth in his eyes as he gazed at her sent excitement skittering through her.

"Devlin, you're such a great guy. Why aren't you in a serious relationship already?"

"I was—at least, I tried to be—about a year before I met you."

"What happened?" Had Devlin had his heart broken?

He stroked her back. “She and I had known each other casually for a long time. We worked together and that can be a problem so, even though we were attracted to each other, we didn’t act on it. Then she left the company to start a new job. A bunch of us took her out for drinks to say good-bye and”—he shrugged—“I asked her out.”

He glanced at her and she nodded her encouragement.

“Because we knew each other pretty well, having spent a lot of time together at work,” he continued, “we moved forward with the relationship at a fast pace—too fast, as it turned out. After four months, I found myself asking her to move in with me.”

“And did she?”

He sighed. “No. She got that deer-in-headlights look and said she needed to think about it. After that, she was ‘busy’ ”—he said the word with finger quotes—“a lot. We saw each other a couple more times, then she broke it off with me.”

She nodded in sympathy, wondering if he still carried a torch for the woman.

He shrugged. “It was a learning experience. Now I know to take it slow.” He smiled at her. “If a woman is worth being with, she’s worth waiting for.”

Aimee laughed in the background, then ran toward the blanket and plopped down behind Sandra.

“Hey, Devlin. You’re hogging Sandra.”

Sandra felt soft fingers against her back, then felt her bathing suit top release. Aimee tugged on Sandra’s shoulder until Devlin released her and she rolled onto her back.

Aimee pulled the fabric until it slid away from Sandra's breasts. Her nipples pointed to the sky.

"Well, that's a pretty picture." Devlin grinned.

Aimee stroked down Sandra's stomach, then tugged at her bottoms.

"Hey, why do I always get naked first?" Sandra complained.

Aimee let go of Sandra's bikini bottom. "Okay." She turned around, putting her back to Sandra. Sandra unfastened Aimee's damp top. When it fell to the blanket, Aimee stood up. So did Sandra. She tugged Aimee's bottoms down her hips then to the ground. Aimee stepped out of them, now naked.

"Here, let me help speed this along." Devlin grabbed Sandra's bottoms and guided them down her legs.

"Why don't you two go and remove the guys' bathing suits?" Devlin suggested.

Sandra moved to James and smiled as she tugged his wet bathing suit down, revealing his cold, shrunken cock. She stroked her hand over it.

"Sandra, I think we'll need to warm up their cold members."

Sandra wrapped her hands around James and stroked him. Aimee immediately took Craig into her mouth.

Craig smiled broadly. "Oh, baby, that is warm."

Sandra crouched down and took James into her mouth, and he immediately began to swell. Soon he filled her mouth and she licked his cockhead.

"Why don't you grab those cocks," Devlin said, "and

lead them this way?" He picked up the bags they'd brought with them to the beach.

Sandra stood up, one hand wrapped around James' hard erection, and followed Devlin through the woods. He led them toward the other cottage, then around to the other side of the building. Hanging from a big tree were two wooden swings. Devlin dropped the bags beside the swings, then unzipped his and pulled out some black straps. He tossed two to Sandra.

"Fasten these around Aimee's wrists and ankles."

Sandra took the soft leather straps and did as instructed.

"Drape Aimee over one of the swings, then attach her wrists to her ankles with these." Devlin handed Sandra two strong metal clips. He also handed her a towel. "You might want to lay this over the swing first."

Aimee walked to the swing and, once Sandra laid the folded towel over the rough wood of the swing, Aimee leaned over. Sandra clipped the rings on the wrist straps to the rings on Aimee's ankles, essentially holding her doubled over the swing, her back end totally exposed.

Craig whistled. "Now that's a lovely sight."

"Sandra, her breasts look cold. Why don't you warm them up?" Devlin suggested.

Sandra crouched down and dipped her head under the swing, her own naked back end sticking up in the air, and smiled at Aimee's upside-down face, then stroked Aimee's breasts. She leaned toward one and licked it. Then she sucked the other nipple.

She felt a male hand stroke over her behind, then glide

along either side of her exposed folds. Then over her slit. Her eyes fell closed and she sucked harder on Aimee, eliciting a moan.

"Come back up here," Devlin instructed.

The hand slid away and Sandra backed out from under the swing.

"I think Aimee's been a pretty bad girl this weekend, bringing all these men here and carousing around with them. You need to punish her."

Sandra stared at Aimee's exposed ass. She glided her hand over the curved flesh, then smacked Aimee's butt.

"You'll have to do it harder than that."

Sandra smacked again a little harder.

"Again," Devlin said.

She smacked again.

"Harder," Devlin insisted.

She smacked harder this time. Aimee's soft pale flesh turned a rosy pink.

"Now the other one." Only Devlin spoke. The other men just watched in fascination.

Sandra smacked Aimee's other cheek. That one turned pink, too.

"Now . . . kiss it better."

Sandra crouched down and kissed Aimee's heated cheek. She kissed and nuzzled, then nibbled with her lips, knowing it drove the men to distraction.

"I want to watch James and Craig fuck her. First, get her ready for them," Devlin instructed.

Sandra's nipples tingled at his words and the images they

elicited. She stroked her fingers along Aimee's slit. The folds were already slick. But this was as much for the men as for Aimee. Sandra licked along Aimee's slit, then eased away and dragged her fingers along the opening. She glided her fingers inside. In her peripheral vision, she saw that Craig had his cock in his hand and pumped it.

"Master, she's ready for a hard cock."

"Let me see." Devlin stepped beside her and ran his fingers along Aimee's slit. "You're right." He crouched down and licked her slit.

Aimee moaned.

Devlin stood up and stepped to the side.

He gestured James forward. James, holding his own hard cock, walked forward, his gaze on Aimee's exposed ass.

"Sandra, take James' cock and slide it into Aimee."

Sandra wrapped her hand around James' hard cock, stroked it, then guided it to Aimee's opening. She pushed the cockhead inside. James glided forward and Sandra watched his cock disappear inside Aimee.

"Stroke James' balls while he thrusts into Aimee."

Sandra moved behind James and she slid her hand between his thighs and cupped his balls. He moved forward and back, driving into Aimee. Craig moved closer.

"Grab Craig's cock and stroke him, too."

Craig moved beside James and turned toward Sandra. She grabbed his big cock and stroked while James continued to thrust into Aimee. Her hand still cupped his balls. His thrusts sped up and his balls grew firm. Aimee's sounds of pleasure increased. Suddenly James groaned and drove deep into her. She moaned loudly.

Sandra kept stroking Craig's cock. Devlin stepped behind Sandra and cupped her breast, then he drew her away from James, toward the other swing. He draped her over it, her stomach resting against the wood. Craig moved behind her and Devlin grabbed Craig's cock and pushed it against Sandra's dripping slit. Craig drove forward, impaling her.

The feel of his long, hard cock driving into her made her gasp. Devlin moved in front of her and pressed his cock to her lips. She wrapped them around his cockhead. Craig drew back, then drove forward again, pushing the swing and driving her deeper onto Devlin's cock. She wrapped her hand around Devlin's cock and sucked. Her mouth slid up and down on the big cock as Craig drove into her again and again. Pleasure swelled within her and she groaned, then moaned as an orgasm plummeted through her. Craig's cock pulled free.

Devlin pulled away, and he walked behind her. His cock pressed against her opening and he pushed inside. His cock filled her even more than Craig's had. She squeezed him, welcoming his erotic presence. He drew back and thrust into her again. During his next thrust, he slapped her behind. She gasped, then moaned as another orgasm rocketed through her. He drove forward again and again, slapping her bottom a couple of times, sending her orgasm into a cataclysmic explosion of sensation. He grabbed her hips and drove deep, then groaned as he released inside her.

"Oh, God. You are so fucking sexy," he murmured.

Then he pulled her from the swing and sat down. He lifted her and pushed his cock to her ass. He lowered her onto him, slowly impaling her ass with his huge cock. She stretched around him. Once he was fully inside, he tucked his feet inside hers and widened her legs. James knelt in front of her and pressed his cock to her vagina, then drove forward. His solid chest pressed against hers, sandwiching her between the two men.

James pulled back and drove forward again. He began to fuck her, every forward thrust pushing her hard against Devlin, which pushed his big cock deeper into her ass.

Within moments, she moaned in intense ecstasy, then wailed at the top of her lungs. Pleasure tore through her in an explosive orgasm. When James finally stopped driving into her, she collapsed against Devlin, wondering how she could possibly survive such potent pleasure much longer.

And wondering once she returned to the city after this weekend if she'd ever have the chance again.

Sandra flopped into bed on her own that evening. After a day of hot sex, all of them decided they needed to stretch out and get some sleep. It was strange being alone after being touched and kissed—and fucked—so much today.

Being alone like this is what she'd return to after the weekend. Although there were still a few weekends left in the summer, once Aimee closed the cottage for the season, Sandra would miss the carefree atmosphere she'd found here. Allowing her to be wild and free. To enjoy sex with multiple men. To have total erotic freedom.

Would she see Craig and James again? It would be weird seeing them away from this environment. Inviting them to her apartment. Or going to their places.

But she would still have Devlin.

She sighed.

In addition to the pleasures of being fucked by three men, the main thing she'd learned this weekend was how special Devlin was to her. His loving and encouraging nature had helped her accept this wild side of herself right from the beginning. He was a great friend. A sensational lover.

Could he be even more to her?

Did she want him to be?

Her thoughts kept her awake for quite a while as she stared out her window at the night sky, filled with twinkling stars, but finally she dozed off.

A while later, she became aware that someone was behind her. A warm, solid body spooning with her.

She was sure it was her Fantasy Stranger.

Twenty-three

Heat washed through Sandra, pooling in her groin. She felt a cock stir between her thighs.

God, it felt good.

"I want you to fuck me," she said.

He nuzzled her neck as his big cock slid back, then pushed against her vagina. Slowly, it glided inside.

He thrust forward, impaling her. She gasped at the intensity of the sensation. Tightening internal muscles, she squeezed him, then pivoted her hips forward and back, driving his cock deep into her every time.

He grabbed her hips and thrust deeper still. Harder. She felt his cock swell and she squeezed it again. His hands slid to her breasts and he cupped them tightly. Her nipples ached. Waves of intense pleasure washed through her, rising toward a tumultuous flood of bliss. She could feel it. So close.

She gasped as an orgasm rocked through her, then catapulted her to the edge of paradise. His hand released her breast and slid down her stomach to her clit, then stroked. Her pleasure intensified and she wailed as ecstasy exploded through her.

Finally she collapsed against the solid chest behind her, gasping for air. His rapid breath rushed past her neck, lifting tendrils of her hair, tickling slightly.

A part of her felt guilty, being here with her Fantasy Stranger but not Devlin. Devlin knew about her Fantasy Stranger, of course, but it felt so intimate lying here in his arms. So close. So wonderful.

She felt her heart swell. Her Fantasy Stranger always touched her with such tenderness. She always felt loved in his arms. She knew it was James or Craig, yet lying here with him, it felt nothing like when James or Craig held her in their arms.

Which totally proved the power of the human mind. And fantasies. The Fantasy Stranger embodied her idea of love.

And she could revel in it without feeling she might go down the wrong path, as she had with Eric. Because the Fantasy Stranger wasn't real.

She drew in a deep breath and rested her hand over his as it cupped her breast.

"I love the way you touch me. The way you make me feel."

He leaned forward and nuzzled her neck tenderly. "Do you love *me*?" he murmured softly, his voice hoarse.

"Yes." The word slipped from her lips before she could stop it. She hadn't wanted to admit that.

He'd never spoken to her before as the Fantasy Stranger. He'd spoken so quietly, she couldn't tell whose voice it was.

His cock slipped from her and he drew her onto her back. As she saw the shadowy figure above her in the darkness, she realized she wore no blindfold. He prowled over her and his cock pushed against her.

"I love you, too."

It was Devlin's voice. She gasped as he glided inside her.

She wanted to dive away and escape, but his big cock thrust into her again, stirring the pleasure still spiraling through her from her previous orgasm. His cock filled her deeply again. She squeezed, then clung to his shoulders as she moaned at the intense pleasure . . . building . . . filling her whole being. Then blissful sensations cascaded through her and she flew into ecstasy, trembling in his arms.

His cock erupted inside her.

Finally she caught her breath. She was too aware of his solid chest against her cheek, of his arms around her body . . . of his cock still embedded inside her.

Oh, God, it was Devlin.

Devlin was her Fantasy Stranger.

Sandra squirmed out of his arms and pushed herself to her feet.

"Sandra, where are you going?"

She grabbed her robe from the chair as she raced out of the room, desperate to get away from him. She had to think. She heard his footsteps behind her as she slid open the deck door and raced into the darkness outside. She hurried down the deck stairs, hoping he wouldn't follow.

"Sandra. Wait. What's wrong?"

She heard his footsteps on the deck.

Stopping on the beach in front of the cottage, she stared across the glistening water. She wasn't going to run away into the darkness of the woods.

Hands on her hips, she turned to face him. "You are the Fantasy Stranger?"

"That's right."

"You lied to me," she accused.

"I didn't lie."

She glared at him. "You didn't tell the truth."

"If you had known who the Fantasy Stranger was, it would have ruined it." He stepped toward her. "Sandra, I don't think that's why you're mad. In fact, I don't think you're mad at all."

She stared at him, the blood pounding through her temples, her breathing hard and erratic. Why was she mad? Because he'd played a role? Because he hadn't told her about it?

Or because he'd done it so well?

"I think you're using anger to distract yourself," he said.

She bit back her question—*From what?*—because she didn't want to hear his answer.

He stepped forward. She took a step back.

"You said you loved me," he said.

"I was in the moment. It just came out. I didn't mean it."

"Now I think *you're* lying."

"It doesn't matter." She gritted her teeth. "The person I said it to isn't real."

"He is real. *I'm* real."

Her chest tightened painfully. She shook her head, desperately wanting to run away.

"Sandra, why did you think I was the Fantasy Stranger? I didn't blindfold you. I didn't bring a yellow rose."

"I . . . well, it was . . . I mean, the way you touched me . . ."

He held his hands open at his sides. "But I was just being myself."

She took another step back.

"Devlin, I don't love you."

He stepped forward and caught her shoulders. "Are you sure?"

She stared at him, willing herself to pull away as his face drew near. But she didn't move a muscle to escape as his lips found hers and he kissed her. Sweetly. Tenderly.

The world swayed around her.

"I can't love you, Devlin."

"Why not?"

Tears welled in her eyes. "Because . . ." She choked back a lump in her throat. "The only time I believed I was in love, I was wrong."

He smiled, his eyes glowing in the moonlight. "But what if, this time, you're right?"

Her breath caught and she stared into his eyes, lost in the glittering blue depths, her head shaking.

He cupped her face between his hands. "Sandra, what are you afraid of?"

"What if . . ." She sucked in air and started again. "What if I'm right and . . ."

"And what?" he prompted.

She stared into the fiery depths of his eyes and the heat washed over her, making her feel wanted. Needed. *Loved.*

And it scared her because she remembered when Eric had looked at her like that and how much it had hurt when that heat had faded away.

She trembled. "And . . . I lose you?"

He hugged her tight against him, stroking her hair gently. "Oh, God, Sandra. You'll never lose me."

"You can't know that. Your feelings might change."

"They won't. I promise you that." He drew back and stared into her eyes again, his blue eyes intense. "But even if you don't believe that, you should still take the chance."

"Why?"

"Because being afraid to love is no way to live."

Her heart pounded. She'd been so proud of herself when she'd recognized that what she felt for the Fantasy Stranger wasn't real love. Because the Fantasy Stranger wasn't real. But now that she knew the Fantasy Stranger was Devlin, she realized those feelings *were* real. And they were a reflection of what Devlin felt for her.

She'd met Devlin at a time when she'd promised herself she wouldn't get involved romantically with a man, so they'd become friends, but she'd always been attracted to him. And ever since she'd gotten involved with him sexually, she'd felt the difference when she was with him and when she was with the other men—even James, whom she'd had a strong attraction to in the past. It wasn't the same. What she felt for Devlin was deeper. Stronger.

Could she be in love with Devlin for real?

"Besides, if anything," Devlin said, "this whole experience must have convinced you that you don't have any problem attracting men. As friends. As lovers. Even if you aren't in a committed relationship, you don't need to be alone."

Devlin smiled at her and her heart swelled. Sweet, encouraging Devlin. He seemed to know her better than she knew herself.

She ached to lean forward and kiss him again. To feel his arms holding her tight.

"You really do love me?" she asked.

His blue eyes glittered brightly. "Are you kidding? I'm crazy about you." A deep ache thrummed through her, and her heart pounded with joy because she knew now that what she felt for Devlin was true love.

Devlin stroked her cheek. "I see it in your eyes, but I need to hear it. Tell me."

She blinked back tears of joy, and her mouth broadened in an irresistible smile. She stroked his raspy cheek.

"I love you, Devlin."

He chuckled and picked her up, then spun her around. Their mouths found each other and he kissed her breathless.

When he finally released her, she grinned at him. "Just

my luck. I finally fall hopelessly in love with a man just when I've figured out all I have to do is make a list of fantasies and they'll all come true. Life was just getting interesting."

He chuckled. "You don't think I'm going to stop you from enjoying your fantasies, do you?"

Her eyebrows arched. "Really? Even with James and Craig?"

"As long as I can play a starring role."

She laughed and hugged him tight. "Always."

He stroked her hair back and kissed her. At the tender touch of his lips, her heart swelled with love.

As that feeling swept through her, she realized this was totally different from what she'd felt for Eric. This love settled deep in her heart and rippled through every part of her, filling the deepest, darkest—and loneliest—spots within her.

She sighed as she gazed into Devlin's glowing eyes.

Devlin's love completed her. And deep down in her soul she knew she was totally and thoroughly in love with Devlin.

Twenty-four

Devlin awoke to soft lips nuzzling his neck, under his chin. He tightened his arms around Sandra and drew her closer. She snuggled against his chest, then pushed on his shoulder until he rolled onto his back. Then she climbed on top of him, sitting on his stomach.

"Good morning." She grinned down at him.

"Good morning." He smiled and his gaze wandered to her naked breasts. He stroked his hands down her sides, then over her hips, loving the feel of her curves.

He couldn't stop smiling. Last night Sandra had admitted she loved him.

As if reading his thoughts, she said, "So you love me, right?"

His smile broadened. "Yes, I do."

"And you honor my desire to keep living out my fantasies?"

He raised an eyebrow at her odd wording, but said, "Of course."

She grinned impishly. "Great. Do you also agree to *obey* me?"

He chuckled. "I do."

She hopped off him and sat on the side of the bed, then opened the drawer in the bedside table. She riffled around inside, then pulled out some black leather bands and dropped them on the side of the bed. She wrapped one around one of his wrists and fastened it, her delicate fingers brushing lightly against the sensitive skin on the inside of his wrist as she fastened the buckles. He held up his other wrist for her and she fastened one there, too. Then she held up a leather collar.

He sat up so she could fasten it around his neck. She stood up and drew the sheet, which had fallen in a heap around his stomach, down to his hips, then stroked her hand over his chest and down his abs. The feel of her soft touch on his body sent heat thrumming through him, especially as she stroked lower.

She grinned. "You look sexy." She walked to the dresser and returned with a brush, then brushed his shoulder-length hair thoroughly.

"Good. Now stand up," she said.

He pushed back the covers and stood up. She dragged her gaze over his body, lingering on his groin, watching his cock begin to swell, then she opened the drawer on the bedside table again and pulled out a leather leash. Once she clipped it on the ring on his collar, she tugged on it.

"Follow me." She walked to the door. "Oh, wait." She handed him the handle of the leash and trotted to the dresser.

She opened a drawer, then pulled out a white T-shirt and

pulled it on. It draped loosely on her body, hanging halfway to her knees. She went to the bedside table again and returned with a carabiner clip and fastened his wrists together in front of him, then took the leash again and tugged.

She led him down the hallway and into the living room. Aimee lay stretched out on the couch, reading a book, a mug of coffee on the table beside her, her feet in James' lap. James gently held Aimee's bare foot between his big hands, stroking. She wore a pink bikini and James wore his boxers. Craig sat in the armchair sipping his coffee, staring out across the water. He, too, wore only his boxers. Sandra smiled at the sight of the sexy tiger tattoo on his arm.

Aimee glanced at Devlin, her gaze gliding the length of him. His cock twitched at her perusal.

"You taking him for a walk?" she asked.

"No, but I am taking him out to play. I'm going to be Mistress Sandra. Want to join us?"

Aimee grinned. "Absolutely."

Sandra reached for Aimee's coffee mug, and Aimee handed it to her.

"You mind?" Sandra asked.

"No problem."

Sandra took a sip, then held the cup to Devlin's mouth. He took a sip of the warm liquid. It had sugar and cream, and he usually took his coffee black, but he welcomed the dose of caffeine.

Sandra put down the mug and tugged on the leash, then led him to the kitchen area. She picked up a pen from a cup on the counter and walked to the fridge. There, held up by a pineapple-shaped magnet, was the cocktail napkin with the list Sandra and Aimee had made. Six items were ticked off.

✓1. Be held captive.
✓2. Experiment with bondage.
✓3. Make love to a sexy stranger while blindfolded.
✓4. Have sex with two men at the same time (maybe more).
5. Be a love slave.
6. Have a love slave.
✓7. Be a voyeur.
✓8. Try exhibitionism.

Sandra ticked off number five. Clearly, he was about to fulfill number six.

She grinned at him and tugged on the leash again, then led him to the door and slid it open. They stepped out into bright warm sunshine. The birds twittered in the trees and a soft breeze lifted tendrils of his hair and swirled them across his face.

He followed her around the house to the outdoor shower, the other two men and Aimee trailing behind. Sandra turned on the water and tested it with her hand, then unfastened the leather bands from his wrists and neck and tossed them aside, onto the grass.

"Okay, step into the water."

"Yes, Mistress Sandra." He stepped under the warm water and it streamed over his body.

Sandra picked up a bar of soup and began rubbing it over his body. As the water flowed over her, her white T-shirt clung to her body, becoming transparent. Her breasts appeared clearly through the fabric, the nipples pushing outward.

The feel of her hands on him, the sight of the warm water flowing over her nearly naked body, and the thought of her commanding him to do erotic things to her sexy body sent hormones flooding through him.

"Aimee, come give me a hand."

Aimee stepped under the water, too, and began stroking his soapy body. Both their hands wrapped around his growing cock and they stroked. Aimee crouched down and took his cockhead into her mouth, and he sucked in air. Sandra kissed his chest, then sucked one of his nipples into her mouth. Heat flared through him and his mouth went dry.

Sandra stroked over his ass and swirled her soapy hand over him. He wanted to run his hands over her breasts, to feel the tight nipples under his fingertips, but he left his hands hanging obediently at his sides.

Aimee drew his cock deeper into her mouth as she stroked his ass, too. Sandra kissed down his stomach and licked his cock as Aimee drew her mouth free. His hands balled into fists as both women licked his cock with their warm tongues, up and down.

James and Craig watched beyond the spray of water, their hands inside their boxers.

Sandra stood up and Aimee followed suit.

Sandra glanced up and down his body. "Okay, you look nice and clean." She turned to the other men. "Craig and James, bring the armchair from the deck. Aimee, go grab some towels and . . ." Sandra whispered in Aimee's ear and she nodded.

Sandra's hand curled around his erection and she stroked while they waited for the others to return. Her touch was heaven.

A moment later, the men came into view again carrying a teak armchair from the deck, complete with cushions. They set it down on the grass facing the shower. Aimee dropped a basket of towels beside it, then carried one to the shower. Sandra led Devlin out of the water.

"Go ahead and dry him off," Sandra said to Aimee.

Aimee patted his body dry, paying close attention to his groin area, which caused his erection to swell even more. Sandra fastened the collar around his neck again, and the wristbands, but did not fasten his wrists together again. She tugged the leash and led him to the armchair.

"Sit."

Once Devlin sat down, she coiled the leash around the back of the chair. She reached into the basket of towels and removed a plastic bottle. She handed the bottle to Aimee, who smiled and squeezed clear liquid onto her hands, then knelt in front of Devlin and began to stroke his cock quite thoroughly, totally coating it. He thought he'd go insane with the erotic stimulation of her slick warm hands.

"Now don't touch," Sandra said.

He ached to touch it. Or, better yet, to have Sandra

touch it, but she wandered back to the shower and stood under the water. Aimee stripped off her bikini and joined Sandra. Aimee drew Sandra's wet T-shirt upward and tugged it over her head. Devlin's cock twitched at the sight of her naked wet breasts.

Aimee rubbed the bar of soap between her hands and handed it to Sandra, then began stroking Sandra's breasts. Sandra foamed up her hands and set down the bar of soap, then stroked over Aimee's breasts.

"Hey, guys," Sandra called to James and Craig, "come and join us."

The two men stripped off their boxers and flew under the water. Soon, the four of them were soaping one another, stroking their slick bodies. Male hands stroked over the women's breasts. Feminine hands stroked big hard cocks. Except for Devlin's. His stood erect and ready but all alone, aching to be touched.

Finally, Sandra stepped out from the water, her wet body glistening in the sunshine.

"You three keep playing. Devlin and I will watch." She walked toward Devlin, then grabbed a towel from the basket and dried off, gently dragging the soft fluffy towel over her naked skin, driving Devlin insane with wanting to touch her. His cock ached, wanting to slide inside her.

Once she was dry, she stood in front of him and, resting her hands on the wooden arms of the chair, leaned toward him, her breasts right in front of his face. As much as he wanted to lean forward and suck one hard pebbly aureole into his mouth, then run his tongue all over it, he did nothing but stare at the puckered pink nipples.

"Don't you want to do something?"

"Yes, Mistress Sandra."

"What do you want to do?"

"I want to kiss your breasts."

She grinned. "Anything else?"

"I want to suck your nipples."

"Well, do it."

Excitement skittered through him as he leaned his head forward and kissed her left breast, then licked over the nipple. He opened his lips and drew the hard nub inside his mouth, then sucked.

"Oh, yes. I like that. Now the other one."

He released her hard bud and shifted his head, then took her other nipple in his mouth and sucked. He wanted to stroke her breasts and pull her body tight to his, but he hadn't been given permission by his Mistress.

She drew away. "That's very nice. Now I think I'll sit down and watch the fun."

She turned away from him, then her hand curled around his cock and she eased herself down, pressing his cockhead to her back opening. He groaned as she lowered herself more. Slowly, his cockhead pressed into her heat. She continued sitting, pushing his shaft into her, until finally she had him totally immersed, his cock squeezed by her delightfully tight passage.

She leaned back against him, resting her head on his

shoulder. Under the shower, Craig and James stroked Aimee's wet naked body.

Sandra could barely keep her eyelids open, wanting to sink into the blissful pleasure of Devlin's cock inside her. Stretching her. Making her insides ache for more. But she watched Aimee and the two men under the spray of water in front of them.

Aimee wrapped her hands around each of their cocks, then crouched down in the shower and took one in her mouth, bobbed up and down a couple of times, then released it and took the other in her mouth and did the same thing. Sandra watched, her insides aching, as Aimee alternated between the cocks. Aimee turned the men so that Sandra and Devlin could see them from the side and took Craig's big cockhead into her mouth. Then she took James' cock and pushed it against her mouth, too, and guided it in. Her mouth was stretched wide, but she had both cockheads inside.

She released them, then stood up. Craig pressed his cockhead to her vagina and pushed inside. As Sandra watched that long cock impale Aimee, heat rocketed through her. As much as she loved Devlin's big cock inside her, she wanted another cock inside her, too. Craig caught Aimee under the knees and lifted her. The water sluiced over the tiger tattoo on his bulging arm. James stepped behind her and pressed his cockhead between her cheeks, then eased inside. Aimee groaned.

"Stroke my breasts," Sandra murmured.

Devlin obeyed immediately, his big hands covering her breasts and squeezing gently, then stroking. Oh, it felt so good.

The two men began to move inside Aimee. In and out. Aimee moaning and clinging to Craig.

"Oh, God, yes. Your cocks are so big." Aimee gasped.

"Devlin, touch my body. Lower." Sandra arched her hips, then moaned as his cock shifted inside her.

One of his hands slid down and he stroked her slit. He found her clit and teased. Very lightly. Barely a touch at all. She watched the men thrust into Aimee. Oh, God, it was so sexy watching her friends enjoying one another's bodies as they put on a show for her and Devlin.

Aimee moaned, then wailed in orgasm. James groaned, and a few seconds later, Craig grunted. Sandra's eyelids fell closed and she arched against Devlin's hand, which caused his cock to stroke inside her, and she moaned.

"You want a little help over there, Mistress Sandra?" Aimee asked.

Sandra sucked in a deep breath. "Yes, that would be great."

Aimee soaped up the men's wilted cocks, then washed them thoroughly. When the men stepped from the shower, their cocks were semierect. Aimee dried herself off and walked to Sandra, then knelt in front of her and stroked her stomach. She leaned forward and drew Devlin's fingers from Sandra's clit, then licked the little button. Devlin stroked both Sandra's breasts. The sensations thrumming through her body sent her heart rate accelerating.

Aimee stood up and pressed her breast to Sandra's mouth. Sandra captured the hard nipple. Aimee pressed her other breast to Devlin's mouth and he sucked deeply. Craig and James stood on either side of the chair and shifted Devlin's hands away from Sandra's breasts, then began to suck on her nipples. Sandra gasped at the intense sensations.

"I'm just in the way here." Aimee backed up, stroking her own breasts, then grabbed a towel and sat on the grass, watching them.

"Want us to fuck you, Mistress Sandra?" Craig asked.

"Oh, yeah," Sandra answered, in almost a moan.

James pressed his cock to Sandra's slit, then glided inside. Waves of delight washed through her. He thrust in three times, then slid free. Craig pressed his bigger cock to her slit and slid inside, stretching her wide. He stroked a few times. She moaned when he slid free, but James took his place again.

Sandra's breathing accelerated as the two men shared her. Back and forth, driving inside her, augmenting the feel of Devlin's huge cock inside her ass. Little bursts of pleasure erupted through her. When Craig thrust into her again, she grabbed his shoulders.

"Fuck me until I come," she demanded.

Craig smiled and thrust deep again. Devlin nuzzled her neck as wild pleasure seared every nerve ending. Craig thrust again and again. Devlin's cock shifted inside her, stroking her back passage.

Blazing heat catapulted through her, and she gasped as intoxicating pleasure exploded within her. The big cocks continued to stroke her insides and she wailed as rapture blossomed inside her. Both men roared as they joined her in orgasm. She rode the intense wave of bliss.

Slowly, her senses returned to the real world, and to the incredible sensation of being sandwiched between these two hulking men. Craig kissed her lips, then withdrew.

On the towel, James glided into Aimee, thrusting fast and hard. He moaned again in orgasm, stiffened, and groaned his release.

Sandra took a moment to catch her breath. She couldn't believe she'd found three such loving friends to help bring her sexual fantasies to life—and a man like Devlin who loved her and was willing to share in these erotic adventures.

Life was *good*.

Craig offered his hand and helped her up. Devlin's cock fell free and she missed it immediately.

"You were all very good slaves." Sandra turned around and smiled at Devlin. "Especially you. As a reward, I set you all free."

Devlin grinned, then stood up. He peeled away the bands around his neck and wrists and tossed them aside, then he grabbed Sandra and pulled her into his arms. She melted against him as his mouth ravaged hers, his tongue diving inside her mouth and plundering. Suddenly he leaned forward and she fell over his shoulder.

He stroked her ass, sending tingles through her body, as he carried her toward the shower. Warm water streamed over her as he set her on her feet. She watched hungrily as he soaped up his cock, stroking it until it was rock-hard again.

Then he dragged her against his hard body and kissed her passionately. With his hands on her shoulders, he guided her backward until she felt the slate wall against her back.

She gasped as his big cock drove into her.

His cock filled her like no other. He thrust into her again and again. She clung to his shoulders and moaned as an orgasm began and just kept on going as he filled her again and again with his giant cock.

Finally, when she'd nearly fainted with pleasure, he spiraled inside her and erupted. She clung to him, moaning at the feel of him filling her with his heat.

He nuzzled her neck, then kissed her.

She stared at him with wide eyes. "Wow."

He grinned. "Just to remind you who your main man is."

"Oh, don't worry. There's no doubt in my mind." She stroked his cheek and smiled. "And I will love, honor, and obey you. Because I love you, Devlin."

"And I love you."

Sandra could see the joy in his eyes as he squeezed her tight in his arms. She knew it wouldn't be long before he asked her to marry him. Especially with her not-so-subtle hints.

She also knew she'd say yes.

Keep reading for a sneak peek at
Opal Carew's next novel.

Secret Weapon

Coming July 2012 from St. Martin's Griffin

Sloan Granger hung up his uniform, then closed his locker. He was still getting used to life on the police force in the beautiful town of Kenora, Maine. He'd moved here two months ago and didn't regret the decision to leave L.A. at all. It was quieter here, more relaxed, which meant he could focus on more important things than the stresses of the job.

Derek Jameson, still dressed in his own uniform, walked into the locker room.

"Hey, Sloan." He opened his locker a few down from Sloan's, then sat down on the flat wooden bench and untied his shoes. "Any big plans for the weekend?"

"Not really. You have something in mind?"

He and Derek had taken in a movie last week and they'd played squash together a couple of times.

"That depends. Are you seeing anyone right now?"

Sloan raised an eyebrow at the question. "No. I've been too busy settling in." But Sloan knew exactly the woman he intended to start dating. In fact, Janine had been the reason he'd chosen to move to Kenora.

Janine and Sloan had history. They'd grown up together and, if things hadn't gotten screwed up because of devastating events, they would be in a relationship right now. But fate had kicked them both in the butt and sent them in different directions. Janine had moved to Kenora six years ago. Mostly to get away from Sloan. He knew that. And he was here to fix it.

"Great. I was wondering if you were free on Friday night."

"Are you trying to fix me up with someone?" Sloan asked. "Because I'm really not interested."

"First, this isn't a fix-up . . . exactly . . . and second, if you're not interested in what I'm about to suggest, you need to have your head examined."

Sloan sat down on the bench, too. "Okay, I'll bite. What's on the table?"

Derek leaned toward him. "I go out with this really hot woman and . . . she really likes pushing the envelope, if you know what I mean."

"So you're suggesting what exactly?" Sloan hadn't been with a woman in quite a while—how could he since all he could do lately was think about Janine? He intended to win Janine's heart, but a wild, no-strings hookup with Derek's girlfriend, probably sharing her with Derek, would be a hot, incredibly sexy experience. And with no lasting repercussions.

"She has this fantasy of having sex with a stranger. We've done it where she's had a blindfold on and we pretend she doesn't know me, but she'd like to try the real thing. I told her I could find someone I trust, and who would be discreet."

"So it would be just her and me?" That would be a bit weird. Making out with a total stranger, knowing she was Derek's girlfriend.

"No, I'll be there. Watching. And getting involved if that seems comfortable once things get started. She'll be blindfolded, at least at first, to heighten the situation. That should make things less awkward, too."

"Sounds like you have this all planned out. You do this a lot?"

"Not the stranger thing. This is the first time. But we've done threesomes before."

Sloan grinned. "Wow, you've got a really hot one there."

Derek grinned. "Hot in looks and attitude." He pulled his wallet from his pocket and flipped it open to a picture of a beautiful brunette with an angelic smile.

Sloan's heart stopped as he stared at the picture of Janine.

Red hot erotic romances from OPAL CAREW...

TWIN FANTASIES

SWING

BLUSH

SIX

SECRET TIES

FORBIDDEN HEAT

BLISS

PLEASURE BOUND

Visit www.opalcarew.com to sign up for Opal's newsletter, view book trailers, and much more!

AVAILABLE WHEREVER BOOKS ARE SOLD

St. Martin's Griffin